CHROMOSOME 8

CHROMOSOME 8

By Peter Holt

ibooks

DISTRIBUTED BY PUBLISHERS GROUP WEST

A Publication of ibooks, inc.

Distributed by:
Publishers Group West
1700 Fourth Street, Berkeley, CA 94710
www.pgw.com

ibooks, inc.
24 West 25th Street
New York, NY 10010

ISBN 1-59687-153-9
First ibooks, inc. printing December 2005
10 9 8 7 6 5 4 3 2 1

Printed in the U.S.A.

Of bodies changed to different forms.
—Ovid, *Metamorphoses*

Prologue

On the empty shore of an ancient sea one small fish changed the Earth.

The little fish had fins shaped like lobes, a stiff tail, and a soft body. Evolution had withheld the gifts of armor and speed, and so she was easy prey for any of the hungry sharks, placoderms, or arthrodires that prowled the blue depths of a primeval planet.

In a dim corner of her tiny brain she understood this and so she kept to the shallows, even though the warm water was poor in both oxygen and the small trilobites that were her favored prey. Her kind had once lived in the clear cool deep but had been driven steadily towards the lethal shore by predators. Now they had their backs to an evolutionary wall and could retreat no more, for just above loomed the silent land, so far colonized only by a few mosses and ferns and proto-pines. No animal could survive the desiccation and hard sun and raw gravity. Like countless species before and after, the time allotted to the little fish and her kind was almost gone.

But on they fought, in waters to be known four hundred million years later as the Pacific Ocean.

On a late spring day, the fish was hunting near aqua wavelets that crumped onto bone-white sand. Though she was a young adult she had not yet reproduced; she lacked the energy to ripen her load of eggs and her body cried out for the food that would bring life to her young.

She circled a boulder of dead coral and her eyes, glittering like green opals, focused on a rare bounty. She slid into a dense mat of seafloor algae. She began to stalk. Despite her hunger her instincts told her to be patient. She was.

Finally, when she could creep no closer, she braced the lobes of her fins against the sand and lunged. The horseshoe crab also leapt, but not as fast, and the fish's needle-toothed jaws caught a crab leg halfway into the eyehole of a bleached thelodont skull.

The contest began. The fish pulled and the crab pulled, dragging her against the sharp edges of its shelter while batting her blue-green snout with a black claw. Fins blurred. The crab edged outward. The fish sensed victory and redoubled her efforts, pushing into her energy reserves. Then, by blind luck, the crab twisted its body and locked its shell into her skull. The little fish could not know that the battle was over and her meal lost.

She continued to pull as lactic acid etched her muscles while her vision dimmed and her body stiffened. Finally, the sharp hunger for oxygen outweighed the blunt need for food and she released the crab and ascended, mouth gasping and gills flexing. There was not enough oxygen in the thin water, but in this ecological slum there never was, and so the fish's race had developed a crude trick millennia before. It was the only way they could live.

She poked her pale snout through the blue skin of the sea and sucked a gulp of raw air into her swim bladder. It felt strange and painful, but the pain it caused was less than the pain it alleviated as the oxygen diffused into capillaries and on into her cramping body.

She gasped air again, her grape-sized brain clouded by fatigue and hunger but not dim enough to miss a silver glint that resolved into a five-foot bullet-headed placoderm, one of the most feared predators of the day, launching itself from the deep. The other small fishes vanished and she was alone. She fanned her fins to duck for the shallows but the placoderm followed. She wove through a low ridge of lumpy corals and the placoderm accelerated. She scanned for a hole or notch but there was nothing.

She ran into shallower water than she had ever dared. Waves jostled her while terrifying vibrations announced that still the placoderm closed.

She turned to parallel the beach with dorsal fin exposed, muscles burning, and the placoderm seconds from a meal—and then it happened. The trough of an approaching wave scraped her belly on the sand and a moment later a fat swell rolled both hunted and hunter high onto the beach.

Stunned, the fish lay mired in white sand, fins digging small trenches as she frantically tried to return to the sea from which no animal had escaped. Her gills strained wide and collapsed. The weight of suffocation bore down.

Other fish would have died here. Two meters away the pursuing placoderm was on its way to a flopping, choking death. But the meek little fish opened her mouth and sucked another burst of air into her swim bladder. In closing, rubbery lips clamped by chance around a tussock of greens. She was used to sea plants that were tough or spiny or poisonous. But with no predators the land plants had no need for defenses. They were unguarded. They were succulent.

The fish trembled and lay still, as if aware that while her glistening blue-green skin dried she huddled at a crossroads. The sea called, a familiar but hungry dead end.

The alien land beckoned with food. And a vast future.

She paused a moment longer then began to feed, gasping with her air bladder repeatedly. In the days and weeks to come she would often return to the water, for on land her organs sagged, her skin dried, and oxygen hunger squeezed. But even her simple brain could remember where the food was.

The food allowed her to breed, and she laid her translucent eggs in the shallows under the ultraviolet hammers of the sun. When her young hatched she cared for them, and before her tired body gave out, she even taught them her trick. As it happened, some of her off-spring were even better at it. And so began the conquest of the land.

With new generations new genes formed, rewriting again and again the genetic code governing what once had been a swim bladder. More blood was shunted to it, the better to carry oxygen. Muscles came to cradle it, enabling it to inhale and exhale. Old structures such as gills and fins faded away as their genes fell silent in the rabble of new expression. These genes were shut off by removing or inactivating their tiny "on" switches, known as promoters. But in a curiosity of molecular mechanics, the genes themselves remained intact, like abandoned cars stripped only of their keys. Tucked away deep in the nucleus of every cell these relics were faithfully replicated with every cell division, down to the last detail. Every cell nucleus carries within its invisible depths not only an exact blueprint of what is, but of everything that has been.

Within a few million years animals had conquered the shore and spread into all their many-splendored forms. But no matter how different, whether dinosaur or dog, sparrow or shrew, all those creatures carry within their cells the molecular relics of that great leap so long ago.

The little fish and all she was lives on.

*The thing that hath been, it is that which shall be; there is
no new thing under the sun.*
—Ecclesiastes 1:9

Chapter 1

Three hundred and ninety million years after their distant ancestors
fled the sea, two humans returned in search of an even older mystery.
Their changed bodies could no longer tolerate the ocean so they would
ride in a bubble of titanium hung with thrusters and lights, pierced
by ports and a hatch, and graced with the name *Omega,* painted on
the stern in neat block letters.

Standing in the hatch at the pilot's launch position, Devon Lucas
rested one hand on a fist-sized bolt while the other blocked the glare
from the two-hundred-foot research vessel *Aurora.* Beneath short red
hair, her lined green eyes studied the steel cable that lowered the
research submersible like a metal spider toward the luminous blue of
the waiting South Pacific water, so clear that it didn't look substantial
enough to support several tons of metal.

But it did.

When the yellow hull kissed the sea Devon released the steel hook
from the big eyelet behind the sail, dropped through the single hatch,
and pulled it shut. Her ears popped and, as always, her nose twitched
at the sudden exchange of fresh salt air for stale sweat and plastic
and ozone.

The round cockpit was crammed with displays and equipment. She
placed one foot on a black-taped junction box and dropped into the
left seat, on the way down brushing shoulders with the scientist who
would be her passenger.

He was tall and either lean or gaunt, with short iron-gray hair and
pale skin. He had joined the ship two days before at the Pago Pago
re-supply and since then had rarely ventured from his lab. She knew

that he was a geochemist from Princeton and that his name was Dr. Henry Winston, which was vaguely familiar, though that meant nothing. Each year she piloted hundreds of scientists to the ocean floor, most of whom chattered incessantly and dropped names as a South Pacific thunderstorm throws raindrops.

A set of Australia-bound swells heaved the little sub into the corkscrew lurch that had earned it the nickname "Pukinator," and Devon saw her passenger swallow and tighten an already white-knuckled grip. With no interest in seeing again the runny eggs served an hour before by the galley, she began the final checklist. She had done it a thousand times and was no less careful this time than she had been her first. Her fingers swept from the floor to the ceiling and left to right while she mouthed memorized words. Batteries. Oxygen. Scrubbers. Thrusters. Hydraulics. Fire suppressors.

The cast of Dr. Winston's jaw when seen from a certain angle, plus the way his hand was gripping so bloodlessly tight, brought up a submerged memory.

"Didn't we dive the mid-Atlantic rise together? Two, three, years ago?"

"Four. I wondered if you would remember."

Devon read the next item on her list, then twisted in her seat with fingers poised on the self-test switch for the robotic arm circuitry.

"Apparently you're not a man of your word," she said dryly.

"What?"

"Didn't you swear, last time, that you would never dive again?"

He nodded ruefully. "I hated it last time. Really, really hated it."

She couldn't help but wonder what could bring him back. Many people found the claustrophobic confines of a tiny submersible deep beneath the sea to be uncomfortable or even oppressive, but a few found them intolerable and Henry Winston had been one of these. His return seemed as likely as someone with a fear of rats taking a vacation tour of the Calcutta sewers.

"This must be important," Devon surmised.

"You could say that," he said carefully.

She waited but he said nothing more, and so she turned to the last diagnostics while the safety divers ottered past the viewports. The acoustic telephone delivered the final dive clearance and she acknowledged it with two clicks on the transmitter. She then performed her final pre-dive task: She pressed a finger to her lips and then to the photo taped just below the back-up depth gauge, planting a kiss squarely across Alice and Bonnie, eight and six, while silently promising Alice again that she would be careful, as Alice demanded her mommy do before each dive. Then she turned to her passenger.

"Maybe you should fire your travel agent," she suggested.

Henry was looking at a few striped fish hovering among blue spears of light that plunged to meet in the violet gloom below, where vague shapes shifted in the depths. He took a deep and methodical breath in a way that suggested much practice.

"I can't," he said softly. "After today I'll need a trip to Stockholm."

Devon's hand stopped just above the ballast lever that would drop them toward the bottom. Her ex was a biochemist who often joked about his own future trip to the city where the Nobel Prize was awarded.

She pressed the lever and with a bubbling hiss the viewports filled with foam that cleared to pale blue water. *Omega* slipped beneath the waves and settled, and the light took on a pure filtered quality. Henry drew a black laptop from a nylon case.

"How long till we're on site?" he asked.

She did the math in her head. Thirteen hundred feet. So thirty minutes, more or less, she told him.

He nodded, pulled a paper from his shirt pocket, and fired up the computer. His two index fingers flew like frantic beaks as he input data from what Devon recognized as the ship's daily water sample.

Devon looked on in amusement. Now she had truly seen it all. Once panic-stricken at the thought of being underwater, Henry Winston was now too busy even to notice as the sub sank and the steel cloud of the mother ship dwindled and the hue of the water deepened.

"You couldn't do that before?" she asked.

"I did do it before. Now I have to do it again, with the data from this morning."

"But we're taking water samples." She tapped the dive plan, wondering again what he was up to. It was odd enough that he would come back for more underwater punishment; stranger still was the apparently trivial mission.

"We have to take the right ones. Everything depends on it."

The sub held as rock-steady as if riding the blue rails of light that shot downward, with the only sense of motion coming from the dust-like particles falling up past the ports, the steady progress of the depth gauge, and the color shift of the light. The hull emitted small squeaks and groans as the sea squeezed it, and it was usually these that un-nerved even the stoutest of hearts.

But Henry seemed unperturbed, though he occasionally glanced up and several times turned down the brightness of his screen as the sea darkened from pale blue to deep purple.

Finally the sea strangled the last of the light and the chill of the deep crept in. Devon slipped on her battered Patagonia pullover and Henry matched with a brand new model faced with Gore-Tex. She checked their position and descent rate, called the ship to report all well, and stared into the infinite black, a region where the sun had never shone. Tiny glints of cool blue and green and pale purple formed silent constellations, winked out, appeared again. The lights could have been small and close or huge and distant. Henry was watching them.

"Squid, and maybe an anglerfish," Devon said in the hushed tones that always seemed appropriate at depth. The lights drifted off as the sub whispered downward.

Two minutes later the computer beeped and Henry pushed it away and straightened. "Hello, history," he said softly. On screen was a circular diagram that could have been a crude map of an old village with a fortified wall around simple structures.

"What's that?" Devon asked.

"A miracle. The original miracle. You don't recognize it?"

"I didn't think so at first, and now I'm sure I don't."

"No reason you should, but people have been looking for this for a long time. This is your ancestor. Mine too. Everyone's. The first life on Earth. The first cell. It was born at a place like this one and it's what we're going to find. Shouldn't we be there soon?"

Devon had an eye on the sonar.

"Actually—"

She flipped a row of switches to power up the sub and touched the button for the thallium iodide floodlamps. Three artificial suns exploded.

Henry gasped. At the bottom of the sea lay the offspring of a fairy-tale castle and a polluting underwater factory. Tapered spires of orange and black shot clouds of smoke that glowed with red and yellow flecks. Piles of jagged rocks lay in broken heaps like shattered battlements. Razor-edged ridges and knife-slashed canyons scarred the floor, smeared ochre and yellow and black. Blown stone swelled into bells and arches and tubes.

The creatures were even stranger. Albino crabs scuttled and fought while blind shrimp wandered the valleys and gathered in rings around vents. Strange pale fish, some eyeless, hunkered on the periphery. Groves of six-foot tube worms waved like wind-blown wheat. Mussels and red-blooded clams clung to scorched rocks above the jellied mats of bacteria that carpeted the sea floor.

"I suppose you're going to tell me life started here, at a hydrothermal vent?" Devon asked.

"I am," Henry replied, but despite his promise he said nothing more.

Devon waited. She was a rarity among sub pilots, not only in being a woman, but in holding a Ph.D. in oceanography. For most scientists the sub was a simple conveyance, a glorified bus that let them collect samples and get back to the real work of lab analysis. But Devon had realized that she preferred the diving, the seeing of places never before seen by human eyes, to staring through microscopes or plotting graphs, and so she had made a mid-career shift. That change had been for moments just such as this one. Before her lay a place unexposed to light since the ocean basins filled. It was waiting to be explored. And it was her hand on the stick.

She pushed the throttle lever. With an electric hum the yellow hull snaked between two ochre towers and through a dense black cloud which had started as a pool of superheated water in a magma chamber somewhere far below, and which, after leaching minerals from the Earth's crust, erupted from the sea floor in one of many scalding jets. As the hot water suddenly cooled in the deep, the minerals precipitated and painted the depths in vivid color. Such sites had been discovered less than twenty years before and Devon loved them above all others. They were just so strange, so unearthly.

The sub crested a low ridge and hovered over a miniature valley ringed by ranges of black-spewing mountains.

"I don't see any ancient life," Devon said. She'd visited vents many times, and although one never got used to the strange creatures, she did recognize most of them.

"Maybe you do," Henry replied cryptically, then gestured at a small smoker to starboard. "Let's sample that one, please."

On site the scientists were in charge, within the limits of safety. Devon slid the sub forward then switched to another pair of joysticks and unlimbered the mechanical arm from its folded position.

"This water is over two hundred degrees," Devon pointed out.

"And that's why no one else has found what's in it, Devon. No one's looked. But the answer to the question of how life began is right here. Evolutionary theory once held that life began with random collisions in cool primordial puddles. But my calculations show that the conditions were all wrong. Too cold, too slow. Down here, they're right. The right mix of methane, ammonia, heat, and traces of catalysts like platinum. Of all known hydrothermal vents, only this field has the right mix. From the samples I analyzed on the way down I can tell we need a baby jet, one that will have higher concentrations of certain minerals. Just like early Earth. That gives us a long row to hoe but there has to be one here. We just have to find it."

Devon stared out at what Henry claimed was her ancestral home and the ancestral home of every living thing on Earth. Why not? Other scientists, she knew, thought life had begun in space and rained down like cosmic hail.

"So we're not after water samples?"

"We're after what's in the water. Protobionts. Simple collections of amino and nucleic acids bound up in rudimentary lipid membranes. The basic building blocks of life—proteins and nucleic acids and membranes—will actually self-assemble, given the right conditions. The problem is that the right conditions for one are wrong for the others, so getting all the pieces together is a three-way chicken-and-egg problem. Harder than Chinese math."

Devon looked through the thick glass dubiously. The white clumps of marine snow swirled as gaily as in a Norman Rockwell painting, though this world was as alien as Mars.

"Really?"

He fixed her with a steady gaze. "Really. I wouldn't have come back down for less."

When the first sample bottle was stored in the metal chin rack, Henry directed them to a new location, and then another. The arm reached out and filled bottle after bottle from jet after jet while Henry scribbled notes and whispered into a tape recorder. For hours they sampled around the vent community. Finally Devon moved into a hover twenty feet off the bottom, wiped her forehead on her polypro sleeve, and flexed her wrists to loosen forearm cramps. Henry stared at the rack of sample bottles in dismay.

"None of these are quite right."

"You can't be sure till you review them," Devon soothed.

"Yes I can."

She glanced at the timer. "We still have half an hour."

"Good god. Over that way." He jerked a thumb. "Just think—years of therapy to get ready for this and then not finding my little critter. What would I need then? Restraints. Electroshock. They might have to bring back lobotomies." He aimed two index fingers at his eyebrows and stirred.

They traversed two gullies barely wider than the hull and swooped low above a paddy of tubeworms. Devon waved at a set of perfectly shaped volcanoes that would have been at home on the planet of the Little Prince.

"None of these?"

"We have a lot of imperfect samples. We need to spend our time finding the right vent, not sampling the wrong ones." They floated across a smooth ochre plain upon which stood hundreds of large white crabs that turned to watch the sub, raising their pincers and slowly shifting on bony legs.

Henry pressed his face to the port, bringing himself within inches.

"We seem to have admirers. They look tasty."

"They taste like rotten eggs," Devon said. At least once per cruise, in the name of knowledge, some scientist insisted on trying to eat the deep-sea creatures, which were infused with the hydrogen sulfide stench of their environment. The rivalry between scientists and crew was good natured and intense, and as the curious diners spat on their plates, Devon inevitably noted that scientists were nothing but big babies, since both insisted on putting everything in their mouths.

The terrain became more jagged, with slashed valleys and knife-edged crevasses, fanged volcanoes and tomb-like caverns, all slathered with more orange and less black. Devon scanned her panel. Batteries low but within limits, oxygen the same, carbon dioxide high but not too high. She yawed the nose back and forth, sweeping the lights to maximize their view. It made Henry faintly green but he insisted on it. They had just arrived at the end of a survey line and were about to turn when he let out a cry and leapt against the glass, as if trying to escape.

"There!"

Devon followed his eyes and finger. At the base of a steep slope ten meters to port opened a cavern mouth. Its ceiling was fanged with black rock and just inside the lip sprouted the half-meter tooth of a young vent. She rotated the sub to face the dark hole.

"Too dangerous, Henry."

"Come on. Sample. It's big enough."

Omega crept forward and stopped and Devon wiped her hands on her jeans.

"Henry. Overhangs. Bad."

"Devon. Nobel. Good. For you and the diving program, too. How long has this cave been here? Ages? What are the odds anything would happen now? Tiny. Besides, getting a sample would take only a moment." He gestured as if directing a cavalry column. "Onward. Besides, I read that this is as safe as crossing a street."

"People die all the time crossing the street," Devon muttered.

Henry shot her a dirty look and pointed.

"Right in there is a young vent, less than a year old. We've hit a few teenagers but that's the first baby we've seen. And we need a baby. Plus the overhang will have concentrated the emissions. In there is *exactly* what we're looking for. Exactly." He punched the bulkhead in emphasis.

Henry sniffed the air theatrically. "Smell that?"

"What?" Devon found no odor of burning insulation or leaking batteries or any other brewing disaster.

"Success. The Nobel. I can smell it."

Omega rose and wafted forward, bright lights playing across the ropy black rock that formed the roof of the cavern. The cave disappeared into dark depths, while the slope above was studded with black boulders. Devon considered. If Henry were even half right, the fame would both further her own career and bring needed money to the diving program.

"Looks a bit crumbly, Henry."

He changed tactics and uncorked all his charm. "Just a quick sample. Please. This could be everything. Not just for me, but for science. Some risks are unavoidable, but you're a good pilot, the stakes are high, and we can do this quick and safe."

Devon gazed at the mouth, picturing the sub within it. The margins were tight but she'd handled tighter. The roof was suspect, but she'd survived worse. It was against regulations but everyone knew what rules were for. Besides, if she really wanted to avoid risk, she would have become a banker. She fingered the mike as she considered asking permission but released it. She knew the answer. She didn't look at the picture of Bonnie and Alice—she knew what her daughters would say, too. But they didn't want a wimp for a mom, either.

"One quick sample. Then out. Deal?"

Henry pumped a fist. "Deal."

The vertical thrusters moved *Omega* to within two inches of the rubbled bottom, then the scimitar blades at the stern turned. Dark walls wrapped the yellow flower in a coffin of black stone and Devon ran her eyes from instruments to viewports, barely moving the controls as she held them off the bottom and away from walls and roof. The rear propeller stopped and they coasted.

"Okay," she said while unlimbering the mechanical arm.

The fissure in the cavern floor was a mere crack among the stone rubble but each second it vented fifty gallons along its jagged length, creating an invisible watery updraft. *Omega* nosed into the current as the mechanical arm reached outward. The yellow hull wafted upward like a slow balloon. Devon, focused on moving the arm with gentle precision, saw the motion too late.

"No," she whispered as she grabbed the stick. Before she could slip them down the fiberglass sail met the stone ceiling.

A crunch.

"What—?" Henry started, eyes lifting.

The roof fell like a hangman's trapdoor, releasing an avalanche of boulders to roar down the slope and across the sub. Water bottles and tape recorders and flashlights flew, and Devon thought of crash test dummies as she was flung in her straps. Three times she was sure they were sideways and in a corner of her mind she knew that the hull could not hold.

As if in confirmation a loud crack sounded but it was only an empty urine bottle shattering. The pink pieces hovered in mid-air before flitting away with the next impact. Then the sub went black and in the pure dark the noise seemed louder.

Devon gripped her seat and Henry gripped her, his screams almost inaudible. She waited for the jet of pressurized water that would cut flesh like a laser but there was no icy burn. She knew she should be disappointed, for a quick bloody death would beat slow blind drowning as the sub filled. She wondered: when it came down to a fight for the last breath, who would win? Or would it even matter, for as the scientist part of her brain pointed out, the final shrinking air bubble would become superheated from the pressurization and would be closer to fire than air.

She pushed away these thoughts as the ringing impacts gave way to raspy gratings, then to a rattle of pebbles, then silence. The sub came to rest canted thirty degrees to starboard.

"Henry, let go of me," she said into the black.

He did.

Now glad for the blindfold drills required of all pilots, Devon felt for the switches and brought up the emergency lighting.

"We're alive," Henry pointed out. He leaned forward, saw that some of his sample bottles had survived, and sighed. He looked around, found that there were no leaks, something Devon had already confirmed, and patted the titanium hull with fondness. "A minor incident, trusty pal."

Devon was already moving levers and switches on the panel. Her face was pale against the rose lighting. The motor whined up and then down.

"Devon?"

"Shut up." The motor ran at a high pitch, then low, then high again. An electric smell filled the cockpit. Devon flipped a row of switches and bubbles hissed skyward. Nothing happened. She let the motor wind down, paused, then again ran the motor at max thrust until the hot smell returned. She throttled down. After a moment she opened a plastic safety cover to reveal a red handle. She pulled on it to extend it a foot, then shoved it. It came off in her hand.

Devon sat back and said nothing.

"Why so glum? We survived," said Henry brightly, trying to fill the void.

She doused the lights and ran the motor at a higher pitch than before. In the blackness the control stick squeaked as she yanked it and the hull thrummed with vibrations. The smell grew more intense, then the motor again whirred to silence and the dim lights returned. To Devon they looked weaker than before, but she knew that was because these were the last lights she would see. It didn't matter that the com gear was smashed and communication cut off.

Devon turned to Henry.

"We survived," Henry insisted.

She bided her time before she spoke, putting one hand to the eye of the viewport, now lidded with basalt. *Omega* had closed her eyes for good, and soon so would they.

"No, Henry, we didn't."

Chapter 2

At that moment on the far side of the Pacific, Marcus Oden was marking on a battered map a spot two thousand miles southwest of Hawaii. The map was already littered with black marks, each a place searched. The blue spaces between the marks remained vast but after six years he no longer hurried. He was, however, methodical.

He folded the map, slid it into a battered duffel bag, and stepped outside. The last mark had gone onto the north side of Fangamatu Atoll in the Phoenix Islands; next would be the east side. It lay forty meters away, glinting in the tropical morning as low lines of breakers marched up to the reef fringe to commit blue-and-white suicide. The rising sun forced a bronzed hand against salt-stiffened blond hair, to shade eyes of gunmetal gray ringed by a razor edge of violet.

Marcus glanced over the room to check that he had forgotten nothing. The bare concrete floor supported a cot, several mounds of dive gear, wrenches scattered around a toolbox, and a spare microscope. A portable freezer filled with samples and enzymes was connected to a jury-rigged solar panel by frayed wiring and black tape. The only items that might qualify as decorations—though they were not—were the two framed photos. The larger showed an athletic blond woman on a racing sloop, and the smaller a red-haired, green-eyed woman looking back from the hatch of yellow submersible. An inscription on this one read: *Marcus—Mine goes deeper. L, Devon.*

Satisfied, he glanced at the Casio velcroed to his wrist and saw that the tide would soon turn. It was time. After trotting down the short path of crushed coral that led from the rusted Quonset, past palms and plumeria to a narrow beach of rough new sand, he kicked off his boots and dropped his shirt to reveal a torso remarkable for the carnage it had survived. Scars tracked bronzed skin as if a drunken god had taken up etching, first with a sailfish bill, then with a rough shark snout, and finally with a sea wasp's tentacles. At least, Marcus would sometimes note, he had lost no limbs, unless you counted the left little toe taken by frostbite on Denali, which he didn't.

He gathered up mask, fins, and a hard black backpack vented with slits and bearing a sapphire-blue decal with the letters OSI in white astride the prongs of a green trident, the logo of the Ocean Sciences Institute. Coiled inside the backpack was an experimental artificial gill, cobbled together by Marcus from biomodified membranes, plastic tubing, and a laptop processor, all of which allowed it to strip dissolved air from seawater and deliver a breathing blend customized for depth.

He submerged the backpack in the lagoon shallows, watched a white needle's wavering trip from red to green, and drew two test breaths through the mouthpiece, then checked the tiny scuba tank strapped to the side. With the pack shouldered he sloshed across the knee-deep reef flat to the blue brink of a hundred-foot underwater wall, donned mask and fins, and jumped.

The world of air and weight and miles of visibility swapped out for a foaming wrap of bubbles that cleared to bright corals and darting fish. His plan was to spend ninety minutes swimming a carefully plotted transect over the ocean floor, venturing as deep as 120 feet but with a view to 300, which would earn another mark on the map. Another search completed.

Instead he was back in twelve minutes flat. In just twelve minutes this corner of the South Pacific had undergone a complete makeover; the calm sea had fled before relentless lines of heavy swells that rolled up to the atoll like blue bombs, each hesitating as if gathering strength before detonating into white foam. From the shore they were scenic and spectacular; to a diver the vast amount of water in motion was both challenge and threat.

Marcus fought towards the island using hands and feet to kick, pull and even drag himself. During the strongest surges, when thousands of tons of water raced to get off the reef flat, he could do nothing but find a handhold and dangle like a flag in a hurricane.

The whole process would have been simpler if he didn't have to get his snorkel above the water to breathe. But the experimental gill on his back had failed at depth and the tiny scuba bottle had been exhausted getting him to the surface, and so now he had to breathe in the old fashioned way pioneered eons before by whatever creature had first breathed air: by getting his head, or at least his snorkel, above water. He drove forward during the lulls in the surge, hung on gamely as the sea tried to blow him back out, and stole gasps whenever he could.

When he finally reached the coarse sand he crawled to a block of coral tossed ashore two years earlier by a typhoon and collapsed, back bent and breath heaving.

A huge man beneath a leaning palm watched serenely with eyes that were dark coals in a swarthy face framed by a black mane. A Hawaiian shirt decorated with palm trees and topless women spanned the distance between innocent grin and piling-thick thighs in khaki shorts. Nick Kondos had fewer scars than Marcus, but he blamed several of the ones he did have on the bedraggled creature that had just emerged from the sea.

"Another disaster?" Nick asked.

"Another failure," Marcus corrected with a wheeze. A surprise wave tried to blast him from his perch but succeeded only in tilting him. He fixed a long and wary gaze on the Pacific, which so often made a mockery of its name, then rose and moved up the beach. He shrugged off the backpack and let sixty wet pounds drop to the sand.

Nick lifted the damp mass effortlessly.

"Marcus, how many times has this thing almost killed you?"

"Three."

Nick's bushy eyebrows raised.

"Three this month."

The big Greek's eyes creased at the corners. "And you wonder why I call it Marcus' folly."

Marcus tipped his head and tapped, knocking water from one ear, as a bare hint of a smile played across a face of rugged regularity with a strong nose and firm stubbled jaw. The geometric weave of the Polynesian tattoo ringing his left biceps flexed with each tap.

"Don't you also call airplanes the Wright Brothers' Great Mistake?"

Nick let the pack thump to the sand. "The Earth's surface is perfectly nice. There's no reason for going up in the air or down in the sea. As for this thing," and he prodded the pack with a toe, "maybe humans aren't meant to breathe through fish gills."

"But we fly with bird wings," Marcus said dryly.

"Two wrongs don't make a right. What happened this time? The usual?"

Marcus didn't answer but led the way up the path and set the pack on a crude wooden table outside the Quonset hut painted with a now-faded Ocean Sciences Institute emblem. Beneath it on a table stood the big box of an ancient Zenith shortwave. During their visits to Fangamatu, which occurred four times a year under an ecological survey contract with the Kiribati government, they called this their office.

While unsnapping the plastic closures of the backpack's clamshell lid Marcus described the dive. At ninety-five feet the gill was working better than any previous version, sifting enough molecular oxygen from the sea to let him breathe with ease as he kicked along the deep wall. When he slipped down another fifty feet to examine a banded sea snake, which turned out to be a member of a rare but not unknown species, the air stopped as if the barnacled hand of some bearded sea god had turned a valve. With one breath he got a lungful of moist air and with the next he was sucking vacuum. It was like trying to inhale glass. He switched to the tiny emergency tank and ascended. The current had picked up and it fought him, followed by the surprise set of breakers as he approached the beach.

"I think you saw that part," Marcus finished. The last snap released and he lifted the black lid to reveal twisty pink coils, raw but fragile-looking assemblies shaped like bottle brushes, and tiny capillary tubes.

Nick leaned closer. "I saw it. By Zeus, for a gill that looks like guts."

"Spoken like a true geologist." Marcus held a scalpel to the sun and eyed the glittering edge.

"Where are the proteins you made?"

"Not made, modified. From the bluefin tuna gill. They're implanted in the matrix here and here." The steel tip pointed.

"Clever monkey. Though nearly a drowned monkey."

The scalpel dipped and removed several gelatinous slivers. Marcus placed these on slides and stained them with a few drops of Aniline blue. While letting the dye set he connected a gauge to a data port and switched on an old laptop computer. The gill used an artificial membrane and modified hemoglobin to sift oxygen from seawater; Marcus had used the genetic sequences to develop each in what he described in grant applications as molecular biology meeting applied engineering. Or, as Nick countered, meddling biology colliding with attempted engineering.

Marcus and Nick had worked together in the South Pacific for almost six years, with Nick's background in geology and geophysics complementing Marcus' biological and engineering skill. The two scientists were the entire Ocean Sciences Institute, which enjoyed a small but solid reputation. Working close came easily to them, for theirs was a friendship first forged as college rivals in football and track. Their first actual meeting involved neither a handshake nor a smile but a bone-crushing tackle, after Berkeley defensive back Marcus Oden intercepted a pass and, deducing that a large and surprisingly fast Stanford tackle had the angle on him, veered and tried to run him over. Both were helped off the field and the picture made the papers. They later roomed together in graduate school, and then Nick taught at CalTech while Marcus did a tour with NASA, which had been looking for biochemists with flight backgrounds.

The Ocean Sciences Institute was born in tragedy when Marcus' wife vanished in the South Pacific along with her sailboat. Marcus had come to look for her, and Nick had come to help, and though in the vastness of the South Pacific they found no sign of Callie Oden, they did find many uses for their talents. Their work on harbors and fisheries had immediate and visible impacts, and ended up in the pages of journals such as *Science* and *Nature*. With contracts and grants they scraped by somehow; as Marcus said, fish and fowl don't pay but the work needed doing. Flying, diving, and island-hopping seemed unlikely for Nick, since the big Greek made no secret of his aversion to leaving the planet's surface in any direction, and when he had first come he had said he would stay for only a few weeks. Those had stretched to years.

Marcus frowned at the diagnostic program and slid the slide beneath a dissecting scope.

"The usual?" Nick asked, hunched over to peer from the side.

Marcus rubbed his eyes and nodded. "Matrix again. Collapsed and crystallized. Getting the O-two out of the sea is only half the battle; it also has to go into gas form. I've got some ideas on modifying the DNA code to change the tertiary protein structure just a bit."

"Maybe what we need isn't in DNA," Nick said.

"It isn't."

"What?"

"That's why I'm modifying it."

"Improving on hundreds of millions of years of evolution?"

"Right."

Nick took half a step back and crossed his arms. "Marcus, exactly how many impossible tasks are you pursuing now?"

A pause as Marcus contemplated either the gill or his answer.

"You would say at least two. The answer is zero."

Nick tilted his head to fix a calculating gaze on him.

"You're right. I would say at least two. This gill, and the search that is the reason for the gill. Just so we understand each other, do you think anything is impossible?"

Marcus looked at him. "Well. Some things are hard."

Nick shook his head and opened an old ice chest that appeared constructed from silver duct tape and glue. He extracted two green bottles and opened both, handed one across, then drained half the other in a swallow and winced. The bottles had once had once held beer but had been refilled in the Royal Tongan bottling plant with a suspect solution that wasn't quite soda and wasn't quite juice, but at least was cold, liquid, and most importantly of all, present.

"Marcus, do you ever think you might be doing all this for the wrong reasons?"

"Never." Marcus drained his bottle and set it aside, seemingly impervious to the mischief of the Royal Tongan bottlers.

"The Ocean Sciences Institute is just the two of us, and we have projects on a dozen islands. We spend half our time commuting in that ancient relic of a seaplane." Nick waved at the lagoon, which in contrast to the ruffled violet outside the reef wore a smooth aqua. The faded planks of an old pier walked across the water to an even older PBY Catalina flying boat. With its high wing mounted atop an ungainly pylon, twin radial engines, primitive snout, and dual fuselage observation blisters, the plane looked as flightworthy and modern as a pterodactyl. Then again, Marcus claimed that pterodactyls had been very good flyers, and Nick had to concede that the plane worked well as a sort of flying RV that carried their science gear, two hammocks, and a crude galley. It had one white wing and one blue wing and the fuselage bore long sections of primer-gray paint striped by lengths of silver 200 mph tape. Hand painted below the cockpit was "Va' Alele"—Polynesian for flying canoe, the islander word for an airplane.

"And all this is because you're still looking for her, Marcus. But it's been six years. Six. Years."

Marcus set down a miniature Phillips screwdriver and took up a pair of needlenose pliers.

Nick was undeterred. "You look at that map every day. You add a mark every chance. The gill is just a tool to search more places. We even just bought that old funky deep-diving deathtrap so you could search more places. You don't give up. You haven't given up. But you have to. It's time."

"No it's not," Marcus corrected quietly.

Nick finished his bottle and reluctantly took another, his eyes full of self-pity that their beer supply had run out days before. But his tone softened. "This isn't healthy. Your pursuit, I mean. As for this Tongan junk, anything this funny tasting probably is healthy."

In the lagoon beyond the flying boat the local pod of spinner dolphins returned from their morning hunt for the daily frolic in the protected water. Bullet-shaped bodies spun and flipped before landing with giant splashes. Pairs arced side by side. As Nick liked to point out, especially to cooing tourists—on those rare occasions when they reached islands accessible to cooing tourists—dolphins were far hornier than Flipper ever let on; randy males had even been known to attempt couplings with human females.

Marcus aimed an electrode into the gill matrix and kept one eye on the computer screen.

"Someday you'll realize you're not my mother, Nick. Until then I wish you'd bake cookies instead of lecture. We're doing good science on all our projects, work no one else would or could do. We're helping people all over. We've got no bureaucracy, no administration, no requisition forms, and no staff meetings, just us doing what needs doing. Yes, we run projects on a dozen islands, and we accomplish more than organizations ten times our size. At first we scrounged for grants; now governments and agencies come to us. We've got the kind of jobs all scientists want."

"I know all that. And don't forget I was raised by a Greek mother—some of it rubs off. But Marcus. People die. You have to move on. Callie is gone."

Marcus set down the electrode and looked up. "We don't know she's dead."

"Callie and her boat and everyone on it vanished six years ago. We do know. You have to stop looking. Find someone else. What about Devon, the sub pilot off the *Aurora?* She seems to have the same underwater death wish as you. And she was catting around with you when we were last over that way."

"Nice girl," Marcus shrugged dismissively, already back at work with the pliers.

In disgust, Nick lobbed his bottle into a steel drum where it shattered with a merry tinkle and reached for a new one. He knew that the distance was not the problem; despite the huge reach of the South Pacific many of the foreigners—the *palangis*, as the natives called them—managed to know each other. Marcus and Nick had drunk with the Harvard-trained lawyers revising the Palau constitution, worked with the San Diego cannery experts based in Samoa, met enough of the missionaries to avoid the rest, and bunked with coral, fisheries, and agricultural experts on a dozen islands. While the rest of the world relied on email and faxes, they used an old-fashioned shortwave radio. A satellite phone was beyond their budget, and there was no phone and no Internet on most islands.

"Marcus, after half a decade its time to live."

"I do live."

"It's time to move on, then."

Marcus glanced into the lab where the afternoon's work awaited. "Like you said. I don't give up."

"Maybe you should."

They looked at each other in solemnity, then Nick grinned and Marcus shrugged and they clinked their bottles in a spontaneous toast.

"Why do I bother?" Nick sighed. "You can't help it. It's in your genes. I know that. And I can't help talking about it. That's in my genes. We're just the victims of our DNA."

Marcus settled into his chair and flexed the soreness from his shoulders, then put a hand on the gill and looked across the sea.

"Maybe not."

Chapter 3

In a borrowed shed at the foot of Tanua's wharf, Linc Cafferty set down an archaic dial phone that despite its beige bakelite worked all too well. The *Aurora*'s chief engineer had the look of someone torn from a caveman movie and shaved in the dark with a dull blade before being wrapped in Goodwill leftovers and plunked onto an oceanographic research ship in the middle of the South Pacific.

His beady eyes, shaded by a protruding suborbital ridge, avoided the faces assembled before him in favor of studying the grimy tennis shoes encasing his size seven, triple-E feet. Just visible through a sooty window was the *Aurora*, her white bulk destitute and forlorn without her yellow baby, *Omega*. The mother has lost her chick, Linc thought. It was ten hours since the sub went into the water; five since it became clear it would not return.

At first it had seemed like a blessing that the accident had happened here. After all, Tanua was part of American Samoa, a place which even had phone lines, and so at first it had seemed that the chances of getting help were unexpectedly good. At first.

The crew waited as he placed call after call across the oceans on static-filled lines. The US Navy, the Royal Navy, Scripps, Woods Hole. The Russians. Even the freaking Chilean Navy. Now for the first time in hours he ended one call without immediately dialing another. He sat hunched until the soft murmurs died away.

He looked up.

"Seven days," he announced.

He was met with a stunned silence.

"A week," he repeated.

A wan geophysicist named Stanislaw Tatum, an unenthusiastic veteran of many a research submersible dive and a self-professed coward who insisted on familiarizing himself with every risk of venturing beneath the sea, spoke first. For the last six months he had been stationed on the isle of Tanua, but he had served on *Aurora* and knew his ship-borne colleagues well.

"But Linc—those Navy rescue subs. They can be deployed anywhere in the world within forty-eight hours. Two days. That's what they say."

Linc rubbed a hand across his pudgy face, leaving a track of dirt and grease. "They can. And one will be. Within forty-eight hours, a Navy Deep Submergence Rescue Vehicle will have landed in Pago Pago. A mere four hundred miles away. It will take a week to get it that last four hundred miles—our little *Aurora* isn't big enough for a rescue sub designed to evacuate a nuclear attack boat. A week to get a big enough ship, with the launch and recovery gear, in place."

The silence thickened and the walls sweated. Giant bugs clattered against the flickering fluorescent tubes. The sky opened, as it did several times a day, to drop rain on the tin roof with the force of a million ball bearings. Stanislaw fidgeted. He looked left, right, and left again, smoothed his thinning hair, and only then asked the question. The din drowned him out the first time and he had to raise his voice to a near shout.

"But—can they last a week?"

Linc waited before he shook his head once with eyes lidded and stony. "Two, three days max. A week . . . No. And that's best case. Assuming that all the emergency equipment works. We don't even know what's happened down there."

Linc pushed away a platter of dough balls fried in fish oil that the locals called *pankekes*.

"We don't even know if they're alive," pointed out a Canadian meteorologist.

"We heard no implosion sounds. What we heard suggests a landslide or rock fall. We have to assume they're alive, but trapped."

"Lordy lordy," groaned Stanislaw.

"If the US Navy can't get here, we simply need to call someone else," announced a British phytoplankton expert.

"Is there anyone else?" one of the two Houston soft corals taxonomists asked.

"Only a few navies have rescue capability."

"Barking mad. What a stupid—"

Linc raised his hands. "Worldwide, there are several dozen research subs. Only the US Navy, the British, and a few others have dedicated rescue craft, but I've checked the location of every other sub. Because at this point we'd take any help at all. But no one else can get here any sooner. The US Navy's not just the best bet, it's the *only* bet."

"There's something else we should do," said a computer programmer known to all as Casper, who sported a pallor worthy of a Nome night clerk despite the South Pacific sun.

"Call Marcus and Nick," Casper continued.

Linc looked at him blankly.

"The Ocean Sciences Institute? Two guys with an old seaplane? Eight hundred miles away? What could they do?"

Casper shrugged. "Maybe nothing. But I've worked with them and they've done a few projects that people said couldn't be done. And we'd hate to find out, too late, that they could have helped."

A hydrocoral taxonomist rubbed his chin. "Wasn't Marcus with NASA? And the other guy—the huge one—a prof at Cal Tech? They're not dummies. Though you wouldn't know it by looking at them."

Stanislaw Tatum smiled in spite of himself, in spite of the situation. "I've heard Nick say that there's a direct correlation between a man's intelligence and the ugliness of his Hawaiian shirts."

Linc managed a half-grin. "If so, then Nick's the smartest man alive."

The rain stopped as if a switch had been thrown and in the sudden silence Casper cleared his throat. "That's not what I meant, though. We also should call them because of . . . Marcus and Devon."

Linc's pencil snapped in his hand. "Oh crap. Weren't they just—"

"They were friends. Very good friends. Maybe more, or maybe they would have been more. Who knows? But after what happened to his wife . . ."

Linc nodded, then let out a long sigh as if his body was deflating. His face said he dreaded delivering news that might crack an ordinary man's psyche, that might make an ordinary man think the sea held a personal grudge against him. The only consolation was that Marcus

Oden was not ordinary; though, in truth, Linc was not sure he had not cracked long ago.

Linc opened the worn notebook containing shortwave frequencies.

Chapter 4

Gastro Nister paddled a one-man outrigger canoe across the clear lagoon embraced by Tanua's coral arms. He used the same steady rhythm that had propelled the ancient Polynesians across the bright Pacific while Europe was still scratching and itching its way through the Dark Ages. With coral-white hair that brushed sun-bronzed shoulders, he could have been one of those ancient voyagers, but the near-violet blue of his eyes betrayed roots that lay elsewhere.

The canoe was small but the outrigger, or ama, would stabilize the craft in all but the roughest seas, when it was necessary to remember to 'lean ama' to plant that slim strand of koa wood firmly on the back of Tangaroa, the Polynesian sea god.

Gastro shipped his paddle and scanned his world. The island was a green tooth embedded in a seamless blue void melded from a soft lapis sky and a powder sea. The swell was low and the waves were curves of glass.

He rapped the paddle against the canoe hull, once, twice, and then in quick succession two more times. He paddled further, watching bright corals and electric fish, and rapped again. At a flash below he smiled and balanced the paddle across the bulwarks of the canoe.

Katya's head appeared fifteen meters away. His daughter waved then backflipped with the ease of an otter. Gastro felt a surge of fatherly pride. At twenty-four she was embracing her womanhood and showing the same lithe grace that earned her mother an Olympic gymnastics medal and the heart of a precocious medical student.

Gastro removed a square of wood from beneath his feet to reveal a clear plate surrounded by heavy dabs of caulk. He owned what was perhaps the world's only glass-bottomed canoe. Blue barrel sponges and banded sea snakes scrolled beneath but Gastro saw only his daughter, either through his underwater viewport or directly when she surfaced. She breathed easily and Gastro held his own breath as he watched. Finally he let out a sigh of relief. Over a decade after the miracle, the wonder remained fresh. Fresher than ever, perhaps, given its longevity.

Katya edged into the blue mist, dissolving away, but Gastro knew she would return. While he waited he ran his eyes over Tanua—the volcanic cone of black rock, the lush slopes, the shockingly white beaches. It was, he realized once again, a kind of paradise. It had great natural beauty and no pollution, and so far man's occupation had left few scars. Even the main town of Sava nestled comfortably and discretely against the low hills. As on many islands the native life was curiously barren; there were no large native mammals except for the fruit bats with their fox-like faces and four-foot wings and cat-sized bodies. The parallel which interested Gastro most was that Tanua did have a native serpent—the Tanuan boa. How it had arrived was a mystery but here it was. Jungles, fruit, and a serpent, he mused. Perhaps those Polynesians who believed the actual Garden of Eden was on one of their islands were more correct than they could have suspected. Prescient, even. There was already one miracle afoot on Tanua, though its genesis lay miles and years away.

Two weeks before Katya's tenth birthday she had been returning with her mother from the San Francisco Zoo—one of her very favorite daytrips—when the accident happened. The details had always been fuzzy but Gastro was not of the sort that required them. Three other cars, at least one driver impaired by alcohol if not outright drunk, a litter of bloody wreckage off an embankment.

Katya and Ekaterina had arrived at the trauma center, which by macabre coincidence was in the same hospital as Gastro's thoracic surgery and across the street from his genetics lab. When he saw his wife's skull and spinal injuries he knew that at best she would be a shadow of her past self. At worst, well, it was not clear what the worst was. The worst might be the best.

In the hospital chapel Gastro met the driver who had caused the accident, a man whose own son had died. Although Gastro knew intellectually that this tattooed creature who likely owned several motorcycles had not intended the accident he was surprised at the forgiveness in his heart and together the two men prayed. It was the first time in thirty-six years that Gastro had appealed to a greater power. It was also the last.

Ekaterina died three days later. Through his anguish Gastro knew this to be a blessing in many ways, for Ekaterina's life would have been one of too much pain for a woman he loved so much.

At least he still had Katya. She was in critical condition with burns and a broken femur but she was expected to survive, and largely intact. Gastro and Ekaterina had emigrated from Romania together and neither had a taste for socializing; their family unit was small and tight and paring it by one-third was daunting. But at least there were still two; through the logarithmic math of familial relationships two together were infinitely stronger than one alone.

Then Katya had come down with pneumonia. The infection should have yielded to standard antibiotics like ampicillin or vancomycin but did not. The infection worsened and Katya's lungs began to fill with fluid. Plasma began to leak into her alveolar sacs and collapse them, leaving no room for air. Katya's rosy complexion began to edge towards blue.

Gastro understood the prognosis. Within the span of one month he would lose both wife and child.

Losing his only child to a respiratory ailment, after a career spent fighting just such demons, was too cruel even for a Romanian accustomed by breeding to suffering.

When Katya had a mere forty-eight hours of life left Gastro made his decision. He entered the hospital late at night with the simple bottles and tubes he needed and set up at Katya's beside. The procedure would almost certainly work; of that he had no doubt. It was less certain whether success was better than failure.

He realized that his decision was for himself as much as for the nine-year-old waif lying helpless in a hospital bed, but he saw no option. He sedated her with Demerol and Pavulon and saw her tightened features relax, then watched her take the ragged inhalation that might be her last breath. When she exhaled he trickled a liquid perfluorocarbon down her windpipe and into her lungs. The Teflon-like liquid could carry oxygen and carbon dioxide and would displace the plasma that was clogging her lungs. But it was still a liquid and when it hit the lungs it triggered instincts that not even anesthetics could suppress. Katya stiffened and convulsed with the drowning reflex, fighting to climb above the level of the liquid as eons of evolution had trained her little body to believe it must. Gastro felt tears well in his eyes as he held her down and his own fluid dripped onto her face as the perfluorocarbon flooded her lungs.

The spasms passed and he attached a standard ventilator to oxygen-ate the perfluorocarbon. The liquid constantly evaporated and he set up an automatic drip to replenish it.

Katya's lungs might be too damaged to sift oxygen from the air and might even be too scarred to heal. But Gastro vowed that she would not die for such minutiae.

The task seemed trivial though it was not: one-fifth of the atmos-phere was oxygen and it was merely necessary to transport a tiny bit of that across a thin barrier of skin and into Katya's blood. Different organisms used a host of devices for this; some insects simply let oxygen seep through gaps and crevices, an approach workable only with the geometry of a tiny body. But there were two other approaches endorsed by evolution: lungs, and the aquatic equivalent, gills. Neither presented an immediate solution and Gastro knew he would have to focus on regeneration and healing, perhaps all the way to the molecular level. It was the cruel joke of an irreverent god, he would muse late at night while drinking a fine cabernet, that the merest lizard could re-grow what it lost while supposedly advanced humans were doomed to wear their injuries forever. Perhaps someday humans would evolve as far as lizards.

Until then there was the perfluorocarbon.

Katya rose again below the canoe with her dark hair floating in a halo. As he watched her his eyes welled with tears. She was not the same and never would she be the same but she lived. And perhaps she was better. He saw her lips purse and then grin and knew that once again she had read him. She made the chopping gesture that meant she had a serious topic to discuss, then, while still underwater, flashed the signs she still preferred though no longer were they necessary.

When she finished Gastro wore his surprise on his face. Coming from anyone else he would have instantly refused the request but he had a weak spot for Katya; not only was she his sole remaining family she was also, like her mother, an expert at manipulating him. Even so what she wanted was too dangerous though admirably charitable. Life honored life, he had taught her. But not this time. Not this way.

He flashed his answer back to her.

She shook her head in anger and Gastro saw more than a trace of his beloved Ekaterina. The same arch of the neck, the same flash of the eyes. He would have thought Katya was imitating but she had been so young when her mother was lost.

No, he repeated.

Katya flared, eyes afire, and her hands shot signals that were chiding and impatient. She enjoyed inventing not only curses but also the signs to express them and after a series of anatomically evocative moves she finished her tirade with three words. Life honors life, she reminded him. The abyss awaited them all and it was the duty of the living to preserve living. To move life forward.

Gastro paused and Katya hovered as a neon cleaner wrasse inspected her tanned left knee. He agreed with her argument and respected her sentiments. Of course he did, he reminded himself. They were his own. But the application to these facts troubled him. Then again perhaps as Katya sometimes teased he had become too conservative in his old age. What, he asked himself, would he have done twenty years before? One did not win battles by retreating; one only avoided defeat. He was too old to avoid defeat.

He nodded to himself and presented a different signal.

Katya thrust her head into the sun, smiling, then plunged into the blue below, rolling beneath the canoe and waving. Gastro held her gaze until she turned away then he began paddling towards shore. He did not look back. There was no longer anything to see.

Chapter 5

"I hate this," Nick said from the tight confines of the right seat of the cockpit. The throttle, mixture, and propeller controls hung from above like demented steel fruits, while the view ahead over the old Catalina's broad nose showed a frightening slice of sea far below and the suspended anvils of isolated thunderstorms all around. "Remember what happened to Icarus?"

"An aviation pioneer who had a good life and a quick end."

"Glenn Miller? Aerosmith? Patsy Cline?"

Marcus flipped a row of overhead switches to transfer fuel between wing tanks and keep the big plane in trim. "All famous, all singers. You, in contrast, are just a gravel-voiced ex-professor. Perfectly safe."

Nick snorted and glanced over his right shoulder at the plane's blue wing. He couldn't see the white one. "Their planes probably had wings the same color."

"And what good did it do them?" Marcus replied. Then, to derail a pointless conversation of exactly the sort that Nick enjoyed, he eased the yoke forward to lower the nose and gestured.

"There's Tanua."

Thirty miles ahead and two below a green pyramid held apart the sea and sky. Beside it rose a black spire. The view brought to mind the shortwave call received from this very place the night before: There had been an accident. No one knew exactly what or why, yet. Two: Devon Lucas and a scientist. Yes, they had called the Navy, and yes, they were coming. A week. A week. There was a problem with surface transport. Yes, they knew. They understood what it meant. They didn't have any choice, did they? One doesn't just swim a thousand feet down.

Afterward Marcus lifted the shortwave and threw it, it seemed to Nick, over the moon, which hung low and full on the eastern horizon. That this was a mere illusion was confirmed seconds later when the radio exploded on a coral boulder. A few hours after that the sky pinked and Marcus firewalled the throttles and the Catalina lumbered into the air, bound for the green fang of Tanua eight hundred miles to the east.

"Allow me to consult the bible," Nick said with forced levity as he pulled the Lonely Planet guide to the South Pacific from a canvas pocket on the bulkhead. That something had happened to *Omega* was terrifying. That they were going to do something about it was worse. He dusted off the tired guidebook and, despite his inner dread, tried to hit his usual flippant note as he began turning pages.

"Where should I start? The restaurants? The hotels? The fabulous shopping?"

"Tell me about the harbor," Marcus said, knowing he would soon have to put the big plane down.

Nick ran a thick finger down a page slick with humidity and sighed.

"May as well. There aren't any decent restaurants, hotels, or shops. The bay is big and sheltered and should be good for landing, but don't expect a five-course sunset dining experience unless you're missing one from your six-pack." He grinned but received no response except seeing Marcus run his hands over the controls in the pre-landing ritual that always made him nervous. Though he disliked flying he particularly disliked landing and taking off. He felt that he should like landing, since it involved returning to earth, but he knew it to be just one slip away from crashing, which tended to ruin it for him. He returned to the book.

"Tabu is the local name for that island with the black spire just to the north of Tanua. At low tide it actually touches Tanua. Officially they're one island but the islanders don't see it that way."

He turned a page. "This area has the usual long and bloody history. Strike that, an unusually long and bloody history. Tanua lies just north of the kingdom of Tonga, once known as the Friendly Isles despite the tendency of the locals to eat each other and especially, when they could get them, Europeans. Dining habits were about the same in the Samoas and—here's a jolly fact—were particularly grue-some here on Tanua. The ancient kingdoms of Samoa and Tonga fought lots of battles over Tanua, and everyone from the losing side would be slaughtered every time it changed hands. So Tanua is also known as the Isle of Long Pig—you remember that humans were known as "long pig" for their long torsos and porky taste?"

Marcus looked at him expressionlessly and Nick flipped through the last few pages and summarized. Tanua had no airport and only a weekly ferry. What foreigners were there—known as *palangis* to the islanders—were mostly scientists, often anthropologists, seeking to follow in Margaret Mead's sandals, and a few hardy tourists. Traditional culture ran strong and the island was home to a group of secessionists calling themselves the Matai, who sought an end to all western influence and a return to traditional ways. Nick finished with a list of famous Tanuans—several NFL players, a world sumo champion, a Hawaiian singer—and put the book away.

The cockpit misted with the first fetid hints of jungle, loamy and earthy compared to the clean ocean smell, and Nick half-turned to study Marcus, who, compared to his own shot-putter's bulk, had the lean wiriness of a mountaineer. They had been through many things and Nick knew Marcus to have a knack for doing things that couldn't be done; he held degrees in biology and veterinary medicine, and after a year with NASA waiting for a flight that never came, he now spent his days piloting a vintage seaplane around the South Pacific.

Though neither would admit it, their friendship was stronger for the rivalry that preceded it; after their first meeting on the football field they became better acquainted in the more genteel sport of track and field. Then in a deft midnight raid in their senior year, Marcus stole the Axe, an icon of their schools' rivalry that was awarded each year to the winner of the football game, from its place in Stanford's sports pavilion and faxed a picture of it and the day's newspaper to Nick. Two days later there was another night raid and the Axe reappeared in Palo Alto in the hands of a large Greek. A return fax followed.

As grad students they roomed together and, on a solid foundation of intellectual and athletic rivalry, grew a bulletproof friendship. Marcus came to realize that Nick enjoyed playing the part of the big affable oaf, but that under his garrulous exterior was a razor sharp mind and a deep compassion. Nick found in Marcus a mix of brilliance and bravery, perhaps with a large dose of recklessness. Since Callie had vanished, that streak of recklessness had broadened, and now Nick felt like he worried as much as the proverbial Greek mother Marcus accused him of becoming.

Even so, he could not hold his tongue.

"Marcus, this is a bad idea. Let's not do this. I've got a funny feeling."

"You always have a funny feeling."

"I often do," Nick admitted, then waved at the cargo bay. "But this time with good reason. That thing is at least twenty years old and probably hasn't been wet in ten. It might not keep you dry in the shower. We haven't tested it. And you're going to try to go down a thousand feet in it."

Marcus removed a pair of sunglasses from a shirt pocket and slipped the frames under his headset. The twin shields faced Nick.

"No choice, Nick."

Marcus held his gaze and Nick searched his face, as if he would be able to detect the difference between the self-sacrifice of a rescue and the self-destruction of a death wish. He tried a different tack.

"Marcus, how long have we known each other?"

"Since Big Game day, sophomore year of college. About 3:12 pm, if I recall."

Nick winced at the memory of the vicious tackle.

"Right. College, plus grad school, plus six years here in the South Seas. Long enough for me to be worried about what you're up to."

"If you have a better idea I'm listening."

Nick laid a great paw on Marcus' shoulder. "I just hope this is really about a missing sub. And not something else."

Marcus double-checked that the gear was up and the Catalina configured for a water landing. From above, Tanua was roughly circular with a bite missing from its western edge. He picked up the wind direction from blowing palms and rolled wings level, flying downwind away from the bay. The black finger of Tabu passed off the left wing.

"This isn't about Callie or even Devon; this is about a sub and two people who need help only we can give. What happened to Callie doesn't matter, and my relationship with Devon—or lack of one—doesn't either."

"It's just that it wasn't far from here—"

"That Callie's boat was lost," Marcus finished. "Maybe a hundred miles, more or less."

"You feel guilty that you weren't there. There was nothing you could have done. It wouldn't have been any different if you were there."

"Probably not." But six days after the *Nefertiti* vanished Marcus was in the South Pacific. He took a leave from NASA and borrowed the old flying boat from a friend of his father's in Hawaii and retraced the *Nefertiti*'s route. From a hundred feet, from a thousand feet, from five thousand feet.

He found nothing. But what was supposed to be sojourn of a few days was now in its sixth year. In his third week, while refueling at a small island near Nuku 'alofa, the lethargic islanders mentioned that the fish from their reef were sick and so were they. Marcus donned his dive gear and toured the reef. The cause was simple; a broken pipe spilling sewage. At the next stop the islanders asked him about an epidemic of parasitic worms on their fish and he looked at their samples. He identified the parasite and explained which fish would still be safe to eat, and a small reputation began to grow. Marcus became a minor celebrity when he cured the King of Tonga's pet elephant of a troubling cough and in return received the title to a tiny atoll with a square mile of land with groves of mango and coconut, leading some to call him King Marcus. Emperor, he would correct them.

Within a few months he put the life savings that would have been the down payment on a home into buying the plane and forming the Ocean Sciences Institute. Nick complained bitterly but immediately joined up. In six years he had not left and sometimes it seemed like he had lodged at least one complaint on every one of those two thousand days.

The plane banked and the blue horizon cut diagonally across the pitted windscreen as the green island swelled.

"Sometimes I think you're the Greek, not me. This is like one of those myths. Searching far and wide, high and low, for year after year."

"Here we go," Marcus said, dropping the flaps and rolling onto final. The deep indigo at the center of the bay was ringed by light blue that was in turn edged by pale green frosted by the brilliant white of the beaches.

Marcus touched a rudder pedal and dipped a wing to slip past something that broke the water. A head. He glimpsed a girl's face with wet dark hair, bright green eyes, and full lips rounding in surprise. For a moment the features seemed familiar and his autonomic nervous system gave a jolt that shot flutters from his spine to his fingertips. But it was not his lost wife.

"See that?" he asked.

"What?" Nick replied.

"Nothing." Somehow Nick never saw the weird things the ocean threw at Marcus. This girl, for example, who for a moment resembled Callie. She had to be an excellent diver to be out so far and down so long he had not seen her before. Nick, unaware of swimming females, was thinking of an ancient black-toothed village chief and fisherman in the Cook Islands. The old man, so thin his head looked like a black-painted skull, took Nick by the arm, led him to the beach, and pointed seaward with an arm bone.

"That," the old chief rasped, "is an open grave."

The flying boat's hull thumped onto the water.

Exactly thirty-five minutes later the *Aurora* cast off her moorings and sent into the blue sky a cloud of black that hung like a charcoal smear on a watercolor. The last twenty-five of those minutes were used to transfer a large crate from the Catalina's hold to the ship; the first ten were needed to convince Linc Cafferty to do it. After heaving the stern line Marcus joined Linc and Nick on the fantail, where they stood over the pine box. Marcus ran his eyes over the smooth blue of the bay, over which stood black peaks dabbed with bright green. There was no sign of the girl.

"Didn't mean for you to come. No need for a geologist and biolo-gist," Linc was saying again.

"Stow it. By pure dumb luck we just bought exactly what you need," Marcus said while edging a pry bar beneath the lid of the crate.

Linc shrugged.

"By the way, where are your deck hands?"

Linc cocked his head and regarded Marcus. In his battered shorts, hiking boots, and ripped tank top he looked more like an athletic castaway than an expert field biologist. Then again, Linc recalled, most field biologists tended to look like some flavor of misfit. In contrast, with his usual aloha shirt draped across enormous shoulders, Nick looked like a vacationing professional linebacker, and Linc had never known a geologist to look anything like that.

"A few are missing. Maybe they couldn't get back—we did leave on short notice. But we have enough of a skeleton crew. We're not going far."

A massive Fijian with skin almost black turned away from the winch he was oiling. An incongruously tiny pendant sparkled at his throat.

"They wish to avoid more trouble," he said in a soft baritone that plowed though the lap of waves and the luff of the wind. "But it is too late. There is no escaping it now." He continued serenely up the deck, oiling machinery.

"Well that's cheery," Nick said.

"Everyone's a bit on edge," Linc said and took up a hammer to join in ripping nails from the crate. "Especially the islanders."

"Breadfruit," the diminutive Stanislaw Tatum said.

"Breadfruit?" Nick asked.

"Breadfruit. It's one of the things I've picked up in the six months I've been here on Tanua. This year the breadfruit trees have been bearing triple, rather than single, fruit. Single fruit are normal. Double are considered a sign of a hurricane year. Triple are even worse. They mean that something very bad will happen."

"Like what's happened?" Marcus grunted while levering the pry bar.

The little geophysicist smiled. "No. Not at all. Something much worse."

Marcus lifted his head from the crate to look at water that was shading to violet beneath whitecaps spawned by a freshening breeze.

"Who was Devon with?"

"Henry Winston. Princeton geologist."

"Met him at a conference in Seattle," Nick said. "Good man. I thought he hated diving."

Linc nodded and shrugged at the same time.

"Bet he really hates it now," Nick muttered.

"Nick," Marcus said, and pointed at the box. Most of the nails were out and Marcus had levered up the lid a few inches. Nick slid his hands into the gap and his shoulders bunched. The remaining nails shrieked.

"Just remember this wasn't my idea," he said as he set the lid aside.

"Wasn't mine either," Marcus agreed softly.

Two islanders gasped and stepped back. Looking up from the crate was a metallic head pierced by round ports, atop a metal body with big round knee and elbow joints. Half medieval suit of armor and half spacesuit.

"An honest to god Jim suit," Linc said. "Named after Jim something or other, who made the first one decades ago in Britain. I haven't seen one of these in twenty years."

"It's a bit of an antique," Nick said.

"A classic," Marcus suggested.

"Where'd you get it?"

Linc looked at Nick and Nick looked at Marcus.

"An oil company," answered Marcus. "They used it for rig maintenance for years, then mothballed it a while ago. We picked it up cheap. Our budget is a bit tight."

"So I've heard," Linc replied, turning sternward to eye the heavily patched flying boat in the distance. "When did it last dive?"

"Ten years."

Linc's mouth actually fell open. "Jesus. And the last maintenance?"

Nick and Marcus exchanged a look.

"Jesus," Linc repeated. "Ten years again, eh? You know how to work it?"

Marcus nodded after a pause. "I got a dry check out; not much to it. No power and no thrusters. Two simple hand controls for the pincers. Just wear it and walk, as best you can. I was going to start with shallow water trials at our Kiribati site, and then use it for deep biological work and observations. This particular suit went to fourteen hundred feet fifteen years ago."

Linc was shaking his head and pulling on his beard. "And you want to take this eggshell down twelve hundred feet and hang a cable onto *Omega*? You know the pressure down there is over five hundred pounds per square inch? You know if the suit leaks—"

Marcus raised a hand. "I know. Nick never lets me forget. At that depth if the suit fails I get crushed so fast I don't even get to drown. But no one else here fits, and no one else has trained at all. So I'm elected."

Linc shifted from foot to foot, his thick brow beetling, then placed hands on hips and thrust his chest forward.

"You sure about this?"

Marcus smiled though his eyes held cold. "No. But let's do it anyway."

Linc scratched at chin stubble that defied all attempts at shaving. "Alright. Let's. Before you come to your senses."

The squat engineer dredged up what he remembered about a Jim suit. The joints were oil-filled and would stiffen with pressure. The faceplate tended to fog. The whole thing, in essence a wearable submarine, was bulky and clumsy and claustrophobic. But it could work.

Linc pulled out a piece of paper marked with the blurry lines of a sonar map and sketched on it a big X and a few crosshatches. "This is the sub and this is the main vent field where they were collecting samples. Some of the jets are over three hundred degrees centigrade, hot enough to melt Lexan and some metals. The gradient is steep so the water cools in just a few inches, but you can't hover. So watch your step or you might get a hot foot."

The ship swept past a small outrigger canoe paddled by a lone white-haired man. The *Aurora*'s wake rocked the frail canoe but the paddler rode the swells with ease and did not even bother to take them bow on. He turned as the ship passed and Nick saw the white gleam of the ship reflected for a moment in the man's eyes.

The man was a tiny figure when the *Aurora*'s engines slowed and the ship took on a new pitching motion. Marcus glanced at the shore, comparing the angle of the town of Sava to the peak of Tanua and the black cone of Tabu, fixing their position by landmarks. It was an old habit.

"Almost there," Linc said.

Marcus unclamped the suit's head and hinged it forward like a huge metal mouth, then wedged himself down the steel throat.

Chapter 6

From his canoe Gastro Nister watched the research ship fly past. A cluster of men stood on the fantail and one, a giant with a thick mane of black hair and a non-Polynesian cast to his features, looked straight through him with eyes like onyx torches. Another, smaller but leanly muscular, worked at some task on deck.

Gastro rapped his paddle against the canoe twice, paused, then rapped again. He did not expect Katya to appear and she did not.

But something strange was afoot. First the white research ship appeared. Then came Katya's request. Followed by the arrival of the airplane—Gastro had not even seen an airplane in years. And now the research ship hurrying seaward with a group of purposeful newcomers.

Gastro rapped again, and again. Katya was headstrong but dutiful and he believed that if she heard him she would obey and appear. At least he hoped so. Her willingness to disobey gave her no reason to refuse, for if she disliked his instructions she would give him a quirky smile then shrug and vanish and do as she pleased. It had happened before. It would happen again.

Gastro stroked the water with his paddle, moving the heavy hull—the ka'ale—through the bright slap of the waves. He enjoyed the solid heft of the koa paddle which had been made in the traditional way by island craftsmen. The ka'ale was made in the same traditional way, by hollowing a log with fire. Though Gastro's long-fingered hands were comfortable with supercomputers, laser scalpels, and micropipettes, they could also recognize the inherent rightness of ancient technologies refined through centuries of craftsmanship.

He rapped once more. Still no Katya. Perhaps she was out of earshot.

Gastro saw the ship slow and turn into the swells. A glint of something on deck. Now he had a bad feeling. He rapped the paddle again. And again. He pulled up the wooden plate but saw nothing but slanting blue beams.

In the water among those same blue beams Marcus sank easily, the cable paying out until the anti-fouling red of *Aurora*'s hull shrank to a clot of coagulation adrift in sun-shot cobalt. The helmet had four round viewports: one straight ahead, one forty-five degrees up, and one facing each forward quarter. Looking down he saw that azure rays pointed the way. Rather, part of the way. He was going beyond them, past where they seemed to converge. Upward he could see the slim strand of steel connecting him to the ship.

"How's it look?" Nick's voice cracked over the cable-borne intercom.

"Like a long away," Marcus replied, taking a breath of air tinged with oil and old sweat. He felt a strange mixture of relaxation and tension; it was always good to be back in the sea and the deeper the better. But the suit was an unknown and he might be about to find the body of a friend.

At three hundred feet he tried the elbows and knees. All had stiffened and the left elbow was almost frozen. He moved the joints back and forth and looked out at the violet tinged world, thinking of Devon descending through these waters just a day before. She had always loved the deep, had claimed to prefer the purple abyss to the bright blue of sky. He wondered what she thought about that now. If she thought at all.

At four hundred feet the joints were moving better. The ship was a barely visible dimness on the mist above.

At four hundred eighty feet there was a deep pocking sound that he felt as much as heard. The suit shivered and he flinched but there was no rush of water and no vise-like squeeze. A shaft of glitter fell away. One of his two lights had shattered.

At six hundred feet the ship was gone and only a deep blue twilight loomed above. Below lay a velvety dark. It was like being lowered from a night sky into a black lake.

The problem with the Jim suit, which was actually a tiny one-man submersible, was that he could not feel the sea on his skin. More than he would admit to Nick, his wife stayed on his mind and these waters might hold what was left of Callie, or might hold the answer to where she had gone. For a long time, perhaps even before she had vanished, he had felt that the sea held many answers, and this was true in a scientific sense but it was not this that had drawn him in. Perhaps it was some resonance with ancient creatures that had gone before, or perhaps, as Nick suggested, he just liked to see the bikinis. He had learned to dive as a boy in Alaska, in a patched and leaky dry suit, and even after becoming a pilot and a scientist he felt that simply submerging in the sea gave something to a person that couldn't be gained in any other way. He knew that it made no scientific sense, that the sea didn't actually balance out electrolytes or cleanse one's aura, but he felt it and he left it at that.

At a thousand feet he found himself in a world of darkness so perfect that the helmet ports could have been painted over. He placed his hands against the cold glass, fingertips less than an inch from crushingly pressurized ice water filled with creatures unknown. Even in the twenty-first century most deep sea animals remain unknown; exploring this frontier was one of the goals of the Ocean Sciences Institute, one of the reasons he was building an artificial gill that would allow men to submerge indefinitely, and the reason for buying the Jim suit.

At twelve hundred feet the cable jerked and slowed and Marcus thumbed the switch for the lights. Only the intact one worked and it cast but a pale yellow pool. That was enough to see the bottom rising and a moment later his metal feet crunched onto rock. Three yards to the left a four-foot volcano erupted black smoke mixed with yellow specks, while on the right, a series of orange and black ridges jagged the seafloor. White flecks swirled and pale fish wandered past. Marcus turned and found the suit even more clumsy than he had feared but he was able to see that behind him lay more black smokers and a grove of giant tubeworms beside a field of mollusks. He had traveled less than a mile but arrived in another world.

"Down," he announced.

A long pause from the world of light and air, then: "You're two hundred meters south. Sorry—the current pushed you."

Marcus clicked an acknowledgment and checked his compass then began the rolling gait that would carry him north. The suit was clumsy and heavy and he felt as if he were walking in a full-body cast. Despite the chill of the metal he was sweating within a hundred meters. Four times he found himself in small canyons that a child could have run up but which he could not manage and each time he had to backtrack and choose another line.

Walking the seafloor showed why evolution chose fins over feet. With poor traction and worse mobility he slipped on slopes covered with slimy bacteria and slick limpets and had to detour around pumping volcanoes that could boil him. He tried to skirt the groves of seven-foot tubeworms but they were bracketed by hot jets and he had to plow in. Each worm was six feet of chalk-white tube topped by a foot of bright red flesh, like a giant lipstick. They bunched as tight as subway passengers and at the first touch of a steel claw the red flesh vanished. As each worm ducked, its neighbor sensed the vibration and also hid. Marcus watched a wave of worm fear sweep beyond the cast of his puny light. Sweat dripped into his eyes and he blinked.

He leaned into the mass and some of the stiff tubes cracked and others gripped and tugged. As he stepped, the viewports showed only the splay of worm bodies and an occasional drifting chunk of broken shell or ripped red meat.

Then he was through and onto a carpet of mussels and clams. Two anglerfish and an eel came up as if curious at the commotion and the eel slipped through his legs. After thirty minutes the sonar from above put him twenty-five meters away but the sandy lane he was following ended in a box canyon. The walls were too steep to climb and he cursed the maze. A fish that looked like a big-eyed trout stared at him and levitated as if either taunting or showing the way. He wiped the condensation from the faceplate and staggered onward.

A glance at the battery gauge drew another curse—the decrepit, ancient cell was failing. Marcus eyed his course and punched off the light. For the next forty meters he traveled in blackness pierced by flashes of light. Each flash showed a startled fish or a grove of ancient worms or groups of barnacles or shrimp, some of which had barely changed since the time of the dinosaurs. It was an eerie slideshow in which, sometimes, he thought he saw glimmers or glows.

He looped around, flashing like a lighthouse, until a different glow reflected. One that was bigger and brighter and yellow.

"He should be there soon," said Nick Kondos, eyeing the quivering strand of steel that led from the ship's deck to another world far below.

"You think he'll find it?" asked Linc.

Nick nodded. "He'll find it."

Linc regarded Nick with the same studious gaze that the big Greek was training on the ocean.

"You two are supposedly quite a pair. Lots of stories out there."

"Lies and exaggerations."

"You really met in a football game?"

Nick pulled his gaze from the cable. He prided himself on never telling a tale the same way twice, and he told this story often. But this time he was not in the mood to fabricate.

"We did."

"How do you guys manage to do so many projects?"

Nick's eyes stayed fixed on the point where the cable met the sea. "You know what they say about the wicked."

"But there are just the two of—"

"Got it," cracked Marcus' voice over the intercom.

The sub lay at an angle in another steep-walled box canyon. Rubble lay all around. Her paint was chipped and much of her external gear broken.

After his call to topside Marcus wanted to peer into the ports and bang on the hull but instead he readied the lift cable in a steel claw. A boulder lay before the nose and he used it as a step.

Linc's voice came to him, hollow and tinny after passing through the sea. "Have you tried looking in the viewports?"

"All dark," he coughed, for his air was getting thick. "But the hull looks sound. Stand by."

As he ascended past the main viewport he twisted back and forth to coax the dull glow from his lamp to penetrate. Then the angles worked.

He swore and jumped. From the three feet away he stared at the yellow hulk. The sweat on his back and chest turned cold and clammy.

"Marcus?" A few moments later the call came again, and then again.

Marcus fought the urge to look over his shoulder though he knew the blackness held things. He knew that now more than ever.

"Slipped," he lied. "Attaching cable now. Stand by." He fastened one claw and then the other around broken attachments on *Omega*'s hull and pulled himself up until he reached the top. He finally ran the clip through the ring.

"Ready to hoist," he called while flexing the muscles of his arms and shoulders and stomach in an attempt to warm himself. The dark around him was sucking energy and he gazed upward at a lighter shade of black. The cable grew taut then shivered and the sub began to rise.

They reached the surface together. Nick dove into the water and attached the line from the auxiliary derrick to the Jim suit and within moments they were on deck. Marcus was surprised that Nick had descended into the sea voluntarily and he saw relief in the big Greek's eyes. That would not last, he knew. As he popped the helmet he saw a jubilant crew and had the same thought again.

Omega bobbed alongside the mother ship as a lone bushy figure stood on the small sub, rocking in the swell. Linc fought to reach the hatch and three times he reached it and three times the sea twisted it from beneath his grasp. Then he put both hands to it, braced his squat legs against the sail, and twisted. The handle moved.

Linc thrust his head inside. He did not emerge triumphant; did not lend a hand to anyone below; did not twist and jerk with body language as if talking. He did not move at all. The little man and the little sub rose and fell, rose and fell, rose and fell. Silence covered the crew.

Linc's hands finally pressed downward and he emerged, face blank. No one else rose behind him; the hatch remained empty as the mouth of a corpse. He signaled the crane operator to lift the sub aboard and he rode the slick hull with both hands gripping the lift cable. The setting sun threw blood on an oily sea.

As the sub's muddy skids touched the deck a crowd surged forward, ignoring the crane boss' calls to stay clear. The men pressed against the chin bubble.

They recoiled as if stung.

Some began crossing themselves. A few mouthed prayers. Two collapsed. Toma the Fijian ripped something shiny from his neck and heaved it over the rail.

Nick crossed the pitching deck and peered through the port.

"You knew," he said when he returned to Marcus, who stood soaked and limp by the rail with his hands wrapped around a paper cup of hot water, all he could find.

Marcus nodded, his eyes never straying from a sea fading to coffin gray in the dusk. Neither man looked at the submersible which squatted behind them.

"I don't understand," Nick said.

"I don't either."

"It can't be."

"It is."

"They're gone."

Marcus nodded once. "They're gone."

Chapter 7

Gastro Nister entered his lab long after sunset. He preferred nights, when the cool and the quiet seemed to allow a greater focus. His best work often came at hours comfortable for a vampire.

He slipped on a sweater and added a white lab coat against the chill of a room that was, he knew, the coldest for two thousand miles in any direction. But computers and separation columns, electrophoresis wells and automated pipettes, incubators and cell sorters all worked better without the infernal press of heat. So too did the all-important element of humans. How could one concentrate on extracting eons-old capabilities with sweat running down one's nose?

The lab occupied one building of an old copra plantation in a narrow valley on the forbidden isle of Tabu, and the peeling paint and decaying masonry gave the place a calculated look of abandonment. But things were not what they seemed and the wolf in this sheep's clothing was sleek and mean. Behind hidden double doors and a low-pressure system the labs were sparkling and bright, with black shiny benches, polished floors, gleaming sinks and fume hoods, and everywhere the hum of equipment. Had there been any government inspectors assigned to the islands they would have been startled to learn that these hidden labs qualified for Biosafety Level 4 protection, a level adequate to house Ebola and matched by only a few mainland labs. There were, however, no inspectors.

Gastro rubbed his temples while gazing at a bank of equipment. A two-liter Pyrex flask of transfected *E. coli* would soon be ready for harvesting; a DNA robot of the sort that sequenced the human genome years ahead of schedule was midway through its task; a bank of column chromatography units busily separated proteins. Many procedures in molecular biology typically run for hours, and clever researchers leave their experiments to work for them. Gastro was a master in this and he liked to say that his work had not taken a break in decades. Something was always growing or spinning or consolidating or running.

Normally he would tour each experiment with excitement but tonight he could not. He was too unsettled.

The last days had not gone as anticipated. First had come the white research ship and then a vast old flying boat; if the first was bad then the second was much worse. Nothing could be done now for as Caesar said, some years before being knifed to death, the die was cast. Gastro agreed with the sentiment but hoped for a different outcome.

His eyes flicked to the stainless sink holding what looked like two ordinary water glasses. Each was wrapped in orange biohazard plastic and each would be bleached and autoclaved. They were not ordinary water glasses.

Katya entered the lab with wet hair pulled back around her full-lipped face. She kissed him on the forehead.

"Hello, Papa."

His return smile was fragile and, as usual, she read it and wrapped her arms around him and squeezed until he returned the embrace.

"Papa, it will be fine."

"This has never happened before."

She pulled back to fix him with eyes of deep blue shot with sea green. "It was unforeseeable. But we followed our rules. We did as you always say. We chose to—" and here she paused for him to join her.

"Honor life," they said together.

Her eyes went to the sink. "It is done?"

"It was done before the plane came. But perhaps—"

"No, Papa. That was the right thing. It was as it had to be."

"You know what could happen. To both of them. We have seen it before."

"Too many times," she agreed, then tilted her chin downward to look up at him. "But Papa, they say you cannot make an omelet without breaking eggs."

Gastro's eyes glistened. "I never wanted to break any eggs, Katya. Only to save one."

"And you have done not only that but so much more."

Gastro nodded. He knew that over the years he had come to rely on Katya, drawing her strength for himself and even letting her judgment sway his. Now he wondered if that might have gone too far. What started as the saving of one priceless little girl had led to so much more, to so many more.

Once again she read him.

"Stop worrying, Papa," she chided. "You will grow old before your time."

"Maybe it is my time."

"Nonsense."

He studied her; when he had his eyes on the flesh and blood that he had brought into this world with his body and kept in this world with his mind he knew that he had done only what he must and that it was right. It had taken some time to come to this thinking, and even now the dregs of doubt lived on, bubbling to the surface late at night when giant Tongan bats winged across the silver moon. But those doubts could not survive the flash of Katya's eyes or the glint of her smile. Saving her had been the only thing to do. And having done that, he could not let her be the only one. It would have been cruel to her and even, according to his new philosophy, unfair to Life. Life is change, he knew, and the duty of the living is to spread life. Humans were not outside the process; they *were* the process.

There had been a time when his thinking was relatively undeveloped and it had been forced to evolve when he first found a way to save Katya, for his discovery was for some tastes too extreme. Later he realized it to be less unnatural than common therapies such as heart transplants and brain surgery and in vitro fertilization. More importantly it was the only way, even though it posed both practical difficulties and required a special locale—ideally one far from view but within a political system which was known and therefore controllable.

American Samoa was perfect—US laws but eight thousand miles from New York and five from California. The handful of researchers and administrators might have been a problem but they were on the island of Tanua and so Gastro found his way to the ominously named but pristine island of Tabu. A few political contributions brought power generation equipment and road improvements and Gastro had what he needed.

The islands were a good choice; they allowed Katya to grow up strong and even magnificent, Gastro thought as he took in her tan figure in the usual cotton blouse and wrap. She looked at him with the tolerant smile that said she knew he was being a softie again.

"You will do the first session tonight?" Katya asked.

"Of course. That is how we do it. There can be no turning back once it has begun." He nodded at the biohazard-wrapped glasses.

She kissed him again. "Papa, for a long time there has been no turning back. You have done more for humanity and more for this planet than anyone. Than perhaps any single creature."

He shrugged and his eyes glinted with humor. "Hardly. Though possibly I am in the top three."

It was an old routine but she played her part. "Top three? With who else?"

"With the first fish to take the land and the first dinosaur to find the air."

She nodded. "Top three, then. That's not so bad."

He was supposed to nod and shrug with self-effacement and say, 'Good enough for a Romanian farm boy from Tjarnaslava.'

But as if of their own volition his lips changed the script: "I hope not."

Chapter 8

Beneath a mottled pre-dawn sky the color of a dead fish belly, Marcus and Nick walked through the through the village of Sava, following Linc Cafferty, the *Aurora*'s engineer, and Stanislaw Tatum, the local geologist.

It was the first time they had been out of sight of *Omega* since hauling the empty yellow hulk from the sea, and despite hours of work, they knew no more about what had happened than when her steel skids first met the deck.

There was no question that the sub had been pummeled; the hull was battered and the buoyancy tanks holed and the external lights and equipment smashed. The little craft could never have returned to the surface on her own and all the damage could be traced to the remains of the rockslide Marcus found around her.

But that did nothing to explain the fate of the crew. The sub had only a single hatch and no lock, so opening the hatch underwater would flood the sub. Yet the sub was dry and the crew gone. No theory could explain the vanishings and no theory could explain why no theory could explain it; they combed the hull as if hoping to find a hidden compartment hiding two vanished scientists but Devon Lucas and Henry Winston remained missing. By five in the morning only the four men were left, with the titanium, steel, and ceramic bones of *Omega* around them on the floor. It was hot and damp and the men were sweaty and grimy and there was no more that could be done.

Walking past a storm-shuttered bar, Nick slowed to gaze at the split bamboo walls and hand-lettered sign as if he were seeing a red carpet and a royal buffet.

"After that night a nice single malt would be the perfect breakfast," he allowed. He had spent enough time in the South Pacific to look left and right, scanning for the near-feral dogs that were common.

"Not a lot of choices at this hour," said Stanislaw Tatum, who as the local had been appointed to play guide. "Though I do have some nice tea in my quarters—"

"Food," Linc instructed.

"And drink," Nick finished. "By the way, has anyone else noticed that this town is a bit creepy?"

Bits of dead ships lay everywhere: huge anchors squatted on corners; heavy chains lay like rusting snakes in the grass; stumps of broken masts erupted from black soil like fingers pushing up from a grave. The empty sockets of portholes stared from gardens and fences.

"A regular ships' graveyard," Linc said as Marcus ran a hand over an anchor shaft and read the stamped writing.

"A lot of towns are like this here. Nautical décor and all," Stanislaw said.

"That's not what I meant," Nick said. "The people."

"The people?"

"There aren't any."

Nick gestured and they took in the silent village. Normally at this hour a village would be marking its awakening with the smoke of cooking fires and the cry of babies and this was particularly true of the island's capital. But Sava was silent.

They passed more empty fales, some lit by the blue glow of television. In a few were piled clothes and boxes and abandoned luggage; more boxes and luggage lay on the street, apparently abandoned in mid flight. No stores were opening, no cars traveling the road. The town seemed as empty as the *Omega*.

Marcus glanced at Nick and the big man shook his head and squeezed his brow. It was a gesture he made when things were going in the wrong direction.

Stanislaw guided them past the corner of a small modern post office situated in a one-story brick building with plate-glass windows and a flagpole. Painted on one side in reds and yellows was a shattered canoe beside a huge dripping creature that seemed to be eating the people in the canoe; arms and legs hung from its mouth and a few swimmers seemed to think they would escape but a clawed hand had already encircled them. On the next panel a group of celebrating warriors danced around one of the earthen umu ovens that used red-hot stones to cook breadfruit, taro, pork, or other meats. From this umu protruded a pair of blackened human feet.

Stanislaw placed his back to the murals.

"I don't know where everyone is but nothing here surprises me anymore. The six months I've spent here on Tanua feel like six years, because this isn't a normal place. All the rules are different. You saw the islanders in the crew after *Omega* came up? All that falling to their knees and wailing and chanting?"

"Hard to miss," Nick pointed out. The sight had been unnerving, not because it showed panic but because it had not. It was instead a resignation to some awful fate—the kind of thing pigs might do upon realizing their truck had just pulled up at the slaughterhouse. The men had clustered on the bow, as far as possible from the yellow sub on the stern, stripped themselves to the waist, and chanted while facing the sea.

Stanislaw looked in both directions before continuing.

"There's a lot of what we would call superstition here. And maybe for good reason because there are also a lot of strange things—like the triple breadfruit and the influx of giant bats. There's a local chief who says that an old god is coming back and is royally pissed and these are his signs. Everyone's a bit freaked and this thing isn't going to help. Unless there's a good explanation, which there doesn't seem to be, we can expect some panic. The locals were already wound up pretty tight—lately some of the weirder stuff has been getting unusually weird, even for here."

Nick sighed, both hands now on his brow.

"What weirder stuff?" Marcus asked. He had been walking behind the group, his eyes silently taking in everything.

Stanislaw checked the street again. "Two things. First, the earthquakes have been picking up. I was sent here to chart the geologic faults under the island and so I should know a lot more than I do, but the locals objected to the research charges I was dropping under the bay."

"They objected?" Nick asked, sensing more from the little man's tone.

"In the local fashion. They sank my boat and promised I'd join it if I kept desecrating their waters with my efforts. I was just uncovering what could have been a good paper—a mix of highly stressed faultlines and indications of significant magma movements consistent with an eruption."

"Oh, great," said Nick, looking at Marcus accusingly.

"Meaning, possibly, within ten years, if ever," Stanislaw clarified. "As you know it's an inexact science, particularly since I don't have much data. Anyway, small quakes have picked up from every few weeks to every few days. Could be nothing. Who knows."

"And the second thing?" Marcus asked.

A dark cloud passed over Stanislaw's face. "Yes. The second thing. Supposedly one should not even speak of them: *vaitama*."

Marcus knew a little Samoan and took the word apart. *Vai* meant water and *tama* man. "Water men?"

"Sea creatures. Sort of like leprechauns. They're supposed to be mythical but around here they have the annoying habit of showing up. And unlike leprechauns they mean bad news. No pot of gold at the far end of a rainbow; more like a vat of poison right in your face."

"Stanislaw," Marcus said in a calm tone, "have you seen any yourself?"

The little geophysicist looked away. "I don't know what I've seen. Stick around long enough and you'll say the same thing."

The lip of the sun curled over the horizon to blow a red glow across the island. Parrots screamed from tamarind and kapok trees and a night patrol of giant bats flapped overhead on leathery wings. The earth shivered beneath their feet. It was like being on stage and having the lights and sound effects kick on.

"See?" Stanislaw said. He led the way along a waterfront lined with a ramshackle marine purveyors, a failed casino, and an abandoned cruise ship terminal with the faded remnants of plastic flowers still hanging above its doorway.

"Here," he said before an odd assembly of concrete pillars on a concrete slab supporting a peaked roof of shingles. The building mixed Polynesian style with western materials to the disadvantage of both.

"The Headsplit Bar," Nick read from a hand-painted sign. "What's the specialty—brains?"

"It was once," Marcus said, pointing at a corroded bronze plaque fixed to a wooden post with a nail fat enough to put a man to a cross. The plaque commemorated the massacre of thirty-two captives who were allowed to honor the old gods by having their heads split apart with ironwood clubs and their brains eaten.

Nick rubbed his stomach as if preparing it for battle. "Somehow I'm not surprised this place didn't make the guidebook," he said cheerily. "But you know I never judge a place until it's poisoned me. Let's eat."

The inside of the Headsplit held ship's wheels and portholes and crudely mounted fish. At one table sat a group of island men, seemingly under siege from a litter of cans and bottles that had them surrounded and far outnumbered. The air was rank with sour breath and stale spilled beer and old vomit. The islanders fixed cool stares on the foreigners.

Nick picked a table on the side where the lack of a wall allowed in the breeze. Their Formica tabletop looked ripped from a ship's galley and hammered onto makeshift legs, two of wood and two of plastic. The chairs didn't match—Linc had only a three legged stool—and overhead hung a ship's life ring, stenciled with "Papoose" in faded letters.

They looked to the man behind the bar and he looked away. They looked some more and he looked away some more and Nick finally heaved himself to his feet.

"As the biggest and the hungriest, I suppose it falls to me to shake some grub out of this recalcitrant."

Nick cracked his knuckles spectacularly but the man behind the bar ignored him and stared outside as if turned to stone.

"Oh no," Stanislaw breathed. Nick turned to chide the little geologist about his squeamishness at the stick-shattering finger noise but saw that his head too was turned to the outside. He followed the gaze.

The street was filled with a crowd. It was big and silent and did not look friendly. A black sea of cold eyes stared into the Headsplit Bar.

"Where'd they come from?" asked Nick. "Did someone beam them in?"

A big man now faced the crowd and Stanislaw slipped down in his seat as the giant seemed to rise. He was huge—seven feet and 400 pounds of bronzed Samoan warrior chieftain. The crowd faced him with expressions of mixed fear and reverence.

"I should never have left Kansas," whispered Stanislaw.

The chief was flanked by ten muscled young men who looked like warriors from an old anthropological photo: all were tattooed from nipples to knees, all wore woven mats, all carried wooden war clubs. From their fierce expressions they were looking for trouble and believed they had found it.

"My people," the giant boomed to the gathering. "Behold the enemies. The enemies of our ways. The enemies of our people. The enemies of our ancestors. The enemies of our progeny. The enemies of our gods."

Nick had re-taken his seat. "Actually," he offered to his tablemates in a stage whisper, "I consider myself and Marcus to be the sworn enemies of all gods except Bacchus, Dionysius, and Eros. A man's gotta have his pleasures."

"Even now they joke and mock," the giant said, his voice cutting through the heavy air like the razor edge of a traditional wooden war club.

Marcus and Nick exchanged a look. First the giant and his crowd appeared out of nowhere. Now he had ears in the back of his head.

"Stop it," Stanislaw hissed. "That is Paramount Chief Pelemodo, the Tui of the islands, the supreme chief. He is only rarely seen. And even more rarely is it a good thing when he is."

The air around Pelemodo seemed to fill with the odors of oil and smoke and things that were loamy and old.

"Today the palangis received the second of two warnings. They understood this one no more than they understood the first. You are to bear witness to their intransigence. To understand that their punishment, when it comes and it comes soon, is fully deserved."

"Don't much like the sound of that," Nick muttered.

"Smart man," Stanislaw agreed.

In the torchlight, Pelemodo was the very image of a tribal chief, with oiled skin glistening and a necklace of fish vertebrate rattling. Few of his followers knew of his Yale degree, and none knew of his senior mathematics thesis on higher-order polynomials.

"The palangis have been studying the research submersible to learn what happened to its crew. They have pursued every lead and hypothesized madly but they have nothing. From their point of view it is impossible for two people to vanish in this way.

"How," Chief Pelemodo called out, "could the palangis be so ignorant? How could they be so stupid? How could they not see the signs?"

"How, how, how," chanted the people.

"Perhaps they are arrogant. Perhaps they are stupid. Perhaps they do not care. Perhaps they wish to die horribly."

"Perhaps, perhaps, perhaps," chanted the crowd, now beginning to push and jostle. Nick began searching for a nonexistent rear exit.

Pelemodo raised his arms in a gesture of reigning in control. "But we can find the answers to these questions. The way is simple. To understand why the palangi has acted in this way, let us simply . . . ask him."

Pelemodo drove his palms together with a thunderous clap and then strode to the palangi's table. The lack of a wall let him approach closely. When he moved he floated across the floor and the light filled in features that were cut rough and deep, as if his big face was a blunt tool that had been used hard and often. He seemed to grow more massive for his bulk was not flab but hard muscle overlaid with skin the color of dark honey and etched with blue-black tattoos that coiled around his torso.

"No, no, no," breathed Stanislaw. "This isn't happening."

"Oh but it is, little man," boomed the Chief in a voice so deep it seemed to bypass the ears to vibrate bones and blood directly. He tilted forward and the coils of tattoos on his torso shifted.

"You are the ones who found the *Omega*. You have received the honor of being given two messages," he said. "The same message was sent twice and only a palangi could miss it both times and that is why I am here. The first message was when your *Omega* did not return."

He paused.

"The second was its emptiness when it did."

The wind died and the heat closed in as if the island's thermostat had been cranked. Droplets welled on Pelemodo's face but refused to run or drip.

"And so now I ask you, on behalf of the people of these islands, on behalf of our gods, and on behalf of our way: why did you send a submersible into the very home of our sea lord Tangaroa?"

The table shivered and the low rumble of a small earthquake rattled through the air. "Feel his displeasure," Pelemodo intoned and the crowd murmured.

"We didn't know that Tanua Bay had any significance," Linc offered.

"Ah. Then tell me this. In your advanced culture, is ignorance of the law an excuse?"

"No," admitted Stanislaw in a high voice.

"And though you consider us primitive it is the same here. Ignorance is no excuse. Such a transgression must be punished and so it was. They intruded and they were taken. They were not the first and likely they will not be the last. Our lord of the sea Tangaroa has taken many of your kind."

Marcus straightened imperceptibly.

"Tangaroa took the sub crew?" he asked in a quiet tone. The giant head rotated and fixed eyes like black torches on him. Stanislaw shivered.

"He did."

"And he has taken others?"

"Many. What is a mystery to you is simple to us; everyone on this island understands for this type of thing has happened before. Many times. Many have been taken in this way. Many *tele*. You may disbelieve and you may scoff but you are chained by your thinking in the same way that your Church once insisted the earth to be the center of the universe long after it was proved otherwise. But your ways are not the only ones; the Aztecs had a prophecy that a conqueror would come from the east and it came true. We here also have a prophecy.

When the strange fruits come, when the vanishings begin, when the earth moves, when the vaitama run, these things mean the return of our lord Tangaroa."

"Oh, please," Nick groaned.

"Scoffing, as predicted," Pelemodo observed. "Tangaroa lives in the bay and the submersible violated his home. He responded against the transgressors. Before you dismiss my words recall that your fancy science has no explanation. All you can say is that it is impossible. Yet what is the sign of a god? Doing the impossible. And this god has done the impossible many times. He took our people for many years before the palangis came and now he takes you too. The old legends say he eats some of those he takes and changes other into vaitama.

"I can see that you disbelieve and this is natural since you are polluted by your science. But know that the reason your science cannot explain so many things—more than it will admit—is that your science is wrong. It is like a blind man who believes he can learn everything by touch. But touch cannot see color or things out of reach and so it is with your science. What it cannot explain it deems not to exist. We see things more purely here. And that is why we understand what has happened. What is happening. And what will happen."

"You say Tangaroa has taken the other boats lost between Fiji, Samoa, and Tonga?" Marcus asked.

"You have only to look to see the bones of his victims here. There are many."

Marcus slid his eyes to the sea then locked them onto Pelemodo. "How many?"

"Over the centuries too many to count."

"How many recently?"

"You have a particular ship in mind," Pelemodo surmised, and Marcus' estimation rose a notch. The chief was more than he appeared to be. Possibly much more.

"The *Nefertiti*. A sailboat. My wife was on it."

Pelemodo nodded as if every day he met palangis looking for the victims of his god.

"Yes. Tangaroa has them."

Marcus flinched. "Then her boat is here?"

Pelemodo pointed one arm at the sea and the other inland. "Here or there."

Marcus ignored the stricken expression that Nick was wearing.

"I'd like to see it."

Pelemodo shrugged grandly. "That could be arranged."

Marcus edged forward. "Then please arrange it."

The great head shook slowly. "No. That you will have to do yourself."

"How?"

Stanislaw cringed as Pelemodo leaned far forward, as if he were going to kiss or bite Marcus. Instead his lips stretched into a smile.

"When Tangaroa returns. You can ask him."

Marcus held the Chief's black gaze before leaning forward himself and smiling back. "I will."

From the rear of the crowd came murmurs and then shouts and then screams. People shoved and the crowd split to open a lane from the bush to the sea. Bundles of gray hurtled down an avenue of sand from the forest and each plopped into the sea and vanished.

Pelemodo straightened and swung his head like a turret. "Vaitama. Perhaps those you seek are among them."

Marcus rose but Pelemodo's great fist closed around his shirt and held fast until the last little shape vanished into the sea.

"You have done enough, palangis. Leave the vaitama be. As we shall leave you be. For now."

Pelemodo called to his followers in Samoan and they gathered, with many still gazing at the jungle and the sea. They marched away to a low chant and trod over the path of the vaitama.

Afterward Marcus walked the beach and looked at the water and the frothy edge of the jungle then returned and shrugged. All the tracks had been trampled; there was no telling what they had seen. On the table were baskets of fruit and fried balls of dough and fish heads, for the cook had been instructed by Pelemodo to 'fatten Tangaroa's captives for slaughter.'

"Uh oh," Nick said through a ball of fried dough after seeing the set of Marcus' features.

"Pelemodo is the first person in six years to offer an explanation for what happened to Callie's boat."

"Yeah. And it just happens to be an idiotic one."

"Maybe there's a shred of truth buried in there."

"Zeus' turds," Nick countered.

"He's right about all the ship debris here."

"And that's true for a hundred islands."

Stanislaw had set down his fork and was turning his head as if watching tennis.

"Schliemann followed legends to find Troy," Marcus pointed out.

"Troy wasn't kidnapping people thousands of years later."

"He's also right that Western science doesn't have it all figured out. Someday people will scoff at things we take for granted."

Marcus didn't say the rest of what he was thinking; he was still sane enough to know what would be considered insane. But too many impossible things had happened since Callie vanished and too many seemed to suggest–if not involve–her.

"You don't really think the *Nefertiti* is here," Nick said. Marcus fixed him with a level gaze.

"Nick," Linc offered. "Think of all the junk on this island. The whole boat could be here. We could have walked by pieces of it today."

"And it could take years to find. Don't encourage him."

"Years if I looked for it myself in the old-fashioned brute force way. Turning over stones and browsing rubbish heaps. So I won't."

Marcus rose and went outside.

"Where are you going?"

"To hire some help."

On the far side of the plaza Marcus sat on a black lava stone beside a small boy. Soon they were talking and a few minutes later the boy shrieked with glee when Marcus produced a marble from the boy's left ear and a baby gecko from his right. A small crowd of children gathered around the strange palangi who spoke their language and had magic hands.

"What's he doing?" asked Stanislaw.

"Kids explore places like no one else; he'll find a way to get them to look for the *Nefertiti*. He's done it on other islands."

Stanislaw clucked. "Think he'll accomplish anything?"

Nick turned to him and raised one eyebrow. "I never count Marcus out."

Chapter 9

Paramount Chief Pelemodo sat in his royal fale high on a mountain-side beneath banyan and kapok trees and smiled. The encounter with the palangis had gone spectacularly well. Finding that one had lost his wife in the Tabu Zone served up a chance for a rhetorical feast and Pelemodo felt that he had devoured the entire buffet, table and all. From the faces in the crowd this had been far more convincing than a sermon. The news that palangis had vanished from under the sea had rocked the island and Pelemodo had pumped the wave then ridden it like a Hawaiian long boarder. Even the skeptics now believed.

He looked down upon the green slopes of Tanua and the violet bay, the seat of his true power. As a boy playing in its waters he would never have guessed that one day they would be the key to making Tanua a kingdom. And Pelemodo a king.

The appearance of the vaitama was more than he could have prayed for. Such timing showed that Tangaroa was actively planning his return. Events were accelerating; he could feel it. This was both good and bad for things were going the right way but the pace was threatening to outstrip the preparations.

A drum began to beat in the jungle and he levitated and whispered down a narrow path with his bulk untouched by leaf or vine. Pelemodo could not explain it, but he moved with a ballerina's grace—though he would object to such a metaphor and instead demand a comparison to a dolphin's leap or an octopus' slink.

He floated a quarter mile to a large glade shaded by a high canopy that cast a perpetual blue-green twilight, as if the clearing were underwater. At one end rose a stone mound built eons before and which would have been a first-rate archeological site had the palangis known of it, but they did not and would not. It was one of many secrets the island had kept.

Across from the mound stood a huge fale roofed with pandanus and timbered with hand-hewn koa beams joined in the old way that used no nails or metal tools but only sennit and pegs and ingenuity. Rediscovering lost techniques had been difficult but well worth it; the fale was a powerful symbol of what the old ways had achieved. And of what they could yet achieve.

As always Pelemodo had ordered the torches lit to bring alive the element of fire and so flickering light whipped across two hundred young men. Twisted shadows crawled the stone floor and oily smoke mimed corpses and war clubs and grisly feasts before joining with the sky.

Pelemodo surveyed his followers. He nodded with approval at the calloused feet of those who had given up the rubber sandals of the west to fully embrace the *fa'a Samoa*—the Samoan way. The torches cracked and a breeze pushed frangipani and rotting mango across the rustling pandanus.

There were more recruits than usual and he thought back to the western saying about atheists and foxholes. His goal was to turn Tanua into a foxhole and to that end he fixed his eyes on the line of fish-poison and toa trees that edged the clearing and paused as if waiting for some divine signal. Then he nodded once.

"Talofa Matai," he greeted them in Samoan, and saw pride swell. He had picked the name of his group with care for in the islands rank matters and a matai is a village chief. Most of his followers were young and without status but by joining him they became chiefs.

"You honor me as the rain honors the land, as the sun honors the sky, as the wave honors the sea. You are the last guardians of the Samoan way. Your ancestors salute you and your true gods salute you.

"We are here because our sacred way, the fa'a Samoa, the very fa'a that has nurtured each of us, is under siege by the palangis. They come here with their soulless foods and their money and they take over; that is their way and they have done it in many places. Here they used trickery with the prophecy of Nafanua. Long ago when we were new on the land the goddess Nafanua said that someday from the sea would come a kingdom not of earth but of heaven and that we must enter it. The palangis twisted this to trick our people to think that Nafanua meant the palangis. But the palangi kingdom is not that prophesied by divine Nafanua; their kingdom is not of heaven. Only Tangaroa brings the next kingdom. The true kingdom from the sea."

The Matai cheered and Pelemodo waited to continue.

"We must reclaim our heritage before it is too late. If we do not act the fa'a will vanish like a raindrop into the sea. The palangi has eaten many cultures; ours is stronger but even the hardest cliff will be carved by the battering of the waves. For now our blood is still strong and for now the fa'a survives. Our lord Tangaroa returns and brings with him a new world that is old. The world we were promised so long ago. Today we continue our study of that world, the real world that the palangis have tried to keep from us. High Talking Chief Fuimono will teach us."

Pelemodo looked sideways to a big man wearing almost-blond dreadlocks, with a pocked face and the ceremonial flywhisk and staff of an orator. Pelemodo thought of Fuimono as something of an alter ego; though smaller than Pelemodo and lacking his cunning and guile, and though of obviously mixed blood, Fuimono was loyal, enormously strong, and had the ferocity of a hungry tiger shark. Pelemodo used him for tasks so dirty they might sully his own lordliness, and Fuimono was a man who enjoyed his work. Fuimono nodded to Pelemodo and then to the men, his eyes eager but his face relaxed. The man was, Pelemodo knew, a natural force with the power and patience of a tsunami, and with little guile.

"But first we eat," Pelemodo said and clapped his hands twice. Young boys carried in woven trays laden with boiled taro, lobster, bonito, pork, young taro leaves baked in coconut cream called *palusami*, star fruit, and papaya. As the old ways required, to Pelemodo went the *tuala*, the ribs of the pig, while the orator Fuimono received the *alaga* or flanks.

"Eat and be strong for Tangaroa. And listen. Tonight we talk more of our lord Tangaroa and how he defeated an enemy. High Talking Chief Fuimono, honor us with your words."

Fuimono stood to tell the story of Tangaroa's trip to the island of a woman named Faumea, who had in her vagina eels that killed men.

Tangaroa lured these out and then married Faumea and she bore him two children. While surfing, one of these was dragged to the bottom by the demon octopus Rogo Tumu Here. Tangaroa baited a hook with sacred feathers and drew Rogo Tumu Here to the surface, then hacked off each of the demon octopus' tentacles and finally hacked off its evil head.

"It will be the same with the palangis," Fuimono finished. "First we hack off the tentacle on Tanua. Then the one in Tonga. Then Fiji. Hawaii. All the way back to the head in Washington."

The Matai cheered and Fuimono finished with a piece of old knowledge.

"Once each of us had an *aitu*. We now think of an aitu as a ghost but once each person had a fish or bird or animal that was sacred and this was known as an aitu. When the palangi came he made us eat our aitus! But we will have our aitus again. And this time we will see who gets eaten."

The Matai cheered and Fuimono cheered and from the back of the fale Pelemodo watched them. He looked for intelligence and discipline, and like any commander, he looked for loyalty and malleability. Much would soon be demanded of these young men. But he saw that they would be worthy.

Chapter 10

Marcus crossed the main village of Sava. The fales and streets remained deserted and in daylight the ground showed a litter of clothing and abandoned suitcases and duct-taped boxes. It looked like the scene of a hasty evacuation and it was. The weekly ferry had been stuffed to the gills with fleeing islanders.

Marcus knew that most westerners and scientists would scoff at the fear of an ancient god as pure superstition, and that with degrees in marine biology and veterinary medicine as well as astronaut training, he should be among the first to scoff.

But since Callie's disappearance six years before he had come to see the world differently. He did not believe in an old sea god but he realized that the world was not entirely what it seemed. Had Callie simply vanished without further adieu, the world would have become a capricious and cruel one. But she had not, or rather Marcus could not be sure she had.

On three occasions he had seen what could not be. Once while working on a shallow reef in the Cook Islands he fought a balky remote underwater camera for twenty minutes in rough surge before convincing it to fit its stand. When he finished he turned and found that the rocks behind him had arranged themselves into a giant C. Doubting himself, he took a picture. He never told Nick and never showed him the picture. It happened again off Vanuatu, this time an etching in sand. The third time was on a bluff overlooking the sea on Palmyra atoll. While staring upward at the Southern Cross, the breeze wafted past him a scent he could not describe, but which he recognized as the unmistakable scent of Callie. He crept upwind but in thirty feet the island ended. Again the sand was disturbed as if something had crawled out and then back into the waves. The sea, Marcus believed, held far more than anyone knew.

And so he had not given up. The answer was somewhere out there in the sea; it was merely a question of finding it. He had never shared these thoughts with Nick because that, he believed, would have been too much even for his old friend. It was one thing to put up with a slightly eccentric and possibly obsessed companion, but it was quite another to spend your days and nights lost deep in the South Pacific with a certifiable lunatic.

Marcus opened the squeaking metal door of a building that looked stolen from the American southwest. The walls were three feet thick and cut with ventilation slots screened with rusted metal. A faded sign announced that this was the Coast Guard station, a statement which had been untrue for the several years since the Coast Guard took its one small boat and went home.

The air inside was cooled by banks of dripping air conditioners. Marcus ignored the yellowed sign-in sheet above the empty receptionist's desk and moved down a narrow hallway past tiny offices. Computer equipment was piled haphazardly: gutted cases, disassembled motherboards, broken monitors. Much of it was ancient and the rest outmoded—one of the perks, Marcus thought wryly, of living off grants and working for a perpetually under-funded agency.

He followed tiny sounds until he heard a string of curses.

Beneath a window in the back of the warren he found a disheveled man in his late twenties with the baseball cap and pallid skin of a computer geek. His T-shirt bore the unlikely legend "Institute for the Sexually Gifted," and he was turning a tiny screwdriver inside a grimy beige computer case.

"Casper Jenkins," Marcus said, pulling up a chair.

Casper set down the screwdriver and pushed his glasses up his nose.

"Hi, Marcus." He added a string of cheerful profanity, which targeted the computer before him, then all computers and the Internet, and then expanded to take in Tanua, the Polynesians, humanity, Earth, and finally the local corner of the Milky Way galaxy.

"Impressive," Marcus noted.

"I have a lot of time to practice."

"Good. Think you could use some of it for me to do some research?"

Casper regarded him blankly then looked to the pile of computers awaiting his attention. "Yeah, but I don't know anything about biology or geology or whatever it is you guys do."

"It's not about that. Something right up your alley." Marcus described what he wanted.

"Give me thirty minutes."

Casper was better than his word and twenty minutes later Marcus held a sheaf of printouts.

Tangaroa, it turned out, was indeed the Polynesian God of the Sea, the son of Rangi the Sky-God and Papa the Earth Mother. He was said to live beneath Tanua Bay in his sea fale and in form he was part fish and part man with a head like a blade and body-builder arms and a broad flat tail. His mouth sparkled with rows of triangular teeth.

Tangaroa had a long-running feud with his brother Tane, the forest god, who gave canoes, spears, nets, and fishhooks to fishermen so that they could hunt the sea god's children. Tangaroa took his revenge by sinking canoes, drowning fishermen, flooding fields, and eating away the shore.

Anthropologists considered Tangaroa's bloody-mindedness to be a reflection of life in a place where hurricanes and tsunamis and famine struck often and without warning. Life was often hard and short and for no good reason. Without jet travel and resorts the tropics were no paradise. But Tangaroa was not only cruel; he could reward his followers with the bounty of the sea while wreaking spectacular havoc on their enemies.

With his group of followers known as the Matai, Chief Pelemodo had either reinvented Tangaroa worship or, according to one anthropologist, brought into the open something the islanders had secretly practiced for years. The Matai were not limited to worshipping the god they called The Angry One but also sought an abandonment of Western technology and a return to the old ways. No more TV, no more canned food, no more western churches. And no more palangis, for they also sought independence and the creation of a pure Polynesian state.

Status as an American territory was a vast insult for it meant that the American Paramount Chief, or President, had authority over Tanua. The palangi attitude was clear: Vice President Quayle once visited Samoa and described the inhabitants as "happy campers." On the mainland it was yet another comedic faux pas but in the islands it was more palangi condescension.

Under Pelemodo's guidance the Matai were taking a turn toward darkness. Two Swedish anthropologists studying the group had vanished and it was feared they had come to bad, and possibly very bad, ends. Another anthropological team, this one from the University of Pennsylvania, had written a controversial paper expressing concerns that the Matai favored a return to the days of long pig, a quaint cannibal term for human flesh. The team was roundly lambasted for its lack of sensitivity to the traditional notions of a minority culture.

The next section of papers was the thinnest but the most important. Little had been published about the Tabu Zone, a name coined in the tabloid press when some wag found that flyspeck of an isle in its center. It referred to a triangle bounded by Tonga, Samoa, and Fiji.

Inside this triangle, eleven vessels had vanished in the last decade and the next page held a listing of the missing ships, which were mostly freighters and container ships, along with a fishing boat, a tanker, and of course one racing yacht. It was a knife in the guts that cut no less for having been expected. He turned to the others. The first to vanish was the freighter *Bethany Cook,* lost nine years before with a load of mining equipment and explosives. There were no distress calls, no weather, and in the end no ship. The best guess was that some mishap with the explosives reduced the ship to a flash and a bang.

It was the same with the others. The *Cumberland, Shing Wa, Rio del Oro, Papoose, Maverick Hauler, Cielo di Sarona, and Hamburg Express.* Eight ordinary freighters carrying eight mundane cargoes. Steel, concrete, ore, heavy equipment, grain, textiles. One Philippine fishing trawler, the *Vicky Lee,* gone five years.

And the *Nefertiti.* The smallest of them all. Marcus thought of Callie and wondered what their future might have been. A big house. Lazy afternoons. Weekend chores. Perhaps kids. Callie in worn overalls tending a garden or chasing a squealing towhead. Instead he sat alone in the South Pacific reading a list of shipwrecks.

The second ship on the list was the *Papoose,* a Native American word for child. Marcus, who carried a splash of Cherokee blood in his veins, had always been the Indian in childhood games of cowboys and Indians. To his friends' dismay he made every fight the Battle of the Little Big Horn and all his friends became Yellow Hair.

His eyes lingered on the word. *Papoose.*

With the papers in hand he jogged to the Headsplit Bar and ignored the owner who once again did not emerge from behind the bar.

Still hanging over a table was the old and battered life ring. Still inscribed on it were the letters "Papoose."

Marcus looked again at the printout, knowing what it would say. The *Papoose* was one of the ships lost in the Tabu Zone. And here was a piece of it.

Just as Pelemodo had claimed.

Chapter 11

Gastro Nister entered the clean space they called the demonstration lab with a blank face and a heavy heart. There was no choice but to perform this duty and not even Katya's husky and slightly reedy voice had been able to make him eager despite its usual power over him.

Perhaps that power came from his knowledge that she was so lucky to have a voice. After he had given her the perfluorocarbon so many years before he had found to his horror that her lungs were too badly damaged to work again. Scar tissue blocked the exchange of oxygen and so her cure would require technology that did not yet exist—technology that might never exist.

He would not let her die because of the inconvenience of the perfluorocarbon, which had to be constantly replenished and was uncomfortable. It was a dirty secret of modern medicine that convenience was sometimes more important than life. But not in Gastro's philosophy, in which life must honor life. He had her moved into a special suite in his home and taught her sign language so that she could communicate despite her flooded lungs and useless voice box. He arranged twenty-four-hour nursing care using only trusted help from his native land. He designed a mobile aerator and a custom drip housed in a form-fitting backpack so that she could move around and keep the fluid in her lungs oxygenated. And most of all he worked.

He deconstructed the human lung and traced every element to its developmental roots. He identified the genes for building the complex structures and this work alone would have completed most scientists' careers and earned a Nobel nomination if not the prize itself. But he published no papers and held no seminars. Many times he marveled at the lung and by extension the whole human organism. So simple it seemed possible it could have resulted from the mere random collisions of molecules, but so elegant that the invisible hand of some creator was implicated. Sometimes, while crawling through nucleotides that looped and repeated, he felt as if he were encountering the primeval footsteps of a preternatural god, preserved as clearly as if in ancient mud turned to stone by the eons.

Gastro spared little time for such fancies although his dreams began to focus on primordial times when some gasping fish first crawled ashore. On a whim he looked up the name of that first lobe-finned fish to leave its watery home: *Eusthenopteron foordi*. No one could know on what ancient beach, newly shaved from rocks and young corals, the event happened, but Gastro liked to think it had been nearby and perhaps even on Tanua—or whatever had been here in place of Tanua in an era so long ago the continents had yet to take their shapes.

His research into the regeneration of lung tissue proved disappointing. The genes were there but every attempt to induce their promoters to kick on failed. Failed in vitro, failed in the mouse model. Failed in the chimps. Time was running out and already Katya had hung on longer than he would have thought physically possible. He did not allow himself to imagine the psychological scars.

Yet while the lung genes were recalcitrant, another set of genes, ancient ones from the dim past, were not so fussy. These might date from a time when organ regeneration was not the exclusive province of certain low reptiles, or perhaps from when the highest organisms were just such low reptiles. He opened another front in the battle and found still more elegant simplicity. As well as something more. At first he was stunned, then shocked, and then uncertain. In the end he was joyous.

The something he had found was of a sort that he kept to himself for he recognized that the research community would not look kindly on work in this direction. The research community, however, did not have a daughter in Katya's condition.

He startled his Stanford colleagues by resigning his chair. Saying only that he needed a change, he moved with his daughter to the remote island of Tanua, deep in the South Pacific. He felt a certain trepidation for he was on the brink of something which would be either a tremendous accomplishment or a tremendous failure. The academic community speculated on these odd events for the next six weeks, until the topic of choice became a plastic surgeon's scandalous affair with a nurse who was, most shockingly of all, the surgeon's own age rather than half it.

Gastro knew that everything he had done culminated in the demonstration he was about to give in the bright lab. He began by nodding a greeting to his audience of two—a tall man and a compact woman, both still in the coveralls they had worn aboard their submersible—then turning a steel spigot to fill a clean Pyrex beaker with water. Crystal bubbles swirled and he took a drink then offered the beaker.

"Fresh from mother earth's bosom, naturally mineralized and filtered," he said, as he had many times before. His tone gave no sign of the darkness in his heart.

As usual there were no takers so he dumped the beaker into the acrylic box before him and left the faucet running to fill it. He crossed the lab to a wire cage that emitted animal smells of lettuce and feces and reached in with a gloved hand.

He lifted a struggling body and spread small legs to read a blue tattoo on one thigh. G43.

"Gwendolyn 43," he said and dangled her by the tail before the two-person audience that refused even a drink of water.

"A simple rat, yes?" he asked.

They nodded cautiously.

"Not simple at all," Gastro corrected. "Observe."

He dropped the forty-third Gwendolyn into the tank that was now four-fifths full. Gwendolyn swam like a shipwreck veteran with her pointed nose held high and her legs paddling.

Gastro lowered and fastened the lid. It was perforated with holes so small that no rat, not even one with an endearing storybook name, could pass through. He fit a rubber hose to the faucet then slipped one end through a hole. Water streaming down the sides twisted the image of the rat into something else. Gastro turned and saw wide eyes and pallid complexions and dry lips. The two exchanged a glance, one of thousands they had traded since their sub was trapped in the deep.

"It is not what you think. It is nothing you could even imagine," he counseled. His voice lowered and he turned away. "Though if you really tried you might remember."

The water rose and Gwendolyn with it, tethered to the surface by the need to breathe. The water held within it dissolved molecular oxygen and was even made up of atomic oxygen bonded to hydrogen but none of this would help Gwendolyn. Her head reached the lid with a small bump. Her nose siphoned air from the wide thin bubble at the top. The bubble shrank and then was gone.

"Ah, Jesus," the tall man said, shifting uncomfortably from foot to foot. The woman beside him appeared stunned.

Gastro smiled compassionately. "In life, changes can be awkward. But there is no cruelty here. Just the opposite."

Gwendolyn's legs kicked in small blurs and her tail drew a wake. Her nose slid along the glass and white needle teeth tried to chew through it. She thrust her snout into the corners, hoping to find air where there was none. Where there is life there is hope, they say, but what they don't say is that where there is only a little life there is a great deal of hope.

Finally Gwendolyn's kicks seized and the small body spasmed. Her legs splayed and her tail drooped. A few bubbles leaked from her mouth and she sank tail first with eyes wide.

The audience let out twin sighs and Gastro realized that they had been holding their breaths, perhaps in unconscious sympathy with Gwendolyn. The air conditioner hummed and somewhere an electric chime announced the completion of an experiment.

"My friends," Gastro intoned, "it is not over. It is only beginning."

He pointed and they saw he was right.

Gwendolyn was stirring and her legs paddling once more. But now her nose pointed down and she toured the bottom of her enclosure with calm deliberation.

The tall gaunt man leaned close.

"How—" he began.

"Look for yourself, Dr. Winston," said Gastro. "You too, Ms. Lucas."

Gastro pointed at Gwendolyn's tiny chest, which was pumping water, rather than air, through her body.

"I don't understand," said Henry Winston.

"Me neither," said Devon Lucas.

"Of course you do. You see, I have taken nothing from little Gwendolyn here. Instead I have given her something. Something wonderful."

Devon and Henry looked at him, and he pointed at the sealed water bottle which hours before had filled their glasses with oddly brackish water that was ambrosia to the dehydrated survivors of a wrecked sub. Those glasses were now wrapped in translucent orange.

"And I have given it to you too."

Chapter 12

Marcus walked from the Headsplit Bar with a slow pace and a long gaze. A piece of one of the Tabu Zone ships was hanging in a bar on Tanua. An anchor from a second lay in a lane a quarter mile away, the name *Rio del Oro* stamped on the shaft.

A piece from one ship might be coincidence for the lost ships had plied these waters for years and ships shed bits the way humans drop dermis: small pieces eventually line their paths. But there was more.

Of the faded photographs on the back wall of the Headsplit most were the usual shots of fortunate fishermen and unfortunate fish: huge black marlin and bluefin tuna, a scattering of hammerheads and rainbow runners and a few small jacks.

But in the background several showed a striped smokestack and freighters in Tanua bay. The Headsplit owner, forgetting himself for a moment and being helpful, told Marcus that the power plant below the stack had been built eight years before and that gave a rough time frame for the photos. One of the shots showed a ship with a distinctive blue hull while another an unusual twin-stripe pattern on the funnel and a third a container ship with unique cranes. Marcus leafed through the printouts. The ships matched the *Papoose,* the *Shing Wa,* and the *Cielo di Sarona.* But according to the records, none of the ships had come through Tanua at those times; the last visit for *Shing Wa* had been twelve years before, while the *Papoose* and *Cielo di Sarona* never visited Tanua at all.

Which meant, Marcus knew, nothing. The names of the ships in the photos could not be read and perhaps they weren't the ones on his list. It might be mere coincidence but for a long time he had been suspicious of coincidences that the sea showed.

In the malae that served as a village square Marcus found a group of kids sitting on the ground. Their faces were respectful and patient and Marcus thought he was seeing trash piled around them, but then saw their expectant faces and understood. From the look of it they had found enough scraps to build two entire boats though neither would float long enough for the crew to jump off.

"You are waiting for me?" he asked in rough Samoan and they avalanched towards him with arms out-thrust.

He looked at everything they brought. Binnacles, compasses, cleats, ropes and lines, brass nuts, winch handles. Whatever it was he looked at it, running his hands over the items and holding some up to the light. He looked not because there was a remote chance any of it was from the *Nefertiti*, but because he wanted them to keep looking and acting interested was his end of the bargain.

Finally a single boy was left, younger and smaller than the rest. He lingered twenty feet away until Marcus called him and when he approached his hands were empty until he pulled from his waistband a rectangular piece of wood.

Wood, Marcus thought, forcing an encouraging smile onto his lips. At least it wasn't a hunk of stone. In his fingers he felt a grain that was roughened, as if long submerged but still smooth with varnish and as he held it he wondered how much more junk he could stand to look at.

Then he turned it over.

Later, after Marcus stood up again, the boy told him that he found the chunk of nameboard in a junk pile near the bar. Marcus had him point out the place and looked among scraps of broken chairs and tables—so many that the Headsplit looked to be living up to its name—but there was nothing else.

He found Nick pouring over seismic data in Stanislaw Tatum's geology lab at the wharf and lay the nameplate on the bench.

"Marcus, that could be from a lot of boats," Nick said after inspecting it. The letters "titi" gleamed in gold on blue.

"Could be," Marcus agreed as he opened his black nylon wallet. He handed over a picture without looking at it; he could see in his memory the bow of the *Nefertiti* and the six-woman crew lining the rail. The nameboard was just below Callie's feet. Gold on blue.

Nick compared the photo to the wood scrap, lifting one and then the other to the light, and even scrutinizing the photo with a magnifying glass. Finally he straightened and handed back photo and board.

"Okay. I agree. Looks like a match. What that means I have no idea."

"It means her boat was here."

"That piece could have floated a long way."

"And pieces of the others? Anchors don't drift." Marcus had described the other ships and the other wreckage on Tanua. Nick sighed.

"Sometimes I hate myself for tackling you all those years ago. Look where it's brought me. What are you going to do?"

"What would you do if you were me?" Marcus asked.

Nick looked away.

"You were going to look for that boat anyway. I don't see how this would change your mind."

"It doesn't," Marcus agreed.

Chapter 13

Paramount Chief Pelemodo entered the guest fale in the village of Amu with the calm pace of a king on parade. The big oval was another of those built without the scourge of western materials: red beams of koa wood held apart a roof of pandanus thatch and a floor of packed sand. The vertical columns were hung with ironwood war clubs that bore dents and old stains gone brown with age. These were famous relics of battles past and each had a name and a pedigree. During feast times days could be spent telling the tales.

The light came from the four-foot torches that vented oily smoke and Pelemodo sniffed and glanced upward. The Amu headman dispatched a small boy to the roof to remove a few panels of thatch to let the stinging smoke escape. The old ways were not always simple.

Pelemodo lowered his bulk into the empty space left for him in the center along the wall, a place of high honor with a stout pole behind it for comfortable leaning. The village elders also had poles, while the young men sat on the open floor.

The faces of the other men in the fale—mostly chiefs and elders of some rank, though far lower than his—watched him with expressions of respect and disguised fear. That was as it should be, Pelemodo knew. The lower must fear the upper. Pelemodo had known both that fear and its power. Chiefly titles were the most valuable property in the islands and were passed down like the titles of English knights. The rules were complex and the identity of the next chief often contested. Clan wars could erupt and now there were even, in a uniquely American affront to the old ways, lawsuits.

From an early age Pelemodo was of chiefly stature and so adept at oratory and scheming that he was seen as a threat to the powerful, who had their own children to advance. Pelemodo's father lacked enough of the chiefly power known as *pule* to protect him, and so when Pelemodo turned fourteen and his head broke six feet, it was necessary for him to leave for Honolulu, where he lived with a distant cousin and completed high school. There he showed two traits rarely mixed in the same person: a ruthless enthusiasm for violence that quickly brought him to the top of the Fa'a Boyz gang, and an innate grasp of mathematics that earned perfect scores on the first two tests he took. The disbelieving Japanese math teacher, who was merely a palangi of another color, did not believe that an island boy could handle trigonometry or algebra and forced him to repeat the tests before conceding that he was not merely a clever cheat. An academic scholarship to Yale followed, where he took math and physics degrees.

A week after graduation the Paramount Chief of Tanua died unexpectedly. He had been Pelemodo's primary enemy and he left a power vacuum. Pelemodo knew as well as anyone that nature abhors a vacuum and so he returned to the islands. Within a month two of the other contestants for the title of Paramount Chief met bad ends: one was stoned to death and the other found baked in an *umu*, a traditional oven constructed from an earthen pit lined with hot rocks and covered by palm and banana leaves. In deference to their western masters, the police filled out the necessary forms and went through the necessary motions. Then, in deference to the old ways, the matters quietly went away. Three weeks later Pelemodo became Paramount Chief Pelemodo.

As he surveyed the crowd Pelemodo saw that at least three men bore visible scars of his displeasure and that nearly everyone in the fale had a relative who had been forcefully disciplined. Forceful discipline, Pelemodo had learned, was the only worthwhile kind.

This village of Amu lay at the northern end of Tanua near the hundred meters of sand that at low tide formed a shallow bridge with the isle of Tabu. Pelemodo knew of the palangis living on the forbidden isle and tolerated them because they furthered his own goals. They were the whetstone for his blade.

When Pelemodo first returned from his years away he disdained the traditional beliefs, which in the glare of palangi light looked like curious and misshapen folk tales. But as he re-submerged into the fa'a, he found in it new strengths and new wisdom. He took over his father's small efforts to rekindle the religious side of the old ways. At first it was a means of building a cadre of followers but he made arguments that were honed by his western training and, to his surprise, he found himself being won over. He became the truest of the true believers.

Sometimes he felt that he had long been a pawn in Tangaroa's patient plot for a return to power. By living among the palangis and studying their science and ways, Pelemodo became uniquely suited to repel both. Those years also taught him that he could best attract followers by uniting them against a common enemy. And so the palangis were both a detested scourge and a provocation essential to bring about the next stage. They were unpleasant but necessary, like scaffolding or a vaccine.

With the ring of an ironwood mallet on a pigskin drum the kava ceremony began. One palangi face was in the crowd; this one came from Tabu and Pelemodo permitted it though he felt it inappropriate.

There was one other palangi, however, whose inclusion he did not resent. She served as the taupo, the village priestess and emblem of purity. Katya's hair was midnight black and her skin a Polynesian bronze and she spoke their tongue and knew their ways. Despite her roots, Pelemodo considered her more islander than palangi and he knew a warrior's heart to beat in her chest. He often wished he could have her spirit inside one of his warriors.

The crowd began to fidget, and he let it continue long enough to make clear he was in charge then rose.

"Honored men of Amu. I am here to speak of something more sacred than the first light of morning, more sacred than a first-born son, more sacred than the meeting of two passing clouds or the silent mating of the sea turtle. I speak of fa'a Samoa. Our way. Tonight we honor it with the most sacred of ceremonies."

He spoke of the great old ways which transported their ancestors across the blue sea while the palangis cowered in mud huts. Of the superiority of their culture, of how they could ascend over the foreign scourge and create their own world. Of the coming vengeance of Tangaroa. A breeze blew and smoke wrapped him, stinging his nose and watering his eyes. He looked at the flickering torch that was tor-menting him and spoke on but then in the red heart of the torch a vision appeared that stopped him. He saw the glowing reds and yellows transmute into hordes of bloody people battling and ripping entrails from each other before sinking into a crimson sea that stained the sand with blood.

With effort he quelled the image and scanned the crowd and saw that his silence was considered a rhetorical pause. He had never had a vision before and he eyed the torch carefully, then finished his remarks and nodded at the priestess.

Katya wore a yellow and white *lava-lava* with a red hibiscus behind one ear and she rolled forward by placing one foot directly in front of the other. She dragged a mat before each seated chief and each placed a slim twist of kava root on the mat. Then she walked to the center of the fale and knelt before a sacred wooden bowl that stood on many feet.

Two boys flanked her and one ladled water into the bowl while the other added pounded kava root. Katya's muscled shoulders worked as she kneaded and squeezed the brown mass with a roll of fiber. After a few minutes she tossed the roll over her shoulder to a young man outside the fale; he shook out the strainer and tossed it back to her, and she caught it without looking. The village of Amu did not follow the other tradition for kava crushing, which involved chewing the root and spitting the saliva-spiced mixture back into the bowl ready for serving. She was glad because although she enjoyed the taste, the narcotic buzz might hinder her. She eyed the crowd and saw that all eyes were upon her and again she tossed the strainer and again caught it.

Still all watched, as she wanted. She liked a challenge. No one saw her palm a plastic microcentifuge tube with the dimensions of a 9mm bullet as she kneaded the thick fluid into the brown mass and smiled up at the crowd and they smiled back. Her father would not approve, she knew. But not even he had seen her action from his seat among the medium-level chiefs. The tube was one of a dozen in her waistband, each with a swab waiting in it. With enough deftness she would collect saliva samples from a dozen people tonight, each a key to their biochemistry.

Katya made a gesture of completion then dipped a wooden goblet into the bowl and took it to Pelemodo, who tipped a drop on the floor for the gods then downed the contents and flung the dregs over his shoulder. Next to be served would be the village headman who was seated across from Pelemodo.

Katya returned to the bowl to refill the cup.

She was halfway to the headman when a cloud blotted the moon and the night darkened and a keening and flapping blew through the fale. Torchlight glinted off four red eyes as two cat-sized bats screeched through. Katya stopped with cup in hand. She knew that *pe'a vao* were a sign and that to ignore a sign was to taunt the gods. According to what Pelemodo said were the ancient ways, the priestess was in charge of the ceremony and so the interpretation was hers. But in that power lay danger for *taupos* had been killed for interpretations considered wrong. At the very least, she decided, she would be expected to pause. When after a decent interval nothing happened she could proceed. The two pe'a va flapped into the jungle over a narrow path and she waited.

Something happened.

The brush on the narrow path below the bats crackled and thrashed and a man stepped out.

A white man.

The crowd gasped. The bats went in and a man came out.

"Talofa," the man said, greeting the crowd in its own tongue and drawing another gasp. He was just over six feet, dark tanned, and sandy-haired, in hiking boots, battered khaki shorts, and a blue field shirt. He held a canvas bag which clanked and from which protruded bits of metal and wood.

Katya, still halfway across the fale with cup in hand, considered. She did not recognize the palangi but since she knew everyone on the island that fact alone told her who he must be. She was surprised to find him attractive and would not have expected that to enter into her thinking but it did.

She gestured him forward and he moved to a place beside her father Gastro. The crowd whispered and warriors began to stir but

Pelemodo raised a hand. The man seemed to take it all in with a glance.

"Traditional etiquette," the man said in Samoan, "allows the inclusion of a guest, does it not?"

Eyes turned to Katya and to the Paramount Chief.

"We follow older traditions here," Pelemodo said. "But we defer to the taupo. She has invited you and so you may stay." The Paramount Chief nodded and received the same in return as the man sat.

"Friend," Gastro Nister said to the newcomer in quiet English, "you may be out of your depth here."

"Story of my life," Marcus Oden agreed.

Katya continued the ceremony by serving the village chief and returning again to the dark bowl. She spent a long time kneading the kava and as she did so, she shot a look at the palangi beside her father. She was stalling because she was considering an experiment. Most of her experiments involved molecules too small to see but this one would test something equally invisible.

It would be an insult for her to serve the new palangi ahead of chiefs. But if she did so, it would also be an insult for the new palangi to defy the taupo by refusing. Since the palangi spoke the tongue he would understand the impossibility of the situation if she approached him with a cup of kava. From what she had heard of this man she thought he might find a clever escape and that would be the experiment. The danger was great, however. The crowd held Fuimono and several other of Pelemodo's more violent followers and they might beat or kill the palangi.

She kneaded the kava while considering and then met the palangi's eyes. She had the impression that he could hear her thoughts and knew what she pondered. Then Pelemodo coughed in a way that meant she had delayed long enough. She decided against the experiment and served another chief. When she next looked at the palangi her father was leaning towards him and they were talking.

"You are not from here. And we don't get tourists," Gastro said in a low tone that did not rise above the hiss of the torches.

"Just passing through."

"You are the one who found the sub?"

Marcus looked at him. A slight but striking figure with untamable white hair and blazing eyes. "I did."

"A terrible mystery. How did it happen?"

"I'm told a sea god did it."

"I wouldn't believe the locals."

"You're a local," Marcus pointed out. "What do you think?"

"I'm a transplant. And I wouldn't even hazard a guess. I'm just a retired country doctor and such things are beyond me. But I do hope you find them."

"I'll just add them to the list."

"The list?"

"The list of those I'll find," Marcus said softly.

The doctor studied him for a long while. "You sound like someone who does a lot of looking. We have a saying where I'm from—it doesn't translate well but it basically says: sometimes the looking is better than the finding."

Marcus shrugged. "We don't have that saying where I'm from."

Gastro gave Marcus a long and fatherly look of kinship. "It's too long a story to tell but I once looked for something for years. Everyone thought my search was impossible but I kept it up."

"Did you find what you were looking for?"

"Oh yes."

"Was it worth it?"

"Very much so. What is it that you're looking for?"

"Like yours, that's too long a story to tell."

Gastro smiled and pointed. "I meant in the bag."

"Ah. These are pieces of ships. A hobby of sorts. I was picking up a few here and there and stumbled onto your little party."

Gastro peered at brass and teak. "Any rare finds?"

"Not this time. But I think I'm close."

Marcus noticed that while the taupo at first appeared to be a beautiful island girl, she was actually a palangi. A palangi who was taupo for a ceremony before Pelemodo had to be an unusual palangi. She was slim but not model-anorexic; she had the lean solidity of a woman who could hike or swim all day. Callie had been the same.

The firelight caught the taupo's cheeks and he recognized her from the sea when landing the Flying Canoe. She could indeed swim.

Now Marcus looked once more at the man beside him. He saw a faint resemblance but he was betting the taupo had taken her mother's looks. That was to her benefit, he decided.

"Your daughter is skilled."

Gastro's eyes narrowed but the corners of his mouth twitched up in a combination of surprise and pleasure. "How did you know?"

"I can see it. You're all palangi and she's all islander but it's there."

"Katya is a remarkable young woman."

"She must be to serve Pelemodo."

"You have met him?"

Marcus nodded and then Katya was before them. She handed Marcus the wooden cup and he honored the ceremony by spilling a drop and draining the cup and flinging the dregs. The taupo left but did not return to serve her father.

Marcus raised his eyebrows and Gastro smiled the smile of a father with a headstrong daughter. "She is the taupo. She decides. Today you are honored. Today I am not."

Marcus looked from father to daughter as kava tingled on his lips and sizzled in his belly.

Chapter 14

Devon Lucas awoke with her red locks plastered to her skull and cold sweat pooled in the hollow of her belly. She lay still for a few moments as her thoughts slowly gathered; the sensation was odd, as if her very consciousness had fragmented overnight and could only roughly fit together again.

She rose and padded across a cool stone floor to a tile sink where she drank a liter of water and stood trembling. In the mirror she saw unfamiliar lines cutting her face, bags under green eyes that now bore a strange glint, and a new leanness and muscularity in her body as if some unseen sculptor were reworking the clay that made her. She attributed it all to exhaustion and stress. The sequence of certain death, followed by what seemed like a miraculous rescue, followed by this.

Whatever this was.

The last days had been a strange blur. All in all, though, they beat the alternative of living out the rest of her life—a period of a few short hours at best—in the stifling darkness of a trapped research sub.

Her body shuddered and she felt a hot flash as if a Swedish sauna had erupted around her, then another creepy pulsing twitch swept from her calves to her neck as if some invisible puppeteer were testing a growing control over her body. It was one of many strange new sensations; besides the sinuous twitches there were aches and pains in her chest, a raspiness to her breath, and the bloody and fierce dreams, the dreams of a predator thirsting for hot blood.

She knew that Henry Winston was experiencing similar symptoms but with even more troubling twists, such as the appearance all over his body of oval, purple-black sores, each like a tiny mouth, and a crushing weakness that kept him bed-ridden. In contrast, Devon felt bursts of animal-like invigoration.

The man behind their rescue, along with his exotic-looking daughter, checked on them regularly and Devon did not miss the expressions of concern in his oddly luminous blue eyes. Things were not, it seemed, going according to plan. Which at least was consistent; from Devon's perspective nothing had gone according to plan since she yielded to Henry Winston's demand and nosed the little sub beneath the overhang that had collapsed and trapped them.

When the rocking sub had quieted in the pitch black of the deep sea Henry did not at first realize their predicament; he equated their survival of the ceiling collapse with their survival. But this was true only in the most temporary terms for the sub was broken and trapped, which left them marooned beneath twelve hundred feet of water. Few people are as inaccessible as those trapped beneath the sea; the cold laws of physics put only space travelers and unlucky mountaineers as far from help. Their future was both short and certain as they sat in the blackness: technically it would be a race between dying of dehydration, dying of starvation, and dying of asphyxiation when the oxygen ran out and the scrubbers collapsed, but Devon knew the little sub well enough to know that it would be no race at all. Asphyxiation would win, crossing the finish line long before either of them could even build up a decent hunger or thirst.

At first Devon did not tell Henry this; she recalled his first traumatic reaction to undersea travel four years before, after which he had sworn that never again would he dip beneath the sea or even a swimming pool. The only thing that could make her last moments worse, as she whiled them away in an enclosure the size of a phone booth, would be to spend them with a crazed lunatic clawing the titanium walls.

But eventually she decided she could not keep their fate a secret and in any event, Henry Winston was too intelligent not to figure it out for himself. When he saw that she was no longer flipping levers and turning knobs and running the motors until they screamed, he understood. He understood the physics of their predicament, and that only a tiny number of craft in the world could travel so deep, and that of those an even smaller number could help them even if they were ten feet away.

He surprised her with the dignity of his acceptance; he was calm and almost peaceful, though considerably chagrinned that it had been at his own urging—and despite his previous and now obviously correct instinct to avoid the deep sea—that they had become trapped.

Devon did not completely accept defeat. She explained to Henry that there were two US Navy rescue subs and perhaps a handful of other craft worldwide that could reach them. And it was possible, she said, that one of them might be on a nearby ship, by some lucky chance.

"You don't really think so, do you," he said.

"No," she admitted, after a pause.

How two people spend what must be their last hours cannot be known until that time comes. For Devon and Henry, the time was spent quietly, with shallow breaths in an attempt to conserve oxygen. Devon thought of her daughters, Bonnie and Alice, while Henry engaged in a quiet but profound bout of self-recrimination, but there was no talking and only carefully controlled breathing. This was not a base attempt to prolong life but an attempt to last as long as possible, in the hope that help might miraculously arrive.

As it happened, it did. Though not from anywhere Devon or Henry could have expected.

A mere four hours after being trapped, long after the scrape and rattle of the avalanche had passed, a new sound whispered through the hull. Something soft and filmy seemed to be rubbing up against the titanium, a rubbing punctuated by enough muffled bumps and thuds to suggest that something was happening.

"Huh," Henry said, as Devon remained silent. A conventional rescue would have commenced with the jolly banging of a wrench on Omega's hull, a maritime Hi how are ya.

This sounded like—and probably was, Devon said—some marine creature making a home for itself in a nook or cranny. The sounds continued, and sometimes came from several places at once.

Then finally the whisperings died away and Devon shrugged into the darkness. Her eyes stung with tears but not for herself; it was her daughters that gave her the greatest regret. Here in the dark she could not even see their picture though she could feel it. Despite their wild ride in the avalanche the small photo had stayed taped to its nook beside the auxiliary depth gauge and she ran a finger along its smooth coolness. It was just as well that it was dark and would always be dark; the image of her daughters would not see her gasping last breaths, her eventual slump, her slow moldering decay, and then, someday, the pile of bones littering her seat. Devon knew she was in the last place she would ever be, that the little sub would rest in place for eternity, slowly buried in silt and marine growth, just another bump on the bottom.

It was then that the sub had moved.

The cry of a giant bat drew Devon's eyes to a sky that was pinking over a row of palms through her window. Another dawn had come, one she might never have had. Whether it was hers—or instead belonged to those who had brought her here—was an open question.

A knock sounded on her door and she flinched. Nothing good had come through that door yet. But she set her shoulders and answered.

Chapter 15

With a red dawn at his back, Gastro Nister bounced down a strip of white coral at the wheel of a pale blue Ford pick-up, following the curves of the coast and chuffing over potholes at a sedate ten miles per hour. Many islanders drove slowly for there were few places to go and fewer to hurry but Gastro Nister was the most unhurried driver on Tanua. He rarely exceeded fifteen miles per hour.

The truck bed was filled with crates, and the crates were filled with work. Though the labor he was about to undertake was menial he enjoyed it too much to delegate for it was both an end and a beginning, and a chance to work hand-in-glove with Nature. Whether she would be ally or foe remained to be seen and might not be known for decades or even centuries. He pulled onto a wide slab of new concrete and as he backed around spume sprayed the truck. As Katya had once rudely remarked here, the ocean seemed glad to see him. When the tailgate fell it dangled over froth.

A local myth said that from the next bluff one could call the shark and the turtle. Gastro made no call but his eyes searched the sea. Within a minute he spied the green flash of a sea turtle in a curling wave and in two more minutes a small blacktip reef shark. There were simply, he had long ago decided, a lot of turtles and sharks. It was an example of how a curious fact could be made to fit a myth.

Now to business. Time for Darwin to do his work. The first crate held a rat which Gastro lifted free and studied for a moment before lowering to the sea. Gastro favored smaller animals with high reproductive rates and fast life cycles for these would provide an accelerated evolutionary laboratory. He was testing his creations in the ultimate lab: the world. Hopefully in ten or a hundred or more generations he or his offspring would cull the descendants of these creatures and find improvements never imagined. He expected a high mortality in these early generations that would compete against creatures with headstarts of millions of years, but some might survive.

This batch was the first to use the new np-704 transposon, a clever piece of DNA which could jump from gene to gene. He had kept its jumping legs but loaded its body with the sequences necessary to bring alive a set of ancient genes on chromosomes 8 and 9.

It was well known that the development of body parts from the blob of an egg was controlled by a series of Hox genes. These lay in neat and surprising rows, with the genes for the head next to those for the neck, which in turn lay beside those for the abdomen. This arrangement was complicated by the existence between and even inside genes of vast stretches of junk DNA called introns. Much of this was thought to have no purpose but Gastro had learned that this was not always so. Not all junk DNA was junk.

On the short arm of chromosome 8, at a site identified on the human genome map as a junk region, Gastro had found intact genes hiding like pearls in offal. These used a different "on" switch than any other genes and since molecular biologists find genes by looking for their "on" switches they remained unknown. Gastro found them only by chance while tracing the nearby genes which built the lung and it seemed that even the cells themselves had forgotten them, for though they were intact they were ignored after a brief embryonic burst of activity.

Gastro's transposon flew in like a guided missile and replaced the sleeping "on" switch with another. And the genes came alive. They sensed their position in the body in a way still not understood but which Gastro did not need to understand, and then they switched on other genes which, in a cascade, switched on still other genes. Gastro merely tipped the first domino and from there gravity took over.

Gastro lowered the next rat to the sea. It splashed and vanished and he looked at the crates filled with black eyes that watched him. The others waited their turns. There had been thousands and there would be thousands more. He took up the next one and for some reason glanced at its identification tattoo.

"Godspeed, Gwendolyn 43. Go forth and make this world your own."

Chapter 16

Katya Nister flipped on her computer and logged on to the Internet. She had finished the session with the new recruit and was not due to meet her father for forty minutes, which was enough time to be productive. She let few moments slip away unused and sometimes felt she was living two lives in one span; she slept only four hours a night and spent the others chasing her dream. Once it had been her father's dream, too, or so she had thought. Sometimes she was not sure.

She knew she was answering a call from deep within and she had come to learn that not everyone heard this call. This was strange, for the call was as much a part of her as her heart and just as deeply buried. It sounded in waves; she felt it more in the sea and most when she went deep, though it could also come on land. It compelled her to do things, things that her father might not condone. Perhaps it was nothing more than certain genes seeking their own survival, a possibility she recognized though it changed nothing. She also recognized the more unpleasant possibility that the genes vibrating in her cells displaced free will and that consciousness was a mere pleasant fiction by which genes made more genes. Again, even if true, this changed nothing.

She launched a program she had written and watched as it accessed the databases of a dozen shipping companies on four continents. A blue map of the Pacific appeared with emeralds marking islands and gold veins the shipping lanes. Katya entered a date a month in the future and ruby blips showed ships.

Out of habit she entered a date sixty days in the future, and then ninety, watching the red blips flick over the blue sea. None would pass within three hundred miles of Tanua. The accuracy of the projection degraded over time but the lack of a close pass would hold true for at least six months.

Once, that would have been a problem. Once, she would have ordered several containers filled with textiles or garden equipment or automotive parts to be delivered to Tanua or to an island which would have brought the ship within striking range. Once, the freighter carrying that cargo would have met a mishap that left it on the bottom with its crew ashore and its fate another mystery of the sea. Once, she would have used her software to pick that next victim of the Tabu Zone, and now out of curiosity she looked to see what ship it would have been. The container ship *Port Moresby,* a nondescript Liberian-flagged vessel. From a company database she pulled the names of the Captain and crew and then their medical records. The captain was fifty-eight, so likely too old. But the eleven other men would have been suitable.

But now none of this would be necessary. Katya had a far more elegant solution and far grander plans, plans that her father Gastro knew nothing about. She checked the samples she had taken at the kava ceremony and saw that the preliminary histocompatibility assessment was progressing; soon she would know a great deal about the immunology of everyone who had brought their lips to the wooden kava cup and from there she could make informed guesses about reproductive suitability. Something deep within told her that it would be wise to find a mate soon. At a faint sound she glanced over her shoulder and saw nothing but checked that the door was locked.

It would not do for Gastro to learn everything. In the end he would have to approve for together their work would usher in the next great phase of humanity, and when creating the next speciation, the effect on a few individuals is inconsequential. One had to see the big picture and Katya was all about the big picture, though it was Gastro's focus on the little picture—the little picture being Katya herself—that had started the ball rolling. But sometimes he was stuck to the little picture. It was an inherent but manageable problem.

She sat again at her computer and changed programs, this time to a simple mail application that contained lists of names and addresses from Argentina to Zanzibar and covering every continent and almost every country with a coastline. She read over the roster, taking the taste of each name, savoring entries as different Santiago del Cuesta,

John Brown, Xing Hu Ming, and Ndbidiboro Hallietasi. She felt a kinship with each of these though she never met nor laid eyes on any of them. Unknown to them, their lives were on converging paths; they shared a strange and exciting future, one that would be led by Katya. She would reach out and touch every one of them, and neither they nor the world would be the same.

Chapter 17

With the sun balanced on the eastern horizon like an orange on a blue plate, Marcus kicked through the water. The twin eighties on his back were heavy and, unlike his experimental gill, could not provide an indefinite air supply. But they would work.

Nick had argued against the dive while Marcus attached regulator to yoke and checked fin and mask straps.

"You're looking for her again, aren't you," Nick said.

Marcus slipped into the shoulder straps and took the weight then stepped to his friend. He pretended to flick a piece of lint from a massive shoulder.

"Nick. You know what we found. So you know why I have to do this. I'm no believer in Tangaroa but whatever is happening is happening out there." He pointed to where the coral arms of Tanua and Tabu embraced a blue arc.

"The exact reason not to go out there, in my book."

"We've always worked from different books."

"Marcus. We came to find *Omega*. We did that. Let's get off this rock. Disappearing people. Angry gods. Missing ships. Restless natives. It's making me nervous." He squeezed his brow. "I should never have tackled you. Look where it got me. It would have been better to lose that game."

"You did lose that game."

The Greek hefted a fist-sized rock and fired it out to sea where it vanished with a silent splash. "Do you really expect to find her boat just sitting there?"

Marcus cinched his waist strap and donned his weight belt, six pounds of lead clanking on a black strap.

"No," he conceded. "I don't."

"But at least you'll put another mark on the map."

"At least."

In truth Marcus had two reasons for the dive. The first he had shared with an unconvinced Nick; it was based on currents and submarine topography. The main current flowed from the southwest and followed the west coast of Tanua until it hit the corner of Tabu and turned. The bend of the corner plus the shift from deep to shallow would act as a natural trap. If there was any place to look this was it.

Marcus' second reason was not based on logic and he would not share it with Nick. In Vanuatu on the same day that he found the crude "C" shaped from sea floor rocks, he found something else. On the beach, in the firm sand just above the falling tide, lay another drawing. It was a set of curves beside a perfect cone shell of a type Callie had collected. The arrangement of lines and shell was odd; more so was that the shell was of a species not found within a thousand miles. There were no footprints; only a drag mark between the sketch and the sea. It could have been a freak of tide or bird coupled with an unknown population of the cone shells but Marcus did not think so. To him it was a map in which the line represented a coast and the shell a target and from then on he tried to fit every island to it. Without a sense of scale most shorelines could provide at least a crude fit and so he searched everywhere. But Tanua and Tabu, considered together, were a near perfect match. And today he would dive on the place marked by the shell.

He wondered, and not for the first time, whether he might be crazy.

Thirty minutes after leaving Nick, over an underwater cliff and breathing hard through his snorkel from dragging the tanks through the chop, Marcus gazed down on the tabletop of the reef flat and the wall below it. The smaller fish clustered on the flat and the bigger in the deeps along the wall and at the intersection of these two worlds things grew tense. The small fish bold enough to swim here might find untapped food but also could become food and so flashes and flickers glinted from this seam between worlds where life on the edge proved both rewarding and risky.

When his wind returned Marcus bit the mouthpiece of his old but trusty Poseidon, took a test breath—clean and dry—and dumped the air from the buoyancy compensator. The pressure built and the colors and sounds changed, and once again he was part of the world of the sea. The clouds of bright fish ignored him except for a pair of baby blacktip sharks, which made a single close pass before fleeing like schoolboys approaching a gruff neighbor on a dare.

He leveled at a hundred feet with a shot of air into the BC and cinched his weight belt tighter as he hung suspended over a steep pitch of reef where fat groupers and kaleidoscopic wrasses and parrotfish prowled among eight-foot sea fans and forests of black coral.

He kicked northward with the wall thirty feet on his right and a violet-tinted view downward to four hundred feet and on his left a blue curtain that as always looked stuffed with secrets. He scanned the deep for straight lines among the rounded curves of coral head and sand channel and manta ray.

For years he had wondered what it would be like to find the missing boat. A sense of sad jubilation, he expected. Perhaps sober relief. Tragic confirmation. The hulk alone might not provide any answers for it would likely be a bare wreck empty of remains and perhaps that would be better than finding a grinning skull once fleshed with lips he had kissed and been kissed by. But by location and condition it would speak. Dismasting would tell of a freak wave or storm; a stove-in bow or mid-ship of a collision; a missing keel of a design defect or accident that had turtled and sunk the boat. The location, too, would speak. Of how much progress had been made and how much the team might be hurrying. He knew the itinerary of the voyage in minute detail; knew of the stops at Noumea, Viti Levu, and Nuku'alofa. Knew that on the day the boat missed a check-in it should have been near Apia, but that it had been two days since the last word.

Marcus knew well that the boat might lie in the great depths between islands and once he had the technology to search there he would. In the meantime he searched in the shallows where the sand map hinted where his quarry lay.

He kicked in an underwater lope and with each slow, strong stroke, the rippling tug of the water reminded him of the smooth touch of Callie.

They had met on a hot day in a registration line in San Diego when after a forty-five minute wait, the functionary in charge closed the lone window for lunch.

"I hate when they do that," Marcus muttered.

The woman in front of him turned and flashed a dazzling smile. "You mean like brain scans? I don't know why they keep giving me those."

Marcus examined her. Reddish-blonde, deep blue eyes with a hint of madness, an impish grin on full lips, and along the side of her chin a faint scar. "They can't find it?" he asked innocently.

"Not yet. But they're hopeful about some new micro scan technique." She nodded eagerly. He saw from the papers in her hand, tucked into an old copy of Ovid atop a slim watercolor kit, that she was a med student. He would later learn that she was second in her class and that she had a fondness for ancient texts. By chance they met again two days later at a beach barbecue. The med students were taking on the biologists in volleyball and Callie had a booming jump serve and a deadly spike. Both seemed to target him and Marcus felt like he'd lost two layers of skin diving and digging.

"Maybe we could be on the same team," he said to her afterward.

"You don't mean you're switching to med school," she deadpanned.

"Can't. Too clumsy. People sue. Animals don't."

She looked him over as if buying a horse then held out her arm. "Maybe."

He took it and they floated down the beach.

Nick Kondos watched with his back to the pile of wood that would soon be a bonfire.

Years later, at a quayside bar in Vanuatu, Nick would tell Marcus he had known from that moment that the two would end up together. Just as he knew now that Marcus had to give up the search and move on. He not only wasn't going to find her, Nick would say and keep saying. He was losing himself.

At a spot that could have been marked by the shell on the map Marcus passed a brown flag of algae waving in the current like a dead hand. The coral beneath it was bleached white, killed by its grip. The flag was what marine scientists called a "diaperfish"—a disposable diaper disposed of at sea. Several more were draped on other death white corals. He looked around and saw nothing else and the symbolism struck a chord. After years of searching he had found nothing but ancient creatures felled by baby poop. Marcus realized that Nick was right: it was time to give up. Time to move on. Callie was gone and the long search pointless. The lines in the sand, the moving rocks, the glimpses and feelings and scents, all were but products of an obsessed brain. *Omega* was something else, as was the curious litter of wreckage on Tanua, but those would have to wait for someone other than an errant marine biologist tilting at tropical windmills and finding an undersea garbage dump. This would be the end of the search. The end of the map. The end of the little marks. The piece of nameplate could have drifted thousands of miles and might even be from another vessel, or from none at all, or part of some hoax. It didn't matter. Callie was gone and that was that and nothing would change it.

He felt a little piece of himself close off inside. It would hurt at first but it would wither and die and then fall numb. Perhaps it should have long before. He decided that not everything could be found once lost, no matter how hard or long one searches. It was a realization both unsettling and soothing.

He relaxed into the sea with a calm that had been gone so long he had forgotten it. He let his mind spin forward to the next projects—a geological assessment in Tuvalu, a deep population study off the Yasawa Islands of Fiji, an aerial photo survey of the Rock Islands in Belau.

A dim wall appeared out of the blue mist. This would be the north edge of the bay and the base of the forbidden isle of Tabu. The current slowed and the corals towered. Blue barrel sponges reached nine feet and opened their mouths wide enough to swallow a man. Finger-thick prongs of stag-horn coral stretched almost as high. A few tridacna, the giant clam of lore, held open yard-wide mouths of purple and pink velvet. A huge anemone appeared, its expanse of waving arms pale gray at depth. Within the stinging tentacles lived a troop of red and white clownfish, who added their teeth to its defenses in exchange for protection. They lined up to watch him pass as if he were a float in a parade.

He let the current drift him around the corner to the west. The corals were healthy and untouched and the fish big and tame. There were no craters from dynamite fishing and no diaperfish and not even any coral-devouring crown of thorns starfish. It was an underwater Eden where no one came and no one fished. He hung in tinted space with eyes fixed westward. As always the mist held the promise of something behind its blue veil. Vague shadows seemed to move across it like actors behind a dim screen and far below the floor was shot with occasional rays and sand sharks.

He had already come further than planned but he let the current waft him on. He was enjoying the pristine beauty and savoring the sensation of the end of the search.

At the edge of his vision, held so tight in the blue hand of the deep it was hard to see, linear clutter showed against the curves of coral head and sponge and sand channel. A blink and a squint and the lines remained. He cracked his mask and let it fill with the sea, then opened his eyes to the blur and cleared the water. Still the lines remained. He exhaled and slipped downward and the lines took on harder edges that resolved against the blue mist like a photograph developing. But even from directly overhead the jumble was unclear.

He headed down further until his computer flashed a warning. He hovered at a hundred seventy feet, close to the danger line without specialized breathing gas or spare tanks for decompression.

Another two hundred and fifty feet below him, dim and violet shrouded, lay a junk pile. Timbers, lines, drums, cables, wreckage. It could be a dumpsite for the islanders and it was reinforcement for the point made by the diaperfish: he was finding garbage. From the marine growths he estimated it to be five to fifteen years old.

Beside the dump another set of lines materialized and with eyes accustomed to litter, it took a moment for the image to pop. Then he saw the blunt prow and flat stern and the parallel lines. Three hundred or more feet long. A superstructure, a hull. A freighter sitting upright on the sand.

He arched to let a trail of cool water into his dive suit and down his spine. This should not be here for there were no local wrecks in the data Casper had found. But no database was perfect and the wreck explained the junk pile which had to be debris thrown off during the sinking.

He passed overhead like the sun over the earth and watched the perspective change. As the pointy prow began to fade another shape broke out ahead. Again, the lines were those of a freighter.

Two. There were two.

The absence of one from the database could have been an oversight. Two could not. He saw that he was streaming bubbles into a trail of exclamation points and forced a measured regularity into the beat of his heart and the draw of his lungs. He ascended thirty feet and let the current draw him along its invisible conveyor belt for now he had to see what would be revealed. He was well off his dive plan and the entire return would have to be a step decompression but it was worth it and his computer said it was workable. He wondered again what capricious gods were toying with him. To find such things on the very day he decided to stop looking.

Another shape appeared and he dropped again. Far below lay a shape that was five times smaller with a sharp prow and a curved hull and a raked stern. The sleek cockpit had a swept contour and the shape was that of a racing sloop.

Only one racing sloop had been lost in the Tabu Zone. And this was the exact spot marked by the poisonous point of that cone shell on the sand map on Vanuatu years before. He wondered at the symbolism: cone shells carry a deadly toxin that can drop a man dead before he drops the shell.

He emptied his lungs and piked down but after three hard kicks stopped. Hovering with the blue sun beneath his black fins, he considered. A dive to four hundred feet on air could well be fatal—though it had been done—but it was not death that gave him pause. It was the timing. He did the math, computing partial pressures and breath volume and descent rates. In all likelihood, he would not even reach the phantom below. At three hundred, three hundred and fifty, or perhaps four hundred feet, oxygen toxicity or nitrogen narcosis or both would overcome him. Perhaps only feet from the hull he would convulse and die or, in a narcotic haze, offer his regulator to a passing fish while he tried to breathe water.

Then again he might make it.

He hung suspended and weightless halfway between the air and the sand, feeling the pull of each.

Chapter 18

From the shade of a coconut palm Pelemodo looked over the pretty stripe of sugar sand that connected the villages of Popo and Atau.

Behind Pelemodo stood the survivors of the latest legion of warriors to have spent time on Tabu with the palangi doctor. It was only with Pelemodo's permission that one could go to the forbidden isle and those who went did not come back the same. On the surface they were unchanged, but in their depths dark things had been twisted into new shapes. Pelemodo recognized that it could be seem a contradiction for the champion of the traditional to seek out the new and foreign, but Pelemodo was a pragmatist and would refuse no advantage. Besides, perhaps Tangaroa himself had put the palangi doctor in his path. To ignore him would be to bypass a perfect mango within easy reach. Pointless.

The warriors moved carefully as they served him woven mats laden with taro and banana and chicken and pork cooked in the old way, so that while the palangis would call it raw it still retained its power. The warriors took great care not to touch Pelemodo or his clothes or even his shadow. To do so would assault the chief's spiritual power, known as *mana*, and could earn a fatal rebuke. After lunch they would resume the journey which they conducted in the traditional way: on foot.

Below them a family of eight walked the beach as they returned to Popo after church in Atau.

Pelemodo frowned at the family and felt his warriors pick up the hostility. The family was one of those that did not yet follow the way. The father wore a stiff white shirt, a neat lava-lava of starched navy blue cotton, and rubber sandals. His three sons wore white shirts and white cloth lava-lavas belted with yellow rope, as did the four daughters and wife. Pelemodo knew them vaguely and knew that each would also be wearing a plain wooden cross on a simple chain.

Many had left the palangi faith recently but this family, the Alamoanas, had not. Despite the stories and the terror of their neighbors and the emptying of the churches they stayed.

The children ran ahead with the smaller ones playing near the waves while the older ones prowled the jungle edge but gave a wide berth to Pelemodo and the silent warriors around him.

Pelemodo scooped a handful of blue taro to his mouth and wished the breadfruit crop was ready. He wondered if there would be any at all this year—the ominous triple breadfruit might never ripen. No one knew. There had never been triple breadfruit before.

The father of the Alamoana family was a thickly muscular man known as Niku and he stopped to sweep his wife Maria off her feet and nuzzle her ear. She squealed and slapped at him with enough force for a loud crack to sound.

"Our children are too big. My arms are empty. We need another baby," he said and she shrieked.

He set her feet on the sand and took her in his arms. Niku lived in a communal society and had no expectation of privacy, so his sullen watchers did not deter him. But he neither turned his back on the chief, which would show disrespect, nor faced him, which might send a challenge.

Thin screams cut the air.

The smallest of the boys who had been at the forest popped over a sand dune with tiny legs pounding. Next came one of those near the water, as fast as her little legs could fly. The others followed close behind.

The reason for the panic appeared: a river of small gray shapes that ran from the forest to the sea. Niku charged forward to protect his young but slid to a halt at the sight. Pelemodo rose to his feet and exhaled.

The shapes looked like rats but they did not act like rats. Bundled in tight groups they ran straight for the sea where they seemed to pop to nothingness. Another clot of gray burst from the forest and the river swelled. There were hundreds. Perhaps thousands.

"Papa, vaitama?" cried the littlest girl.

"Vaitama," Niku agreed with a glance at Pelemodo. The girl ignored her mother's warning and stepped close to the creatures.

"Tangaroa speaks to us," Pelemodo called softly to his warriors. The air was thick and heavy and he did not think Tangaroa would go to this effort without more to show. He was right.

The newest burst of animals rolled itself into a ball and even from a distance Pelemodo could sense teeth slashing and claws ripping. The white sand splashed with blood and body parts and many creatures were left either twitching with death or dragging broken limbs or guts from ripped bellies.

Then the vaitama veered at the family and hit the young girl and she was screaming and beating at her legs and grabbing at small biting bodies and throwing them. For every one she pulled off two more appeared and then her father was beside her. He grabbed her up but the gray tide swarmed up his legs and he held her one-handed while beating at them. His own blood and blood from smashed bodies covered his legs and waist and chest and still they came. He tossed her in the water in the hope they would wash off but she screamed louder and he saw the water boiling and went in after her.

The screams of his wife and the other children came as they too were attacked and the copper scent of blood and the raw odor of opened bodies rolled over the beach. A few of the creatures reached the tree line and Pelemodo saw his warriors swing their clubs. Vaitama rocketed through the air like cricket balls with the popping sounds of small bones shattering.

A warrior looked at Pelemodo and the chief understood why. Was it permitted to kill the minions of Tangaroa?

"It is well," Pelemodo announced. "Tangaroa does not mean for these to hurt us. We may protect ourselves."

As suddenly as they had attacked the creatures broke off and flowed into the sea and vanished. Three of the Alamoana children lay face down on the sand surrounded by red pools and the others were wailing. The bleeding parents scrambled between them.

Pelemodo scanned the bodies on the beach and the wounds on his men and on the Alamoanas. Tangaroa moved in mysterious ways. There were many stories of vaitama going vicious but he had not seen it before and for a moment he wondered what the palangi had done. Then he reminded himself that Gastro was a mere tool of Tangaroa. And it was too late to wonder what Tangaroa was doing.

Pelemodo had at his back a cadre of new warriors. He could see that their breathing was quick and their nostrils wide. He made a decision. The time would be soon and so it would be best to blood them now.

On the beach below Niku ripped the crucifix from his throat and hurled it into the sea then collected those of his children and wife and did the same.

Too little, too late.

Pelemodo turned to his warriors and read in their faces eagerness and hunger, and in the light behind their eyes an urge he had never seen before but which some primal part of him recognized.

"Tangaroa has spoken. These are unbelievers. Take them. Finish Tangaroa's work."

Niku and his eldest son fought well but were no match for thirty warriors. War clubs whistled and again the sand ran red.

Chapter 19

Nick waited until Marcus vanished beneath the waves then turned to walk back up the rotting wharf.

On his right passed the rows of dilapidated metal huts that housed old labs and maintenance shops from the days of the Coast Guard; on his left the *Aurora* and then the Flying Canoe. The multi-colored flying boat dipped its wing floats as if greeting him and he gave it the finger.

The water beside the plane churned as a squadron of flying fish burst out and with fins extended skimmed the sea. What goes up, Nick predicted, and one by one they splashed.

Where the wharf touched the island it met another cluster of tin and rust buildings. Beyond lay an open space through which passed the island's road and then the open malae which hosted the markets of Sava. These offered, in Nick's opinion, a staggering variety of food poisonings, most under glass, which seemed to keep the flies in rather than out. Above the village rose slopes of palm, fern, and fig interspersed with cultivated patches and fales that huddled among the trees. Another ten miles up the slope hung the bald peak of Mt. Tanua. A round cloud hung over the peak like the dot below an exclamation point.

Nick thought with a shudder of descending into the depths at that moment, and acknowledged a certain irony in being a descendant of fisherman yet averse to the sea. Perhaps it was because so many of his line had perished upon it. He didn't even like the wharf; too many of the old planks were half-rotten and sagging.

And yet Marcus seemed to find a second home not only in the deep but in the air. It was one of their many differences; theirs was a friendship built on affection plus a mutual disdain for authority and bureaucracy and a solid enthusiasm for science and what it could do. Though Nick was loath to admit it, traveling the South Pacific by ancient flying boat and working on a dozen simultaneous projects was far more rewarding than scrambling for grants and fighting for a window office on some nameless campus. Not only was the science important, their projects often created practical benefits like cleaner water or better food stocks for the islanders.

But Nick was worried that the long and fruitless search for Callie was eating at Marcus like an acid. And so Nick had escalated his efforts to bring some closure to his friend. Knowing better than to try simply telling him to move on, Nick tried more subtle methods such as connecting him with other women. Nick's relationships with women were the opposite of Marcus'; Nick admitted that he fell in love very easily and after three ex-wives—all of whom he still liked but none of whom he could in the end tolerate—he had declared himself retired from the marriage game. Marcus was more choosey. The only one with whom there had been any chemistry was Devon Lucas, the sub pilot with an outer impishness and an inner steel. And now she too had vanished into the sea.

Nick had long mistrusted the sea gods, and now he wondered if they had it out for Marcus as well. Nick considered his friend deep in the same sea that had devoured Callie, Devon, and countless others, and then pondered his own situation on dry land among the hostile followers of an angry sea god.

Nick believed that when the jaws of death are closing in, there's only one thing to do. And so he set off to find a bar.

Chapter 20

As the sun fell into the Polynesian afterworld of Pulotu, which waited beneath the western horizon, shadows lay their dark bodies across the fales of Tanua and the first evening breeze pressed the heat of day out to sea. Drums sounded slow rhythms and the island drew a breath as the time of sa'a came. Among prayer times sa'a has an unusual twist: it is enforced with violence.

In each village the young men took up the traditional weapons of stick and rock. The men saw no irony in beating someone to enforce prayer time, and the return of the old gods meant the end of what little restraint was once imposed by a two thousand year old carpenter from the far side of the world.

It was at this time in the early evening that Pelemodo sat on the floor of his fale like an octopus spread on a beach. The sa'a was no imposition on him, and if he desired, he could light off fireworks with impunity.

The same was not true for the white man before him.

The palangi wore a cotton lava-lava and a western shirt. His white hair touched his shoulders and the eyes that burned hot as an umu stone were averted in an attempt at deference.

"Doctor. Please stop. It is quite ridiculous," sighed Pelemodo. "You are here to tell me of the latest results. So tell me."

Gastro Nister looked at him and shrugged. "We are continuing to improve. We expect a survival rate of almost seventy percent in the latest legion."

Pelemodo considered. "Now we are killing only three out of ten."

"Slightly more."

"When can you start another batch?"

Gastro blinked and seemed to replay the words in his head. "Another batch?"

"Yes."

"Perhaps a month. Six weeks, to be safe. Diverting resources could drop the survival rate."

"Start more immediately. I may also need additional vaitama."

Gastro frowned. "But did you not say last time that there are already too many? That they are affecting the timetable?"

"I did say that. But," and here his tone became both casual and sly, "we are changing the timetable."

"No!"

"My followers are ready and the fear is rising. Events are proceeding faster than anticipated."

"I cannot be ready any sooner than eighteen months. As we agreed."

"Our agreement," the chief said lazily, "was that we would help each other. We have done so."

"Our agreement is that I am to have Tabu for another eighteen months, then I help you take the islands. Legally. Peacefully. By influencing the American government to cede these islands to local control. Abandon a last vestige of colonialism and all that."

The chief fingered the fish vertebrate that ringed his neck and eyed the palangi as if considering more bones for the necklace. "I am not sure we need you. We have a substantial community on the mainland and properly motivated they will raise a hue and cry heard from Washington to Los Angeles."

"Chief Pelemodo—"

A finger wagged.

"Paramount Chief Pelemodo. I am already working as fast as possible. I am hurrying. I cannot move any faster."

"Doctor, your own efforts have played a part in this. You cannot blame me. The time comes and no man may stop it."

"Eighteen months," Gastro insisted. "It must be."

"Doctor, have you considered that you too might be an instrument of Tangaroa?"

As often happened Gastro found himself gaping at the giant chief and wondering whether he was joking. Gastro reminded himself that he had never to his knowledge seen Pelemodo joke.

"No."

"Which proves nothing. Does a rake know itself to be an instrument of human effort?"

"A rake is not alive," Gastro countered.

"An oxen, then?"

Gastro pressed his lips together. One never won arguments with Pelemodo; the best one could achieve was a draw.

Pelemodo continued. "An oxen cannot comprehend that it is a mere tool of human will. Even when a beast of burden mates it but carries out the will of its master, though it cannot know that any more than you can understand your role here. But all is coming together and this is in part due to your efforts. In the years since you came the Matai have grown and the vaitama have been part of that. They are tangible proof of Tangaroa. But now there are so many they are causing panic. Fear is good for it creates an opportunity for control. But panic is bad. It is inherently beyond control."

"Paramount Chief, I cannot bring back the vaitama anymore than I could catch every fish in the sea."

"I did not think you could. And that is why we must change the timetable."

Gastro blinked. He was beginning to feel like a kitten that has been playing with an interesting flexible stick, which has just revealed itself to be a king cobra, leading to the sudden and serial realizations that: 1) it isn't a game and 2) kittens don't win fights with cobras.

"Paramount Chief Pelemodo, it is quite impossible."

"It is already done. I am only informing you."

"Didn't you just ask me to start another batch? If I leave I will be unable to finish it."

"You need not finish. I asked you only to start. Tangaroa will do the rest."

"You are asking the impossible."

Pelemodo smiled a slow smile. "Doctor, did you not once tell me that you had done the impossible?"

Gastro inhaled and stiffened, one finger already lifting in objection before he recognized that he was trapped. He sighed and nodded.

"Then it should be no trouble to do it again."

Gastro had once been of the opinion that Pelemodo believed that all this Tangaroa talk was nonsense. But now, seeing the glint in Pelemodo's eyes and the gleam on his teeth, he merely bowed and backed away.

"Until next time, Paramount Chief Pelemodo."

"Wait." Pelemodo pointed at him and he froze.

Pelemodo's eyes closed and he remained still for sixty seconds as the breeze blew and the parrots squawked. He appeared asleep or in deep meditation, a giant Buddha.

Gastro started to edge away.

"Wait," Pelemodo ordered again with eyes still closed. Gastro froze for another minute then started to move and again was stopped, this time by a single shake of Pelemodo's finger. Gastro began to sweat and he tried to slide his feet with imperceptible slowness over the mats the floored the fale.

"No," Pelemodo whispered.

A drumbeat walked across the village to announce the end of sa'a. People emerged to fetch laundry and prepare food.

"Now go," breathed Pelemodo.

Gastro went. Pelemodo, he realized, had been protecting him. He wondered how long that would be true.

Chapter 21

Devon Lucas was staring at herself in the mirror, trying to identify the subtle changes in her physique, when there was a knock at her door. As always this surprised her; she considered herself a captive and captives expect no courtesy. But the man who brought her here told her that she was not a prisoner but a guest and a soon-to-be pioneer, and he insisted on treating her like it.

She steeled herself and wondered what new horrors this day would bring.

The door opened to reveal Katya Nister, attired in a cotton top, flowing lava-lava, and sandals. Her body was nut-brown, lean, and hard-muscled. Her body, Devon realized, was like the end point of the direction in which Devon's own body seemed to be moving.

Katya summoned her along paths of crushed coral that led to the lab building, which lay across a grassy courtyard from the dormitory building. The whole complex looked like an abandoned coconut plantation, though on the inside the buildings were well appointed. The dormitory building was three stories tall, and Devon and Henry received rooms on the top floor, beside each other, though Henry had not yet occupied his. The first two floors held other people who apparently had arrived under similar circumstances: none, it seemed, had bought a ticket. But these others were uniformly distant and unapproachable; they seemed as strange as the place itself.

Which was, it turned out, the isle of Tabu. A tiny island that abutted the north end of the larger isle of Tanua, and almost touched it at low tide. Katya and her father Gastro had been entirely forthcoming with most information, such as where they were, and had also told her utterly unbelievable things about what was happening here. They also seemed singularly unconcerned about Devon escaping.

And so she did. Late one night she stealthily fled the dormitory. No one seemed to notice but she did not stop sprinting until she was a quarter mile into dark jungle, surrounded by snaps and rustles and squeaks. Her brain told her that Pacific island jungles lack the hazards of Amazonian or Congo rainforests: there are no vipers or boas or big predators; the largest threat might be a wild pig. But her heart thudded madly at some atavistic memory of being a primate in a lion's world.

She forced herself to calm and then continued. At the beach she began working around the island.

She was back in her room before dawn. She had circled the island and then traversed it. Twice. There was nothing but palms and sand and eerie rustles and, on the far side, a grim patch where the wind whistled and the earth was mounded into what had to be graves. Otherwise, not a phone, not a store, not a village, not a hut. Nothing. The closest sign of anything was the nearby island of Tanua, separated from her by a quarter-mile channel which in the silver moonlight was ripping with the current plunging between the two islands. Even if she crossed, an attempt she did not feel up to after her most recent escape from the sea, she had a feeling that she would not get far. And so she had returned.

As they walked Katya cast a long and knowing look at her.

"Nice walk, the other night?"

Devon looked at her with studied blankness.

"Everyone tries. Everyone finds what you did. There's nowhere to go."

"There's a whole other island, actually."

"We have people there too; that's not an escape. But with that high tide you'd have been blown three miles out to sea before you made it halfway across."

"And then?"

"And then I'd have had to come get you." She smirked. "Again."

When the research sub *Omega*, blacked out and with two gasping passengers aboard and apparently trapped for all eternity, had given its first lurch, Devon thought that perhaps her final mental disintegration was beginning with a tactile hallucination. But Henry confirmed that he felt it, too. And besides, the air was not quite bad enough for the hallucination part of asphyxiation.

The sub continued to lurch and rock, and the slithering noises kept coming through the hull. The viewports showed only the blackness of the deep and so whatever was happening could not be seen. Perhaps a giant squid found the bright hull to be a pretty bauble; perhaps some unknown creature of the depths was taking them down even further. With the instrumentation broken they couldn't even tell if they were ascending or descending.

"Devon," Henry said.

"I know, Henry. Go with it. It's not like we have any choice. And besides, it can't make things worse."

How naïve she had been.

The motion took on a steady rocking swing that continued for over an hour. Then the motion changed slightly. To Devon's trained mind, the new rocking felt like being at or near the surface; there was a period and a frequency to the way *Omega* moved with waves and this felt similar. But the ports showed only black; then again they were horribly scratched and it was night. Her heart fluttered at the notion.

But it made absolutely no sense for them to be anywhere near the surface. It was a nice fantasy, but that was all. Whatever was moving the sub wasn't a rescue, or it would have identified itself. No, they had to be somewhere still in the deeps, in the grip of some phenomenon that no one knew. One of the many mysteries of the deep. One that would have to be left to future explorers to discover.

Still, she was curious enough that she called up the red emergency lights. The cockpit was the same terrible chaos—a mess of broken equipment and shattered dials. But the meager light couldn't penetrate the ports. She could see nothing new.

A small metallic noise drew her eye to the circular handle set in the hatch and her stomach dropped the rest of the way to her knees.

The handle was turning.

"I feel like your mom," Katya said. She had to repeat herself to get Devon's attention.

"My mother?" Devon asked cautiously.

"I was the first face you saw in your new life. When you came out of the sub, looking quite surprised to be in fresh air. It was like a womb. The dividing line between your old life and this new one."

"It wasn't supposed to be," Devon said softly, recalling the surreal scene as she and Henry were greeted by small group of people that handed them flower leis as they alighted. *Omega* was in a deep cavern where the light was a dim filtered blue and the wash of the nearby sea sounded. There were ropes and lines tied to her hull but no other sign of how they had arrived. Devon knew well Katya's explanation that it was plain old muscle power but still had trouble accepting it. Once ashore they watched as the sub was sealed up and the lift bags deflated, and *Omega* sank out of sight in the grip of whatever was pulling those long lines.

Katya continued. "And now, again like a mother, I have to look out for you. Help you, in ways that may not seem like they're helpful. Have you met the others?"

"The others?"

"In your dorm. On the floors below."

"A few. Not a friendly bunch, though."

"They'll warm up. You're still too new. Once you've changed you'll be one of them."

Devon slowed and gave her a hard look. "You keep saying things like that."

"Yes, I do," admitted Katya. "This is no joke. It's as serious as life. As serious as death. As serious as evolution."

"I don't understand."

"You will. Come."

Katya led her to a large room in the warehouse-like building, on the opposite side from the combination lab/infirmary where Henry rested. A dozen men and women awaited them and Devon felt all eyes upon her as she entered. It was exactly like starting a new school; she could feel the other kids evaluating her.

Katya made perfunctory introductions—the group included Brazilians, Americans, Australians, and Italians—then left them, as she said, "to get better acquainted."

After a half hour Devon knew less than she had known before. It was like talking to an alien species; her questions were deflected and the answers she did get were vague if not meaningless. The most common answers were along the lines of: "Just wait; it will make sense soon." There was no reason to flee and nowhere to go; when they had arrived they too had thought this way but now they saw things more clearly. They were where they should be. They were serving a greater purpose and that was worth some inconvenience.

Just be patient, they said again and again. It will make sense.

Devon was not willing to wait for it to make sense; she wanted it to make sense now. She asked and pressed and finally cross-examined like a rabid trial lawyer and the answers grew more elliptical and incoherent; the words made sense but the thoughts they expressed were impenetrable. Devon began to wonder if she had encountered some extreme cult with sophisticated brainwashing techniques.

Finally she realized she would get nowhere with the group. And with that, she thanked them and left.

Chapter 22

Nick Kondos blasted into the village of Feoni like an icebreaker assaulting a floe. Chickens scattered and dogs barked and children stared as a Suzuki jeep slid to a halt and disgorged a huge palangi who made an instinctive beeline for the hamlet's lone bar. That it had a mere three stools and two card tables, and also served as a tattoo parlor, was no impediment. It was far from the main town of Sava and the insanity of vanished people and annoyed gods, ship parts and strange creatures. He had first tried the yacht club and found it to hold the usual band of ex-pats: a mix of tax and spouse evaders, low-rate felons, and a few fortyish personal injury attorneys who hit a big case and retired with a first sailboat and a second wife. It was the kind of crowd Nick enjoyed, though he would freely admit he enjoyed most crowds. He had quickly made his presence known and when during a game of darts he clarified that his own olive complexion stemmed from mother Hellas and not Polynesia, he learned of a countryman in the village of Feoni.

And so here he was in a borrowed jeep. It was the kind of purposeless jaunt that drove Marcus mad but Nick figured he put up with enough to be allowed a few.

Nick assessed his countryman as he ordered a pint. Several inches below six feet and ropy with muscle, black hair shot with gray, and dark eyes. According to Nick's source—a local judge with a surprisingly deep thirst but low tolerance for tequila—the man had married a slim island girl after jumping ship years before.

The beer arrived frozen to near slush that quickly melted in the damp grip of the island heat.

"*Ef haristo,*" Nick said.

The barman frowned and squinted. "You speak Greek?" he asked in that tongue.

"Most Greeks do. Though I was born in Chicago."

The man who had abandoned Kiriakos to go by John pulled Nick into a hug.

"You're one of the ones who found the sub, yes?" John asked while studying him when the clench broke.

"Is there no escaping that?"

"Not on this island." John tilted his head outside towards a group of bare-chested islanders. "Maybe not anywhere, depending what you believe."

Nick pondered which way to steer the conversation. A discussion of the merits of island versus mainland women would be enjoyable, as would a lively argument about the attributes of kava versus tobacco, or local beer versus the favorite import, Budweiser. But Nick was also a scientist and he had his own reluctant curiosity. He sighed.

"What do you believe, John?"

The man snorted and wiped the counter. "I believe there's a lot of crazy in this place."

"Such as?"

John glanced outside to where the islanders were now looking in. "You've seen some, I know, and heard more, I'll bet. Plenty to go around. We got as much crazy here as we got heat and bugs. Plenty. Plenty-tele."

A stout woman and two men entered from the back. All three were heavily tattooed and John introduced the hefty woman as his wife Tasi—the willowy island lass had thickened into a stout tree—and the men as her brothers.

"Do those tattoos go everywhere?" Nick wondered.

"It's a rite of passage," John replied and displayed his own arms. "You got no ink?"

"Only in my pens."

"A virgin. How cute," Tasi said. She dropped her elbows to the bar then cut her black eyes at the growing knot of men outside. They now clustered around the jeep and they were big and muscular and no less threatening for their rubber sandals and skirts. Lines crossed her forehead.

"You helped with *Omega*, right?" she asked.

"Am I wearing a sign?"

"No need to. You're marked. Which makes you bad for business." Outside the men looked unhappy. "Maybe for health, too."

Nick met John's eye. "Just one beer. For Thessaly."

John looked to his wife and nodded.

"And while I'm here, tell me about the crazy stuff you've seen. Not heard about. Seen."

John held out the silver cross at his throat. "Look at this. Had it since I was seventeen. Now, not sure it's worth the metal. Things here—" he shook his head. "Millions of people, for two thousand years, maybe wrong. I really think so."

"Great Zeus. You're a believer in this nonsense too?"

"Wasn't, and don't wanna be. But maybe no choice. The islanders converted to Jesus because of a prophecy that something was to come from the sea or across the sea. Now they say they misunderstood and that the something was to come from the sea and not from across the sea. They say the palangis tricked them. They say the prophecy was for Tangaroa. Not some carpenter. Maybe they're right."

He cut himself off and Nick raised his hands in a gesture that invited the rest.

Tasi looked at John and he looked at her and nodded. "Tell him."

"The breadfruit, the bats, a lot of stuff. Who knows what it means if anything. But the vaitama. Real. Very," she said. "Nothing like that been here before. Something going on. They say is Tangaroa. Maybe it is. Many have left the island."

"Why haven't you?"

Tasi's face broke into a smile of relief. "We are. Every ferry for months is booked but we go in two weeks. A thousand tala for tickets but is worth it to get out."

"A thousand dollars?" Nick said.

"All our savings."

"Because of vaitama?"

"Because of Tangaroa," Tasi corrected forcefully. "You don't understand. No kindness, no forgiveness. All revenge. All hate."

Nick finished his beer and waved for another. "I'm sure there are really animals out there. What I doubt is that they're supernatural."

"When you see one you know. Not normal. Not right. Special."

"Then I'd like to see one."

John was looking at him strangely. "Why do you care, friend?"

"Good question. Long story."

Tasi lifted Nick's bottle and set it down. "You should go. If the Matai hear about this—"

"You can say that you were doing your part to convince a non-believer. Listen. I'll give you a hundred dollars for a vaitama that is—special. Not just a regular animal."

Tasi blanched. "You want to buy a vaitama?"

"I do."

"That could really piss off Tangaroa."

Nick shrugged. "He's already pissed. Hundred bucks. A nice dinner somewhere when you get off the island. There's a good Benihanna in Honolulu."

John cut his eyes outside then half-turned away from the open window. "Five hundred."

Nick did not need to feign shock; he was shocked. Not by the amount of the counter-offer but by the fact of it. John thought he could provide a vaitama.

"Two."

"Four hundred, you insult to our homeland," John smiled.

"Three hundred, you Trojan Horse dealer."

"Deal."

"No," said John's wife. "You pay us three hundred to try. We probably get one. But you pay us to try. Okay?"

Nick studied her, saw John shrug, and nodded.

"One more thing," she said, pointing at the tattoo around her middle. "If we find you a vaitama you buy one of these."

Nick finished his second beer, not counting the four at the Yacht Club.

"If you find me a vaitama, why not?"

Chapter 23

Gastro Nister entered his cold laboratory and slipped into a white lab coat while calling up results. During the night he had run a new set of DNA fragments through an agarose gel to sort them into bands by size.

He saw the band he hoped for and smiled. He drew satisfaction from every success, for despite all the progress, terrible failures still happened. In one sense the last two converts had already cheated the reaper's hand; their lives ended when the *Omega* was trapped and any extra days could only be viewed as a bonus. Gastro knew that Death always has a counterpunch and that anyone who dodges one blow should not cheer but duck, for the next cut of the scythe is surely on the way.

Gastro cut the band from the gel with a sterile scalpel. In this few millimeters of agarose he held the critical Hox genes that controlled the initiation of the expression of other genes; they were the keys to the car and lighting them off in the right way triggered a cascade. In understanding this lay the genius of his work, for the genes were both simple and complex and they did not simply switch on or off but had many intermediate positions. The magic lay in switching them on in the right way in each individual.

After being unused for countless millennia one might have expected the old genes to start up roughly and with a cloud of blue smoke but they kicked over smoothly from the start—almost as if, Gastro sometimes thought to himself, they had been waiting for him, though he knew that it must have been some evolutionary pressure that kept them intact all these eons. Apparently at some point a fetus actually relied on its gills or at least on the genes. It was unconventional thinking but once so were the electric light and motorcar. That such things lurked in the genome would come as no surprise to those who studied it for despite having been sequenced no one knew what the bulk of it did. Only three percent encoded genes and most of even that portion was unknown. The remainder was as blank as the dark side of moon and it lay in every cell of every man, woman, and child.

To dissolve the agarose Gastro added a few drops of a buffer that smelled faintly of salt against the cool air, and then put the tube in a microcentrifuge with a balance tube on the opposite side.

The problem was simple to state but complex to tackle. Humans started out as blobs of cells that were neither bone nor blood nor muscle nor brain. The Hox genes understood where in the body they were and what should be built. One of Gastro's challenges was to make new structures grow in the right place, since he was dealing not with an embryo but with a developed adult. This proved simple; another of the old genes allowed healing on a reptilian scale and so Gastro merely tricked the body into thinking it was healing itself by growing the new structures, with the Hox genes guiding what to grow where.

But the system was fragile and errors by the control genes had led to grotesque failures. He shuddered at the memory of budding third and fourth arms, of ribs growing uncontrolled through the skin, of the big tails that sprouted in two cases, and another in which a dense coat of fur grew. The genes carried an infinite range of horrible possibilities; only one arrangement made a normal human and only one slightly better arrangement made one of Gastro's changelings. But he learned from every success and he learned from every failure.

The centrifuge was spinning with a whir when Katya walked in wearing her usual lava-lava, tank top, and floor-slapping flip-flops.

"Would you like to help?" he asked as he put the tube on ice.

"What can I do?"

Gastro shifted in his seat and as usual turned the session into part father-daughter bonding time, part lecture. One of the drawbacks of living on an island like Tanua was the lack of higher education opportunities but Gastro had done much to fill that gap with a sophisticated computer system and regular lectures. Katya had a keen mind and was a quick study but her breadth of knowledge could be spotty.

"I am refining the promoter for these genes, using this program to project the effect of various single nucleotide polymorphisms. Much of biochemistry is simple mechanics—shapes fitting together and interacting. As you know both proteins and nucleic acids are simply chains—one long piece of spaghetti that loops back and coils and folds to assume a three dimensional shape. Forecasting what shape a given sequence will take has been one of the great challenges of modern science."

"Has been?" Katya was smiling.

Gastro patted his computer, a high-powered workstation that had to be smuggled out of the United States as if Tanua were Cold War Moscow. On screen was a complex glob of multi-colored protein.

"This program I wrote does a rather nice job. As you can see I have entered a possible alteration to the sequence of the oxygen-transport membrane proteins we are currently using. The trick is to modify the active site of the protein so that it binds more efficiently."

He tapped and the protein rotated and he pressed a pencil eraser to the glass.

"Now, see how in this one the anterior lobe of this subunit is more rounded? And when we compare the receptor site," Gastro pecked the keyboard and on the next monitor a different molecule appeared, its various regions colored blue and red and yellow and purple.

"You see? This is . . . in you. The fit is not perfect and there was a time when I was worried by it."

Katya was surprised by what he did not say and so she supplied it. "But not anymore."

He tousled her hair. "Not anymore. Should I be?"

Katya's face was serious. "No. It wouldn't do any good anyway."

Chapter 24

Nick found Marcus rinsing his gear and hanging it from a wooden peg in the dive shed. The shed sat among the small buildings at the foot of the wharf with a door secured by chain and padlock and its interior heavy with the scents of diving—neoprene and salt and silicone and mineral oil. The floor was rough concrete and the walls cracked plywood. The only ornate feature was the row of wooden pegs for the gear; each was carved into a misshapen face with a stout peg protruding from nose or forehead or chin. Marcus wore an expression as wooden as the pegs but even more strained. So did Nick, who carried a bucket.

"I've got something for you, buddy," Nick said.

Marcus turned and looked through him. "Nick. I found her."

Nick swallowed. Something in Marcus' tone told him that the answer to the question he now had to ask would upset him. Especially in light of what he held in his hands.

"You found who?"

Marcus' gaze focused and a line appeared between his brows.

"Is that a tattoo? You hate tattoos."

Nick touched the bleeding scab on his shoulder; from behind it peeked a rough image of a bearded Poseidon. "Yes. And I know that seems surprising. But believe me it's not the most surprising thing. Who did you find?"

Marcus flushed his regulator and looked at Nick in a way that made him want to pinch himself to see if it was all a dream. He didn't because that way at least he could hope.

"The *Nefertiti*. Callie's boat. It's here." Marcus described the litter of wreckage and the two freighters and the smaller sharper shape with the raked prow. "I'm going back with the deep gear. First light tomorrow."

Nick ran both hands through his hair and found several white strands and flung them away.

"Marcus, until a couple hours ago I would have told you there's no way whatever you saw could be the *Nefertiti*. And no way the other wrecks could be here. No way."

Marcus leaned his fins against the wall then shut down the hose and began to coil the soft rubber. He knew that although Nick spent words freely he also chose them with care. He stowed the hose and stood to face the larger man. "Until a couple hours ago. What happened a couple hours ago?"

Nick opened his mouth, shut it, and set the dripping bucket onto the rough concrete.

"This. A vaitama happened."

Nick described his meeting with John and Tasi, and their deal, and his surprise when fifteen minutes after John summoned a boy and sent him running off the youth returned with a bucket.

"Here you go," John had said. "One vaitama. Where you want it?"

Nick held out his hand but John and his wife only smiled.

"I meant the ink, man. Your tattoo."

"Show me this vaitama is special," Nick said.

And they did.

Afterward, Nick stared at the bucket while he sat back and pointed at his shoulder.

"What is it?" Marcus asked as Nick removed the cloth that covered the bucket. "Looks like a rat."

"It does. It isn't."

Nick lifted the gray rodent by the scruff of its neck. Black eyes bulged and a pink tongue protruded. With one hand Nick uncoiled a loop of hose, turned the valve, and filled the bucket to the brim. He looked the rat in the eye then plunged it forearm deep.

"Nick—"

"Watch."

Marcus watched. He had personally seen Nick rescue three different kittens from trees and knew the big Greek believed in kindness to small creatures. Which meant that the apparent drowning of a small animal must be something else.

"Jesus," Marcus said sixty seconds later.

"Wrong deity, it seems."

"It doesn't mind?"

"Apparently not. The villagers say there are dogs, cats, pigs. Everything. This one happens to be a rat." Marcus leaned close to the bucket.

"Is it—"

"Breathing water? Apparently so."

"But that's—"

Nick nodded and released the rat. It remained on the bottom with sides heaving and eyes gazing upward.

"Impossible," Nick finished. "That's what I've been telling you for years."

Chapter 25

Katya entered what they called the demo lab, a plain space of tile and bright light where the changelings learned what they would become. A cage of Norwegian rats lazed in sawdust. The steel sink that had held so many water bottles, after Katya developed the water-soluble virus from the injectable clade, sat empty.

A side door opened to the smaller and more cluttered lab that was Katya's own. Here electron micrographs dotted the walls and electrophoresis and HPLC machines shared her one bench with racks of micropipettes. Overhead the shelves of reagents bore labels from Roche, BioPharm, and Fischer Scientific.

In a position of honor over her desk hung a micrograph of a spiked sphere, like the business end of a medieval mace. This was Katya's creation: the water-tolerant virus.

Until recently it had been her crowning achievement. She flipped on the computer to monitor the progress of the fermenter in the basement thirty feet below and waited as electrons flowed through silicon veins and the brain came awake.

Water solubility had simplified the delivery of the virus: a simple drink awakened the lost genes and put a person on the path of a changeling. Katya achieved this by swapping out the fragile lipid coat of the original lentivirus for a protein shell borrowed from a hepatovirus, which already carried receptors for the epithelial cells that lined the gut. The modification deeply impressed Gastro, who named three acclaimed scientists who had made careers out of less. In the end the virus could survive almost a week in tap water.

That was enough for Tanua but not for Katya, and so she continued her work. Whether by nature or nurture she had an innate ease with genes and the tiny precision necessary to work them. Gastro often said that her natural abilities outstripped his and he no longer said that the lack of a formal university environment was a handicap, for she had achieved too much. In fact she had achieved more than he knew.

The substitution of a few phenylalanines and methionines in the protein coat for prolines and glycines toughened it further while an encapsulating polymer that would dissolve in the gut gave an endurance of over three months in water. She knew Gastro was curious about her work but she did not share this advance with him, because from his point of view there would be no point to it. It just happened that his point of view was wrong.

But the virus still had to be taken internally in food or drink for infection. In Katya's drawer sat a stack of plane tickets and a pile of maps with red circles around city reservoirs. Her original plan was to travel the world like Johnny Appleseed but with vials of pure virus instead of a sack of fruit. But reservoir water is purified before the tap with chlorine or ultraviolet and too much of her virus would be killed. Some would survive but it was a chancy way to spread an infection. It was a worse way to spread a gift.

For a while she was stuck because every trick that would harden the virus enough would also ruin its infection rate. Then one day while returning from a deep swim Katya saw the beach palms bend in the trade wind and a coconut fall in the sea and set off for Australia. Every day the wind blew. It carried species and had even brought to Tanua, which like all islands was once a bare rock, most of the life upon it. Why not use it?

Re-engineering the virus for air-transmission was like rebuilding a Mack truck into a glider with tweezers. The protein coat that made up the skin of the virus had to be overhauled, which meant that the genes inside had to change. It would have been impossible without the computer models Gastro had made for extrapolating protein structure from DNA sequence but even so she had to rearrange the chemicals time after time in a brute force approach. For a virus to be infectious by air it must target receptors on cells which come into contact with air. These usually lie in the lungs or nasal passages.

Katya first tried to modify the water virus but after a fruitless three months realized that she would have to start from scratch. Viruses fit their receptors like keys in locks, and rather than re-shape the old key, she would start over with a new key that already fit and shoehorn her genes inside it. The first question was which key to use. She needed a common virus to which almost everyone would fall prey—something not exotic that wouldn't set off alarms; no Asian chicken flu. The solution was obvious and it even had a name that suggested an aggressive animal from Africa, the cradle of the last great human speciation. Rhinovirus. The cause of the common cold.

On her computer monitor she brought up a picture of an icosahedral and deeply creviced blob. She knew the sight would jolt Gastro's heart with either glee or fright. It should be glee but he had edged towards weakness in his later years.

Into this, Rhinovirus 14 of the common cold, Katya had slid the genetic innards of the changeling virus. It now targeted mucous membranes and could be transmitted with a cough, a sneeze, or a touch. Katya kept her one small batch in a double-walled vacuum container in a low-pressure hood in the BSL-4 lab. She did not want it to escape until she was ready.

She was almost ready. On her computer she checked the fermenter that was growing a large-scale batch and saw that in a matter of hours it would be time to harvest. Thirty feet below her in two hundred gallons of nutrient broth the future of the world grew. She wondered who in the end would have done more: the one who found a way to change a person or the one who found a way to change a world. For the price of a few stamps her virus would travel the globe to take root in Sydney, Pyongyang, Brussels, Nouakchott, New York, Portland, Lima, Wichita, Bombay, Caracas—everywhere. At first she considered flying around the world releasing her virus from a spray bottle but this was expensive and inefficient and even dangerous. Customs authorities are often lax but lugging sacks of biological material across borders would be asking for trouble and a foreign jail cell. Besides, there was a way far simpler and more efficient that would have been apparent to any marketing student.

Junk mail.

A stack of crisp dollar bills would each be inoculated with a few billion viral particles. Each would accompany a bogus plea to save rainforests or feed hungry children or contribute to a politician or join a book club; each letter would give away the dollar with a claim of generosity or a request that it be returned with another or used for a certain cause.

The envelopes and flyers would be tossed and the dollars taken and spent. Again and again. Even if a dollar went into a pocket or drawer whoever touched it would be not only infected but infectious.

Katya had calculated that within a month of the mailing there would be a million infections. Without medical care or any idea what was happening survival would be low but even at only fifteen percent there would be a hundred and fifty thousand changelings drawn to the sea.

Katya pulled out the hundreds of new dollar bills. Each was crisp and clean and stiff.

The plan was so perfect and efficient that it seemed possible that she, Rhinovirus 14, and the international postal system had all been designed for just this destiny.

Chapter 26

The two warriors loped through the jungle as if the razorgrass and nettles and wait-a-minute vines were made of smoke. Seventy meters ahead their quarry thrashed from snare to snare.

Casper Jenkins, foul-mouthed data miner and hardware geek extraordinaire, had grown sick of computers and so had taken a hike to seek a waterfall rumored to lie deep in Tanua's interior. Supposedly one could jump thirty feet into crystal water and he was overdue for an adrenaline jolt.

He had not found the waterfall but he had obtained a gargantuan jolt. In a small clearing shaded by acacias he found two islanders doing something unspeakable beside an umu that lofted a greasy smoke. It was like no picnic Casper thought to exist this side of Hell, and when the islanders' eyes met his, he saw something he had never seen but somehow recognized. For the first time in his adult life his fabled gift for cursing failed and he turned and ran. He had been a strong runner as a boy.

Ten minutes later the warriors were still trailing. Their pace was not fast but relentless and they blew through the forest like the breeze, unhindered by the vines and thorns that had ripped Casper into a bloody mass within seconds. The blood smell had reached their nostrils and though Casper could not know it, this sealed his fate.

Casper emerged onto a narrow beach and threw his hands onto his knees and bent. His breath whistled and his legs ached and sweat spattered the coral sand. Panic fluttered in his belly and he wondered if he could reason with his pursuers but then he remembered their eyes and knew he could not. He wondered if he could out-run them and knew he could not.

He looked back and saw only green and for a moment the beach was so pretty and the water so calm that it was impossible that he could have seen what he saw. Then the jungle thrashed and the warriors came. He looked left and right and saw only more jungle and more running and so he plunged straight ahead. He had also been a good swimmer as a boy.

He was twenty meters offshore and swimming with a strong freestyle when the warriors emerged from the jungle and continued their easy lope into the water.

Casper swam hard for another thirty seconds then turned to check the progress of his pursuers. He stopped. The water behind him was calm and empty. No one on the beach. He turned in a fast circle then a slow one. He was alone. Yet he was sure they had entered the water.

He made another circle and this time looked into the sea with a sense of alarm. Again he saw nothing.

He watched the beach while treading water and trying to catch his wind and collect his wits.

He felt something grab one ankle and kicked at it and then the other ankle was bound in an iron grip.

The plop as he vanished was insignificant.

Chapter 27

Devon Lucas answered her door and, as expected, found Katya. It was time for another session.

Katya had become quite familiar, so much so that Devon at first thought that Katya was either a closet dyke or somewhat socially inappropriate. It developed that Katya was merely curious and intelligent to twin faults; she wanted to know what Devon knew and how she had come to know it. Under Katya's questioning Devon's field of submarine piloting was soon reduced to its simple and complex components, as was her graduate coursework.

As always Katya began by examining her body in minute detail. She asked about aches and pains and sensations, and seemed surprised by none of what the feisty little sub pilot reported.

"Dreams? Anything unusual?" Katya asked, her face blank.

"Nothing usual, actually." Devon's eyes narrowed. "You know an awful lot about all this."

"I know all about it. Now come with me. Let's visit your shipmate."

They left her quarters and traveled down the bare hallway to the tiled staircase that opened onto the central green.

Behind them, the cream-colored walls of the dormitory were three feet thick and of something that looked like adobe. The structure had been built by missionaries a hundred years before as a girl's school, and though the missionaries were long gone, the building soldiered on, bruised but unbeaten by a century of tropical heat, humidity, and hurricanes. The old tin roof had lain streaks of rust down the flanks, completing the look of abandonment created by the overgrown grounds and general air of disrepair.

To the left was the plantation's great house, a rambling structure that would have been at home in Savannah; straight ahead was the enormous barn-like structure that once was used for copra drying. From the outside it looked ready to collapse of its own weight.

But inside it was ready for the pages of *Lab Beautiful* magazine. Sealed glass doors complete with overhead blowers kept the island heat, humidity, and bugs out of an interior floored and walled with cool green tile and humming with air conditioners and electronics, glowing with a thousand dials and displays, and smelling faintly of acid, ozone, and disinfectant.

It was part lab and part hospital, which to Devon's mind was another way of saying it was a lab in which humans were the subjects. Four beds lined one wall in a large room lined with black lab benches, deep steel sinks, shelves of reagents, and fume hoods.

Only one of the beds was occupied. She approached slowly, feeling awkward and timid. Beside the prone figure stood Gastro Nister, his white-haired head looking one size too big for his body.

"How is he?" Devon asked, eyeing Henry Winston. He looked more pale and gaunt than she remembered. An oval purple sore glowered on his throat.

"Not good, I am sorry to say," replied Gastro Nister softly, with a pained look in eyes that seemed reluctant to meet hers.

Devon bit down on a scathing reply. "He's rejecting the treatment?"

Gastro shook his head while injecting something pale yellow into Henry's IV line. "Not technically; there's nothing to reject, not yet. He's having a reaction, a strong one. Sometimes the new instructions work fine, sometimes they scramble things up."

"Scramble things up," Devon repeated, using all her will to stop her tongue there. But her will had less success with her fists and she took a step forward before catching sight of a watchful Katya in the doorway. Katya had implacable black eyes that glittered coldly; there was something scary about her and Devon did not care to beat on her hive with a stick to see what might swarm out. She stopped short.

"You didn't have to do this—treatment, as you call it—on us."

"You lost your old life when you crashed. You gained a new one when you were brought here. The terms may not be the ones you would choose, but you gave up that choice when you gave up control of your future."

Devon was familiar with the logic; she had encountered it in Gastro, Katya, and the others who like her had somehow been plucked from various maritime disasters and ended up here. She didn't buy it but she knew that this was an argument she would not win. What surprised her was that while everyone seemed completely brainwashed, there didn't seem to be any brainwashing going on. It was almost as if something in the air or water convinced people to stay.

She tilted her head at Henry, whose expression, even in unconsciousness, was contorted. "What will happen to him?"

"His outlook is bleak," Gastro confirmed.

"Can you reverse the treatment?"

"It must run its course."

"Even if that course kills him?"

"Others have died, for worse things, in this world. Besides, there is a chance he might live, and even if he does not, we stand to learn a great deal. Our project is too valuable to slow down or stop."

"That which does not kill us makes us stronger," Katya offered from the door. "And here, even that which kills some of us makes the rest of us stronger."

Henry let out a rattling rasp and shuddered in his bed. Devon wondered if he had just died but the jagged lines of his heartbeat staggered along on the monitor. His face was even paler. Despite looking like he had just moved two steps closer to death's door his thin chest kept rising and falling and his heartbeat kept squiggling across the screen. But he was fading way.

"Will that happen to me?

"No. I do not think so."

"You don't think so?"

"So far your body is handling everything marvelously. You could be our poster child."

She felt tears welling up and not sure if they were for her or for Henry or the old life which Gastro now said was gone, she turned away. Gastro said it was an engineered virus that was flowering in them. To Devon it was a weed.

"We'll see about that."

Chapter 28

Just before dawn a chime reached Marcus. He raised his head from a balled coat on a dusty bench in the old lab allocated to visiting researchers and realized he had slept. His watch showed that it had been only thirty minutes; after an all-night session of pipettes and centrifugation he was still groggy.

The evening had started with a parade of disbelieving visitors. Linc was first, then Stanislaw, then Cork and several crew from the ship. Word spread and two lawyers, a fisheries expert, an anthropology graduate student, and finally a pair of Brazilian entomologists arrived, all to shake their heads at the vaitama and leave. Marcus finally locked the door and posted a note saying he was working and could not be disturbed.

Which left him alone with a creature that shouldn't exist. He looked at the rat and it looked at him.

"But you do," he said, and took it up by the scruff of its neck. It made only a half-hearted effort to get teeth into fingers, which Marcus took as a sign that it had been handled before. That she had been handled before, he corrected himself after a check. He stared at the rat's inner thigh where the blue lines of a tattoo peeked through sparse fur. G43, read the lines.

Without a CAT scan or X-ray it was impossible to visualize the rat's interior but the gross morphology appeared standard except for—and this was a big except—a series of slits along the rib cage that lay almost invisible beneath the fur.

The slits had to be the key, but a physical exam told him little and he was unwilling to sacrifice the small animal yet so he went to the molecular level for a study that would be quick and dirty since he lacked the time and equipment for anything else. From the Flying Canoe he retrieved a miniature biochem robot that looked like a battered filing cabinet on wheels with an old IBM laptop bolted to the top.

Next came the collection of a cell sample from inside a slit with a needle. The rat objected and Marcus noted but overruled the objection, and the parties reached an uneasy truce with the rat back in the bucket and Marcus' eyes on the needle.

The needle held cells and these, he hoped, would play informant. Every cell is crammed with thousands of chemicals and one of these, known as messenger RNA, carries instructions from the DNA to the movers and shakers of the cell, the ribosomes, which build proteins. By viewing the mRNA at work he could get some idea what these cells were up to, as if studying an unknown factory by looking at what it made—wrenches or toasters or hand grenades. Marcus prepped the cell samples and loaded them into the robot, which despite the name was really a series of test tubes and reactants and hot and cold dips. The robot would purify the mRNA and sequence it.

It was the beep of the robot announcing its completion that summoned Marcus from his short slumber. Of the thousands of species of RNA in the sample, a mere hundred had been present in significant quantity and the robot had finished with the most numerous of those. The first sequence appeared on the screen together with the matching DNA and the inferred protein sequence.

When converted to DNA and with the reading frame supplied by a start codon the first sequence began:

```
ATG AAG GCA TGC TAT GTT GTC GTA GTG GTC GTC
GTT GTA CCT CCC CCA CCG GGG TGG ACC TTC AGC
GAC GAG AAC GTA TAC TTT TGC GAG GGC TTC GAC
CAC TTT GTA AGC GAC TAC TGC GAA GAA AAA CGT
ACT CAA GCG ATG TGG AAA ACT TGG TAT GTT TTC
CTG CTG CGT CCT TGC TTC AGC GAC CTA TAC AAC
TGC CAC GTG GTC CCC TGC TTT CAA CAA
```

Marcus ran his eyes over the letters, each of which identified one of the four DNA bases. The possible combinations were almost infinite and at first he thought he must be even more tired than he realized for the sequence seemed familiar. He read on and as he did so, he mentally converted the codons to amino acids. A string of valines followed by four prolines and a glycine gave it away. The sequence looked familiar because it *was* familiar. He knew this sequence. It coded for part of a gill membrane transport protein that sifted oxygen from water and which he was modifying for use in his artificial gill. But that gene was from the bluefin tuna. It was a fish gene. A fish gene had no business in a rat.

He found a phone jack and plugged in the computer then dialed up GenBank in Maryland and soon was checking the sequence against those compiled by researchers from around the globe. GenBank had more computer power than many small countries and the search was quick. Understanding the results was not.

Similar sequences turned up in the bluefin tuna, as he expected, and in swordfish. But there was also a close match in the chimp, *Pan troglodytes,* and in man himself, good old *Homo sapiens.* Although Marcus knew that humans are mixed from the same biochemicals as mice and microbes, it struck him as wrong for his own species to be caught up in whatever net was being cast.

There were still closer matches in the rabbit, *Lepus europaeus,* and the chipmunk, *Tamias striatus.*

And then the program found an exact match in *rattus norveigius,* the Norwegian rat. Other researchers had found this precise sequence but had not understood it. Marcus didn't understand it either.

The vaitama—he no longer thought of it as a rat—had grown a gill from a gene that all rats—and perhaps all mammals—carried. A gene that somehow coded a working gill. He looked at his own hands and wondered at the cells within them. It was both far-fetched and possible, he realized. Biologists had been aware of it for years. Early in development, every human embryo develops for a short time not only gill slits but also a tail bud and even a coat of fur known as lanugo that sometimes remains at birth to give rise to stories of wolf children. These were vestiges of ancient creatures who vanished long ago. Evolution works like a painter and constantly covers over what came before. But though hidden, what came before remains. Now the paint was flaking away and the distant past shining through. It was well known that humans used only three percent of the DNA they carried;

much of the rest could be a vault stuffed with things past. The reams of DNA considered junk might actually be fossils.

But why the fossils were rising from their genetic graveyard was something else.

He knew what Pelemodo would say; he could hear the deep and mocking tone: Of course there were similarities. Of course it seemed impossible. That is the mark of a god. And not just any god.

Tangaroa.

Chapter 29

Paramount Chief Pelemodo entered the armory of the Sava police station ahead of the island chief of police. The police chief was a Matai, as was his entire department, and the armory thus belonged to the Matai. This quiet fact had not been lost on those islanders not of the Matai, nor was the Matai's tendency to be bloody minded, which would not be helped by having all the guns. This had helped convince many of the wisdom of fleeing the islands in the time of Tangaroa.

For a long time the armory had been acquiring weapons far in excess of the few revolvers the island police could use. It now held shotguns and hunting rifles and old M-1s and Lee Enfields and Chinese AKs plus a few M16s. Many still rested in their crates while others were racked in neat rows. The warm air was thick with Cosmoline and gun oil.

"A palangi smell," the policeman said.

"But also the smell of victory," Pelemodo replied. "We must fight the devil with his own fire. When he is banished down his hole we will throw his tools after him and seal the door. Only then can we return to the true ways."

"The true ways," the policeman agreed.

"Your men are prepared?"

"They are ready. We expected more time to drill but they are ready enough. This is our island. It will be no trouble to take it back."

"The timetable was changed for reasons beyond us. We cannot question the wisdom of Tangaroa."

"And I do not," the policeman put in quickly.

"That is most wise."

Pelemodo strolled the aisles and hefted a few of the AKs before taking a Remington twelve gauge for himself. It seemed like the weapon of a chief for it could slay commoners indiscriminately. He turned to the policeman.

"Be prepared. You will be called. Soon. Perhaps very soon."

"Not today."

"Quite possibly today."

The policeman smiled in a hungry way and Pelemodo knew that all would be well.

Chapter 30

Katya floated through her quarters with a feather duster that banished every dust speck before alighting on a lace doily in a teak drawer. She did not disturb the three large geckos on the walls and ceiling for not only did they eat some of the bugs—though not enough of the mouse-sized cockroaches—but with their reptilian gazes they interested her. They reminded her of something.

Six swiveling eyes tracked her to the window.

From her quarters in the great house she shared with Gastro she could look down on the old plantation tucked into its hidden valley on Tabu. Fifty meters away a converted warehouse held apartments for those who lived on the forbidden isle. The beach was a ten-minute walk but the sea could be reached in thirty seconds through cracks and tunnels that led to underwater caves that connected with the deep reef. Katya had many times dropped into a cool shaft of dark stone that opened to black water. Sinking through the tunnels made her feel as tiny as a single cell wandering a vast vein in a huge body. Both Tabu and Tanua were riddled with the tubes and while there were some who lived in them Katya did not even like to visit. The sense of being an invader in a huge body was pervasive and she knew enough biology to fear an immune response. She knew it to be unscientific but she felt it. She felt it every time. She used them only because their effectiveness outweighed the discomfort they caused.

From beneath her hard bed Katya slid a cherry case. She clicked open the latches to reveal a black .300 Weatherby Magnum mounted with a Leupold variable power scope. The gun was an unparalleled big game rifle, common in Africa, and with it she was a superlative marksman. It bothered her not at all that there was no big game within five thousand miles for the weapon and its capabilities were things of beauty in themselves.

She preferred the strength and ruggedness of the bolt action and after years of practice she could aim and fire it almost as fast as a semiautomatic and with fewer jams. Boxes of shells rested in the case and she pulled out one to admire the sharp tip and energy-packed cylinder and tiny cap that could start it off. The shape was pure lethality.

She checked the chamber then trained the rifle on the dorm and dialed down the scope to watch two Hispanic men walk the yard hand in hand. They were from the *Rio del Oro* and their homosexuality was a great disappointment to her, though not on moral or ethical grounds. She had experimented herself and she believed that simple pleasures should be taken. But she was trying to build a species and having two healthy males opt out of the gene pool was a great loss. She had not given up on them and had decided that in the worst case they would artificially inseminate females. They did not wish to but this would not matter. In the very worst case they would not even know about it. She could think of ways.

She left the lovers and traversed the scope across the dorm windows and said the name of each person as she targeted the rooms. Keith, Santiago, Lucas, James, Chang, Nicole, Ariana, Max, Hendrick, Calli-anne, Ernesto. Occasionally she saw a person and watched them for a moment. All were safe for she used the rifle now only for its scope and not its killing power. She felt maternal as a hen checking her chicks. She worked her way to the top floor and slowly swept the long row of empty windows. These might have been occupied if the death rate were not so high. The ones who had not made it now lay in unmarked graves in the secret burial ground on the far side of Tabu. She had been to that windswept place only once, years before and by accident. The ocean whistled and grunted through blowholes and the mangroves and palms thrashed and the wind hummed. It was an unsettled place with a sense of wrongness that Katya felt before she realized what the turned earth meant. The flowers grew with vigor and brightness and to Katya the red of the hibiscus seemed so rich that blood could have been running straight from the ground into the flowers. Though it was a small island with few places to go she never went back.

She stowed the rifle and wished she could as easily park the memory of what her father called Elysium. Now to work.

While waiting for her computer to boot she studied the wall above it, where a chart of the South Pacific was marked with pencil to note the places where the authorities thought the victims of the Tabu Zone had vanished. It was no accident that these did not cluster and that none lay close to Tanua. The plan had been simple: bring the ships to Tanua by trick or by force and have them lying on the bottom and the crews secured before anyone knew they were missing. Regular radio checks continued until Tanua should have been far behind and only then did the calls stop. The search always centered many miles away.

Almost all the ships were taken this way, except for the first few, such as the sailboat which Katya had happened to stumble on by blind chance in the course of a genuine emergency, and which gave Katya the idea. When she first presented it to Gastro he had been reluctant; his discovery was meant to save one, not consume many. But why save just one, Katya argued? Why withhold from the species what was surely a gift? Great journeys start with a single step, and with that step taken why abandon the trip? Perhaps human intelligence's main role was the taming of genes to allow the conquest of new worlds, such as that beneath the sea. Why leave her a lonely freak when she could be the first of many? When they could begin something fantastic.

This last held sway with Gastro. How, indeed, could he turn his beloved Katya into a freak. And perhaps he was an agent of a greater purpose. Reluctantly, at first, he had joined Katya's mission. If he failed he might be known as a monster and if he succeeded as a genius but it was not renown that motivated him; it was the chance to be a turning point of evolution. To be the architect of a shift as significant as the first slither of a fish from the sea or the first flap of a wing.

The computer completed its internal digestions and beeped its satisfaction, and Katya began. Of course her father knew of the batch fermenter in the old cellar below her lab; it was a thousand-gallon steel vat that could grow massive quantities of special bacteria or viruses. But while Gastro knew it was there, he thought it had been cold and inert for months. In fact, it had been operating for weeks, growing something new. By remote sensor she checked its temperature—a perfect 98.6 Fahrenheit—and nutrient mix, and saw that all was well. She toggled to the logbook in which she recorded the progress of her subjects.

She was worried about the new woman, Devon Lucas. The little redhead had a fiery stubbornness and was, Katya knew, searching for a way out. That was common among new arrivals but this one seemed more resolute, and the now-certain death of her companion, Henry Winston, would only steel her resolve.

With time all the subjects developed an air of acceptance but Katya wanted to review her old notes and see if any had been quite like Devon Lucas. Katya knew that with time the reluctance faded away as the individuals understood what they had become. If you changed a dog into a cat it would become a cat. It would play with string and give up chasing cars. Once a subject progressed far enough into the conversion, that person no longer even wanted to leave. There was nowhere else to be. The understanding of the situation seemed to occur at the cellular rather than the mental level.

Others had been difficult, Katya knew. A female doctor had been spectacularly reluctant and yet now was stalwart. But one bad apple could spoil the barrel, and steps could be taken. Katya pondered and decided that more drastic action was not yet necessary; she would ride things out a bit longer.

There were differences between those who had undergone the change and those who had not; some were obvious and some could not even be described, but those who were changed felt a bond. They somehow knew they were part of something new and special. They shared a common bond, an awareness of an inner newness that was old. Some responded to the call by suppressing its urges; others gave in and these lived in the depths. Gastro himself had not undergone the change—he was too valuable to risk—and she sometimes worried about his dedication, about his willingness to take things to the next logical step, once he learned that Katya already had.

But with Katya's help Gastro had come to understand what their program could mean and what must be done. That to answer this higher call was their destiny. That their god-given role was to change humanity and perhaps save it by giving it the new world of the sea. Even so he was a reluctant savior.

But that was enough.

Chapter 31

Devon Lucas entered Henry Winston's hospital room—she tried to think of it that way even though it was all too plainly a human experimentation lab—after the evening meal. She had just returned from a run, and her body felt oddly jangly. Her lungs burned after only minimal exertion and her chest felt loaded with some appendage that didn't belong there. It was an altogether strange set of sensations, and it went further. Even the light looked different, flatter and more blue, and her hearing seemed not only sharper but more sensitive to higher and lower sounds than she was accustomed to hearing.

She insisted on exercising because she was planning on finding a way out and she knew she had to be in shape to do so. Gastro Nister said that no one had ever escaped, and cryptically added that by the time his guests were healthy enough to flee they no longer wanted to go anywhere. From her contacts with the others this seemed to be true, but she planned on being the first.

She gasped when she saw Henry. For days he had seemed to be almost decomposing, as if his internal structures were being dismantled and only partially reconstructed. The process was accelerating; she could see its progress even in the four-hour space between some of her visits. He was almost always unconscious, save for one or two times when he gazed at her in evident shock and horror then lapsed away again.

Devon had previously noticed an odd lump on Henry's shoulder, and assumed it to be some sort of cyst or abscess, which in light of Henry's other problems was minor. But the lump had changed since her last visit, and now it made her hand fly to her mouth and the bile rise in her gorge.

The lump was bigger and rounder. And it was growing hair. And two small eyes. A nose. And a line that could only be a mouth.

Chapter 32

From the fantail of the *Aurora* Nick Kondos took in a sapphire sea ringed by diamond beaches beneath a sky of lapis dotted with clouds of pearl.

"You know, Marcus," he said, "people scrimp and save to come to places like this for a holiday."

Marcus looked up from hooking the rusted lift cable to the greasy Jim suit. "And we're here for free. You're starting to sound like me."

"I wasn't finished. To tourists, places like this are paradise. Tall fruity drinks. A dip in the sea. The biggest danger a little sunburn. But to us, to me, this place is something else."

"I'll agree with that, brother," Marcus said as he aimed his feet into the suit.

"Death," Nick said. "That pretty beach is actually a pile of maimed coral, that mountain is a time bomb, the sea is a hungry pit, the palms want us to lie beneath their roots—"

"Now you sound like a brother Grimm. Don't get carried away."

"I haven't even started on the Tanuans."

Marcus half-turned and slid in past his waist. "Them, I agree with you. Not a friendly bunch."

"And that thing—"

Marcus understood; the vaitama had been on their minds. "I know. All I could figure was what we already knew. It breathes water. How, I'm still working on."

Nick squinted upward to where a twin-tailed frigate bird circled high above.

"See that?"

"I saw it."

"You know those are considered bad luck."

"And you know that's from a misunderstanding of cause and effect. Frigate birds appear before storms and so the old superstitions blamed the storms on the birds. Now we know the birds live at sea and come ashore ahead of storms. They're running from the storm, not causing it. So seal me up and let's go."

Nick didn't advance but looked over the rail at the blue. "You're sure about this. You didn't exactly sleep last night."

"I'll barely get wet. Less than five hundred feet."

Nick began locking down the helmet. "That's still a long way to fall," he muttered.

"And that's why I'll be cabled," Marcus replied, clacking one claw against the steel line. His belly was fluttering with fatigue and anticipation. He was about to descend on what could be the *Nefertiti*. On what despite the impossibility had to be. His plan was simple: confirm the identify, glean what clues to her fate were available, return and get on with his life. A sense of relief loomed at the closure. The hulk alone might not answer all his questions but it would at least release him from the pursuit of answers if only because there was no other quarry. He felt the enormous weight he had borne for six years, a burden so familiar it had become invisible until the prospect of its removal highlighted its existence. It was as if a backpack filled with rusty iron bars was shifting before being lifted away.

Marcus pointed and clacked his claw impatiently. "Ready."

Nick waved as his friend dropped into the sea. At a level he recognized as irrational, Nick found it surprising that the sea could swallow a man with so little drama. The skin of the water should bulge and heavenly lights flash and celestial horns sound. Instead blue waves marched across an empty place marked only by a quivering reach of cable. For a while there might be a distorted flicker from below but even that was soon gone.

Nick turned a watchful eye on the winch and the cable payout. Toward the island the water graded from deep blue to the pale aqua of a swimming pool and finally into green; on the ocean side it lay in a deep indigo that spoke with dark clarity of great depth.

The frigate bird continued to circle. Bent wings and a forked tail gave it the look of a pencil sketch of a bird rather than an assemblage of flesh and bone and blood that could live for weeks at sea without coming ashore and without landing. Frigate birds fed by skimming the sea and plucking fish and so were perfectly adapted for living above the sea and nowhere else. But—and for this Nick commended their judgment—never did they enter it. He wondered if he should consider frigate birds his personal totem and scanned the island for others. Instead a flash and flicker drew his eye to the horizon.

The shapes, part solid and part flashing motion, slowly resolved in the glare. "Outriggers," he said softly. "War canoes."

Linc followed his gaze but the smaller man could not pick them out.

"How many?"

"Three." Nick watched the flashing of the paddles and the bow wave thrown by each. It took tremendous muscle power to move the heavy canoes so swiftly. The small boats were direct relatives of the larger versions which conquered the Pacific and which bore sails and simple shelters and were navigated in ways still not understood by Western civilization and likely never to be. The ancient knowledge of using star pits on the horizon and reading waves and smelling and tasting the water for navigational cues was being lost as those who once practiced it grew old and died. As the canoes cut through the chop Nick saw an elemental beauty in the craft. Until the canoes pointed their prows at the *Aurora*.

"How many men does a canoe like that hold?" he asked Linc.

"Eight or more."

"And how many of us on board?" Nick asked, already knowing the answer.

"Five palangis. Me, you and Stanislaw, Cork and Harley in the wheelhouse. And five islanders."

The chanting of the paddlers reached them, a low sing-song rhythm that moved with the strokes. Every ten strokes or so all the paddlers called out together and the paddles rose to flash in the sun and switch sides. It was as if each canoe were a primitive animal shifting its many legs back and forth.

"They're coming here," Linc said as the canoes split to circle the ship.

"They are," Nick agreed.

One canoe pulled alongside the low fantail as the others lined the port and starboard stern rails and on some signal warriors leapt aboard. They held long ironwood clubs inlaid with patterns of coral lime and with edges dented and stained. They waited for a big warrior who climbed up last. He shone with coconut oil and wore red-blond dreadlocks and bracelets and anklets of leaves.

He stood no taller than Nick but was far more massive.

"Fuimono," groaned Stanislaw. "The worst of Pelemodo's lieutenants."

Fuimono eyed the winch and moved to the rail to stare downward at the cable vanishing into the depths. When he turned back his face was white and his jaw muscles quivered.

"How many times must you be warned?"

"We'll be done in less than an hour," Linc said.

The big man's voice was incredulous. "You once again intrude on the home of our Lord."

"Less than an hour," Nick said.

"You will be done even sooner." Fuimono turned and called out in Samoan to the men behind him. Four of the biggest surrounded Nick while another two went to Linc and one to Stanislaw. Muscular arms wrapped tight and bare feet splayed wide.

Fuimono stood before the console for the winch. "Tell me how to stop it," he ordered.

"Let me go and I'll bring him right up," Linc said. "No problem."

Fuimono waved a finger. "I did not ask how to bring him up. I asked how to stop it."

"It's too complicated," Linc lied. "I'll have to do it."

Fuimono glanced at one of the young men. Linc understood the glance for he'd seen it in movies, but the young warrior was no fan of television clichés and nothing happened. Fuimono, with a look of exasperation, roared in Samoan and crashed one fist into a giant palm. The youth spun and threw a blow into Linc's ribs. What it lacked in finesse it made up in power.

Linc let out a rush of air and sagged.

"Tell me, pipsqueak."

"I don't recall," he gasped.

The next punch put him on the deck and splattered a ribbon of blood across his forehead.

Linc rose with a queasy look on his blunt face and two warriors grasped him again.

"Alright," he wheezed. "It's a little tricky but I'll try to explain. You have to get the right hand position, like this, with your finger straight out. See? Good. Now, stick that finger right up your ass." This time two warriors slapped him to the deck.

Fuimono left him and brought the winch to a halt by stabbing buttons at random. He called out again and six men fanned into a search of the deck and machine spaces. Fuimono began to pace with his arms waving.

"You palangis are supposed to be smart people. But really you are stupid people. You insist on tormenting Tangaroa. Why anger a god? Why? It cannot go well for you."

The young men ran to Fuimono and presented their finds. The big man's eyes lit and he examined the tools then handed them back with a sputter of Samoan. The men approached the cable. They held, Nick saw, hacksaws.

The realization hit like a pan of ice water and he wondered about the frigate bird and its cargo of ill luck. Without the cable Marcus would be stranded for the suit was too clumsy for long-distance travel. Walking to shore would be impossible. Nick told himself that perhaps he was wrong. Perhaps they were not going to—

"No," he shouted as a blade bit steel. His handlers rocked as he fought and one spun across the deck but another three grabbed him.

"Pity," Fuimono agreed.

The hack-sawer handed his tool off and moved away while rubbing a shoulder. A second youth moved the blade in a blur.

"Let me just pull him up," pleaded Nick. "It accomplishes the same thing."

"It does not," Fuimono corrected. "He wanted to see Tangaroa, let him see Tangaroa. There is a price for such transgressions."

Nick eyed Fuimono levelly. "There is a price for this one too."

Fuimono turned to him and held out a tool belt hung with heavy wrenches. "You also would like to see Tangaroa?"

Fuimono stepped closer. "Yes?"

Nick decided not to say what he would really like to do as a gap appeared in the cable, a sliver of sunlight in the slim strand.

"You're murdering him."

"We are placating an angry god. A god who has been tormented by you and those like you. That is what we are doing."

With a quiet snap the cable parted and the end vanished into the sea as if it had never been. Nick looked to Linc and searched the engineer's eyes. There had to be another way to pull Marcus up. Another cable or another winch or something. But Linc's eyes held only defeat. There would be no other way, Nick saw.

As if to leave no doubt the warriors began unbolting equipment from the deck and heaving it over. The winch vanished as did all of the sampling and trawling equipment that could be freed with wrenches and muscle power. The ocean swallowed it all.

Nick knew that beneath his feet a rain of metal was falling through a darkening blue towards the ocean floor. At the leading edge of the rain was his friend. He wondered who or what would make up the trailing edge. He was still wondering when Fuimono called out again and the warriors gathered with tool belts and ropes and heavy pieces of metal. Fuimono spoke and they came toward Nick and Linc and Stanislaw.

Nick glanced over the rail and saw that the sea was a wide blue mouth. It was still hungry, he knew.

Seven hundred feet down Marcus hit hard on gray sand between a fat stonefish and a tuft of black lava. He tilted and, knowing that if he fell he would be unable to rise, threw a metal claw against black stone. It scraped and slid and he was still falling when he threw the other claw. The pincer caught a lava crack and held and he fought back upright.

He let his breathing slow as silent loops of cable drifted down like soft steel rain. He waited for what he had known would come since the intercom went dead and the suit lurched into a lazy free fall, and then the cable end appeared. In the glow of his one light the cut was clean and new.

He looked upward for a moment before returning his gaze to the sea floor. He could wonder about how and why but there was no point.

He was beneath seven hundred feet of water in a metal coffin with legs. It was at least four miles to shore and he had enough air for perhaps two hours. The math was simple and deadly and so he ignored it as he began the rolling shuffle the suit required. He blotted out how difficult it had been to walk even a few hundred yards to the *Omega*.

The bottom of loose sand and rock was cut by deep channels that were easy to enter but impossible to exit. Marcus realized that he could be driven deeper into the gloom like a creature that could travel only downstream, and so at the brink of each gully he eyed the opposite bank and walked the edge until he knew he could exit. This ate air and time, as did the constant snagging of the trailing cable, but the D-ring between his shoulders was beyond the reach of stiff metal arms.

After thirty minutes he was soaked in sweat and gasping. After sixty he took a five-minute break. Droplets spattered the faceplate and his body ached and his head stung from the thickening air. He was at six hundred ten feet and had traveled no more than half a mile. He was not going to make it. It was not even going to be close. He forced himself to think, to identify another way out. There was always another way. Nothing was impossible. He had never met a situation he could not survive, a record which holds true for everyone living but lasts for no one. He ran his mind over the suit and the sea again and again. Each time the only solution was to reach the surface. Each time the only way was to walk.

Perhaps, he realized, he was seeking the wrong goal. The surface was no closer than the moon but the target of a six-year search lay in reach. Marcus changed course to the left and away from the direct line to the harbor.

He was still too deep. It was still a long way. If he was off by more than fifty meters he would miss it. But he had a shot at seeing the *Nefertiti* again. At knowing Callie's fate. The end would be the same either way but he had the choice of seeing the wreck or not. It was no choice at all.

He trudged onward, a lone steel man in a vast blue gloom.

Gastro Nister knocked and on hearing nothing entered Katya's room. She was gone. The bare wood floor was swept; the computer desk tidy; the bed made. From beneath protruded the polished edge of a rifle case. Gastro wondered where she got the genes that made her a natural with a gun, for he himself had almost been disqualified from national service in Romania because of his clumsiness with weapons. With conventional weapons, he corrected himself.

The windows of her sunny apartment looked down on the dormitory they had built in a converted warehouse. What once housed bananas and pineapples now held a harvest of another kind. He stayed in the shadows and gazed at the men and women who came and went.

His relationship with them was strange. He had expected them to hate and fear him but instead they gave him gratitude and respect and treated him like a wise father.

After the long convalescence and once they understood what they had become, they did not wish to return to what they had been. Gastro had expected a problem with escapees for even one would bring the world crashing down on him and enshrine his name on the world's list of monsters beside Josef Mengele and Japan's General Ishii. He had experimented with subcutaneous trackers and for two years had kept a boat ready. But the changelings did not wish to undo his work and some, to his consternation, took it further. These were ones he rarely saw for they had gone wild and now lived deep.

It seemed that after an adjustment period the changes became not only physical but psychological. The changelings understood what they became and so their goals became the goals of the changed. They did not wish to return to lives as seamen or bankers; they wished to open a new world for their new species.

Gastro knew that he awakened only a handful of genes and he did not think any of these could have affected the mind in this way. But perhaps the mind was a reflection of the genes, and when the genes changed so did the mind. Perhaps the genome shaped the mind directly and constantly, as a cloud shapes a shadow. It was a puzzle but it was undeniable that those who were changed chose to live in a way that would create more of the new genes and, most important of all, they did not flee. It was what Gastro had hoped for and in evolutionary and biological terms it made perfect sense, but Gastro was surprised by the sheer power of a few tiny molecules to guide human behavior. In a way it was disappointing. He did not like to think of himself as the slave of a stack of deoxyribonucleotides too small to see. But he knew that the power of genes to seek a future for themselves was not yet understood.

This was not the only aspect of the new genes; they had also given rise to other behaviors. The picture was complicated and with his focus on improving the change he had spent little time on such details.

Across the green below walked a woman who had been one of the first to join them after her sailboat wrecked years before. Most of the other women on board died but a few survived to Tanua and of those two survived the change.

Those two, plus Katya, had triggered everything. Their successful conversions, the lack of a mate for Katya and the vision of a new race, plus another opportune shipwreck a year later had combined to change the planet.

The woman vanished and the two homosexuals appeared. Gastro searched the green and the paths for Katya but saw no sign. He turned to a tall bookshelf and began pulling lab notebooks.

He had taught Katya to keep good notes and she had done so in neat block script. He flipped pages and in minutes digested months of work. Here she had started with his own injectable clade and modified it for water transmission. As always he admired the sleek elegance of her changes to the viral coat. Here she had tried other protein substitutions. Some worked, some did not, and some worked but not well enough to be worth the effort.

Rather than move forward she refined her technique and duplicated a number of experiments which did not need duplicating here in their relaxed world, unlike in the land of peer-reviewed journals and grants and publish or perish. That was puzzling because if anything Katya usually took a path between points that was shorter than a straight line. Yet here she appeared to waffle and stall. More refinements, more duplications. And more.

He slapped shut the notebook and opened another and found the same. He picked up a third.

He had come to her room to check her books because he wanted to see what she was up to. Her frequent absences plus some of the stories of the vaitama and everything else had made him wonder what someone with her intellectual horsepower might be working so hard to do. For a long time he had been suspicious, and he could no longer ignore his concerns.

He slammed the fake books onto the shelf, for that is what they almost certainly were. Either Katya had become a dullard or she was hiding her true work. He was not sure which he feared more but he knew she was no dullard. And if she were hiding something it could be found. So he would look.

Fifty stories below the surface Marcus placed one metal foot after the other. A manta ray made a low pass and faded away, and three parrotfish gave chase for no reason he could imagine.

He knew that some men might prefer to spend their last minutes reliving past joys instead of fighting to the end in a hot stinking tube but doing so never occurred to him. He struggled around boulders and drowned hills, across gullies and through rock fields, always balancing the need to hurry with the knowledge that if he fell he would be unable to right himself and would die like a beetle stuck on its back in the sun.

At four hundred fifty feet a dim wall appeared at the same time that a pain began deep in his head. For a moment he was confused but he understood even before he saw the twelve-foot screw below the rusted blade of a rudder commanding a course dead ahead. He had hit one of the freighters.

He slogged through gray sand to the stern where high above hung a corroded nameboard. He turned up the intensity of his light but could make out only the first letter: P–.

Coughing in the thick air he blinked burning eyes and traced the rust pattern until the letters slowly resolved.

Papoose. The ship whose life ring hung in the Headsplit Bar.

He turned away with the fire in his head burning hotter. He was close but it was now a race: the gauge he had been avoiding said his air was gone. Around the stern and onward he went with only a glance at the fuzzy rail and another for the silver sky on the far side of four hundred feet of water that might as well be four hundred miles.

In the blue fog a faint shape wavered like the memory of a dream. His heart hammered and not from the carbon dioxide build up as the shape took form. The rigging sprouted corals and sponges that rose like stalagmites. From their height he estimated the growth to be about six years worth.

A rock turned underfoot and he tilted and for a moment hung on a knife edge. Then he recovered with his head cleared by the near tumble. If he fell he would lie beside the boat he had sought so long, blind to it and not even sure it was the one.

He closed in on the hulk of a seventy-foot ocean racer with a deep keel and a shattered mast. A mottling of marine growth carpeted her hull but Marcus was sure even before he staggered to the bow.

She lay on her starboard side, propped over by her long keel to offer up her nameboard from the port bow. Marcus twisted to aim his light then swiped a claw to clear the growths. *Nefer,* it read.

The *titi* lay in his locker topside.

The pincers that were his hands opened and closed with slow clicks. While he had searched three hundred islands, while he had scoured thousands of miles of ocean, while he had poured over charts and studied winds and currents and even consulted psychics and seers the boat had lain here. He moved to where the sloping deck met blue-gray sand and stepped onto the teak, hearing it creak and imagining he could feel the grain of the wood through his metal soles. This was where she had last been. There were many other places she had been, in medical school and before that college and even her parent's home near Mount Shasta but this last place was more connected. He stepped down into the cockpit and rested one claw on the compass binnacle and the other on the wheel. A man with no air commanding a ship to nowhere.

From a narrow shelf at his left shoulder he pulled a paperback. Though soggy and fragile it held together and he craned forward to gaze through the helmet's viewport. Herodotus. Callie's, he knew.

Callie's slim hand reached into his field of view and he jerked and the hand vanished. The hallucinations that would be part of the hard road of asphyxiation were starting but at least it seemed that his might be good.

He opened the book with pincers and a few tatters rose upward like confetti at a tiny parade. For a moment he feared the volume might disintegrate but it held and he was able to see the blue ink of under-linings and old margin notes in a lost but familiar hand. He pressed against the helmet's center viewport to get as close as possible. This was a fresh communication from someone long gone, and though not directed to him, it let him visit with her thoughts in those last days.

Her face appeared, hair rippling, lips pulled to an impish grin, one eye winking. He jerked again and almost fell and then saw only the book and the cockpit.

The headache built as he leaned back and edged into a near sit. The suit was stiff and awkward but he found a tolerable position. Many men wonder on their deathbeds at the choices made but Marcus knew his path had been true. This was where he was meant to be. And so beneath a violet sky of four hundred and twenty feet of water he raised the soft book in steel claws and began to read.

High Talking Chief Fuimono issued orders and the three canoes shoved off clumsily from the *Aurora,* each paddled by two men. The other warriors remained on the ship.

"We go back now," Fuimono told Linc, but the engineer looked at him in defiance.

"You are no longer in charge here," Fuimono said affably. "I am in charge here."

"Then you can drive the boat yourself."

"The Chief does not do, he orders others to do. Do not mistake my tone for a reluctance to spill blood. There will be much spilling of blood in the next days and a little more or less now matters not at all. This boat will go back. Whether or not your head is attached to your body."

Fuimono gestured and three warriors approached. Two held saws.

Linc looked from Fuimono to the warriors then called to Harley on the bridge. The ship turned and a cloud of diesel settled over them and drew curses from the warriors.

Fuimono moved to the stern where a lone man stood.

Nick stared at the exact spot in the water where the cable had vanished, a spot that looked like every other spot. As the ship left it behind he raised his eyes to Fuimono's bulk and to the dozen warriors nearby.

"That was a mistake," Nick said, tilting his head at the place in the wake.

"The victors write the histories and decide what was a mistake," Fuimono said. "The world has changed. It is ours now. Tangaroa's world. Look." He gestured at the island and Nick saw columns of smoke like the black fingers of an evil hand. The fingers touched villages.

"Tangaroa's purifying fire has come at last. This is now the island of the Angry One and his followers. You and your kind are intruders and you will be dealt with as such."

From the rail Nick saw a group of warriors raiding a coastal village beneath a pall of smoke. The small figure of a woman broke and ran from a burning fale. Three stout warriors gave chase and in five steps caught their prey. Sun flashed on swinging machetes but it was not until after the bloody blades stopped biting that a thin scream—all that was now left of the woman—reached the boat and cut off.

Another group of warriors herded a huddle of captives into a stand of tall ferns. A volley of shots rang out and blue smoke rose.

"You will feed many, fat man," Fuimono assessed. "We will dig a special umu for you. Your Adam's apple will roast. Your cheeks and eyeballs I will save for myself. Did you know that the traditional way of long pig is to be put into the umu alive? It ensures the freshest meal. And do not worry that screaming will affect the flavor—in fact it adds spice. So scream all you want." He leaned forward and sniffed Nick. "Tonight, perhaps. It would have been fitting to have your friend together with you on the same palm leaf, but someone else will serve. Perhaps him." He pointed at Linc. The squat engineer raised a middle finger and a moment later was on the deck again.

Nick stood with his back to the rail. Behind was the sea and ahead stood Fuimono and the others. He felt himself to be between open mouths. He had never liked swimming, never liked being in the ocean. He liked being under it even less. What a terrible world, he thought, where it was the lesser of evils.

He flipped himself over the edge in a movement so smooth that he hit the water before the warriors could react. He knew what the propellers would do to him and so despite his disgust, he drove deep below the lethal scythes.

Warriors surged to the rail with several preparing to jump while another ran for the bridge. Fuimono stopped them.

"Leave him. Tangaroa has him and he will either consume him or return him to us." He turned his back on the sea and faced the island and its growing wreath of black smoke.

"It is our world now. And he and all the other palangis are in it."

Fuimono set his face into the breeze and enjoyed the fine metal canoe.

Chapter 33

The next time Devon Lucas saw Henry Winston he was tied to the bed. He was struggling and thrashing and Devon was surprised to see, when she finally shuffled into range, that his eyes were wide open.

All four of them.

She stifled a scream as the twin gazes fixed on her.

"Two heads are better than one, eh?" said Henry's voice with an eerily calm tone, then he hurled himself against the straps as if throwing himself at her. The tiny head on his shoulder screamed.

"Henry—"

"Give me a hand, will you, please?" he said, and his voice was so calm that she stepped forward automatically. She stood perplexed by the web of nylon straps that trussed him.

"Right here, by my chin, your hand." His head gestured toward his chest.

She extended her reach. "Here?"

He grunted and she jerked her hand back. His teeth clicked shut in the air. The little head screamed again, a thin, childlike keening.

"Damn. Again, please, Devon. And hurry."

She looked down at him, trying to reconcile the calm tone with what she was seeing.

"Henry—"

"Hurry, please. I don't know how long I can control it."

"Control what?"

"It. It. It, of course. Are you dense? Hurry now."

The little head had begun rooting and snuffling as if hunting something. Devon was reminded of her own children, as babies, seeking the breast. What she was seeing might be just as simple, but it was nowhere near as pure.

The little head nipped at Henry's cheek and he twitched left and then right in an attempt to head-butt it, but it was too close. It was like a fist trying to punch itself.

"Devon. Your arm. Right now, right here." His teeth gleamed in the light and his long pink tongue waved. His voice was the suave, urbane one that she recognized as both professional and charming; coming from a man with a second head growing from his shoulder as he tried to convince her to feed him her arm was surreal.

"Hurry, please Devon," he urged. "I can't control it much longer. It's getting stronger. We need meat. And blood. Now. Now. Now."

She turned and ran, and behind her heard what sounded like a fight breaking out. When, at the door of the room she turned back to look, there was only Henry there. She stepped outside and in the distance heard the sound of shots.

Chapter 34

Gastro Nister sat in a small room lit only by a quartet of computer screens that fixed him in a flickering crossfire. The fields of molecular biology and computer science had long been on a collision course for the power of the computer is uniquely suited to the parsing of the vast streams of data tied up in DNA. Much of his success, Gastro knew, was due to his ability to program. Some of his code was almost as impressive as his results in the wetware world of carbon and oxygen and blood and bone. Almost.

But now he was using the computers for a more pedestrian task: to review stored video of a string of troubling interactions in research subjects. In the early years he had several times entered the pens to find red sawdust, blood spattered walls, and groups of research animals ripped apart. At first he blamed a combination of shoddy pens and a roving cat or dog but after tightening security the incidents still occurred and finally he installed cameras.

What they recorded was just as puzzling. The first tape was years old and showed an extended familial group of twelve rats. The spacious pen and ample food should have made for a low-stress environment and all should have been well, but according to the digital timer in the lower right corner at 3:55 A.M. on June 21 a young male arose from a sound sleep as if startled. The male arched his back and his mouth opened and his eyes bulged and his whiskers twitched. Gastro thought he was hissing. Another male jumped up and acted the same way. The two circled each other and another rose, twitching, to join the stalk. The space between them narrowed and the three nipped at each other then exploded into a ball of combat in which fur flew and blood spurted and bits of tail and ear lofted upward. Bloody skin stuck to the walls.

The battle swept onto the others and the melee continued until all were too badly injured to fight. All died.

Gastro had a number of similar tapes. He had tried penning smaller groups on the theory that the genetic modifications lowered the tolerance for crowding, but the same happened in a pen meant for twenty with groups of eight, then four, then two.

Finally a solitary female showed the bloodthirsty behavior, proof that it was not prompted by crowding but by something else. Gastro had a growing awareness that he might not know the full bounty of what he had harvested from the ancient genes; the blood hunger seen in some of the animals might be an anomaly or it might be in every changeling, whether animal or human, and only suppressed in the latter. It might explain those who had gone deep, who lived below the island and rarely surfaced. Gastro approved of this stress test of his discovery but recognized that he had no way to monitor the results. No way save Katya, who assured him that all was well. But occasionally he saw or heard things that made him wonder. So far, he had not had the time to look into it further. Perhaps that should change.

Gastro was still watching the video when Katya entered.

"This again? Papa, you should sleep."

The female arched and hissed and stalked then attacked the walls and straw bedding with teeth and claws. She ran and hacked and Gastro thought that a rat in such a state might be able to take a good-sized cat. The fury spent itself in fifteen minutes and Gastro knew that afterward the female acted normally for six months then triggered a violent brawl that left seven dead.

"I do not understand this," Gastro said to himself as much as to Katya. On screen the rat returned to a peaceful sleep.

"They are rats. What's to understand?"

Gastro did not voice the thought that these rats might be the canaries in the coal mine.

"They are not the same as us, Papa," Katya soothed. "Humans have will. Control."

Gastro felt something very large turn over somewhere in his brain. He wanted to ignore it but it was far too big.

"Why would you say that?"

Katya's face sealed and her arms crossed and she took a half-step back. "I am saying only that we are very different. That we should not read too much into them."

Gastro pivoted in his chair and lay his head back against the rest. His eyes were pale blue beneath his spectacles and his hair spread into a white halo as he studied her.

"Or are you saying that it is only human will that allows humans to control this?"

She said nothing.

He leaned forward in his chair with his hands squeezing knees until the blood fled from both and left his bones separated only by thin layers of cotton and skin. "Katya, do you have such urges?"

"Of course not." The old Katya smiled at him with filial warmth.

"And you would tell me if you did?"

Her smile shifted to a playful grin and she punched his shoulder.

"Of course not."

Gastro returned to his screens and called up reams of data to try to correlate specific genetic changes with behavioral patterns.

Katya sighed. "Father, you needn't. It is but a temporary behavior. An anomaly at worst."

"Is it? This temporary behavior tends to have rather permanent consequences."

"Still, it is rare. Father, you should rest. Please. To bed."

He looked as if about to rise but slowly sank back into his chair and scrolled through pages of genetic maps, each a set of horizontal lines marked by restriction sites and gene loci and homeo boxes and critical areas.

"With the right antisense strand, if I can find which gene is responsible, I may be able to deactivate it."

Katya stood behind her father and looked down on his pale neck. She watched as he immersed himslef in his work and his slender fingers massaged two keyboards. Then she crossed the room to a low leather couch where she sat with her chin in her hands. When she spoke her voice was low.

"Unless it's all of them together."

"What?"

"You talked about targeting one gene for deactivation. But suppose it isn't just one gene. Suppose it's all of them. These are from another time, Father. An age before the dinosaurs. An unimaginably different world."

"So?"

"Father. It was a more savage world. Perhaps a little ancient savagery is the price for what we've brought back. Nothing's free, they say."

He stared at her and she stared at him. Then she broke into her wide grin again and her eyes lit.

"Just kidding."

He stood and stretched his arms towards the steel ceiling to let tension flow outward. "By the heavens. How did you get so smart?"

"Just trying to take after dear old dad. Now let's get some sleep."

"Alright, child. Let's."

Gastro followed Katya while the monitors behind played loops of rats tearing each other apart and the walls glowed with reflections of flying blood.

In the hall an island boy ran to them. He had been orphaned and taken in by Gastro and was one of very few islanders to live on Tabu.

"Father! They are killing!"

"Who? Our people?" Gastro cried, with a glance back at the screens.

"No," the boy replied, puzzlement on his face. "The Matai. They say the revolution has come."

Chapter 35

Marcus opened his eyes to a dim light of pale yellow. His body felt numb and the dull throb in his head blossomed into a line of fire that cut from his eyebrows straight back. He coughed against a hard throat and the headache dug in. He recognized it as an after effect of breathing near-lethal levels of carbon dioxide.

The last things he recalled were Callie's handwritten notes, something about the audacity of one ancient king and the cowardice of another. The visions had come and gone and some were of a shape that could have been Callie with hair flowing like a halo and a smile on full lips. Then the pages flowed and he blinked and the book tumbled through the water and when he reached for it the blackness came. There was no gentle drifting away. No light at the end of a tunnel. Just tunnel.

He massaged his neck and rolled his head back and forth, half expecting to hear pops and snaps. The room was simple and austere and his eye was drawn to the only decorations: watercolors of beach scenes. One looked like the La Jolla pier and another like a kelp forest, fluffy green pipe cleaners against a violet background. From one corner a pencil sketch of a face looked back at him with lines that could have been his own.

A thought lowered a chill onto him. Perhaps he was still hallucinating, still trapped on the seafloor and gagging on his own exhalations while his brain madly shuffled memories to create what he thought he was seeing. His hands felt the roughness of the blanket and his lips tasted dry air and his eyes scanned a world that looked hard and real. He would believe in this world until he saw something impossible like an elephant fly or the dead rise.

He surveyed the rest of the room and froze.

The dead had risen.

She stood by the door. Eyes of a clear blue, blond hair cut short around a face of chiseled Icelandic beauty. The pale scar that belonged along one side of the jaw in a unique form of a beauty mark was missing.

Marcus knew that what he was seeing meant that he himself was dead or hallucinating or something even more unlikely. She could not be here, could not be living and breathing. But neither could he. He cleared an achingly dry throat and on his second attempt spoke.

"Hello, Callie."

The figure stiffened and eyes glistened in a shaking head.

"Marcus," said a voice unheard for six years but as familiar as yesterday.

He had never imagined it would be anything like this. He had expected a rush of emotion and perhaps it was there but diluted by everything else. Mostly it felt strange.

He sat up with a tremble and a rush of blood as a few more railroad spikes slid into his skull.

"Marcus," said Callie's voice. "You should have been out another two hours at least. Now everything is complicated."

Chapter 36

Gastro Nister kicked off his shoes and entered the royal fale of Paramount Chief Pelemodo. He ignored the personal guard, most of which was busy slinging stones at a pair of fruit bats, and stormed directly to where the big man sat cross-legged on a mat with eyes closed and the peace of Buddha on his face. Pelemodo refused to use a telephone and so at times like this Gastro had to visit the lion's den. He quelled his anger and reminded himself where he was and how easily he could vanish.

"Pelemodo, what is going on?"

"Paramount Chief Pelemodo did not hear you," Pelemodo said with eyes still closed.

Gastro breathed in through his mouth and out through his nose and found that this had no calming effect at all as he restated his question with the chief's full title.

Pelemodo rotated his head to fix the black bowls of his eyes on Gastro.

"What is going on is what we agreed years ago. I am taking what is mine. As I told you I would."

Gastro drew a deep breath. "I haven't left yet."

"Maybe you should have."

"I need more time."

"You have had all the time that Tangaroa allows."

Gastro was nodding as his eyes took in the war clubs that hung from the columns. Several were stained with a fresh reddish brown that was not mud.

"Of course. But the timing is not why I am here. The revolution was to be calm. Orderly. I've been hearing stories, Pelemodo."

The chief shot him a look of warning.

"Paramount Chief Pelemodo. Stories of savagery." He suppressed a shudder but saw the chief's deep eyes flick with detection and interest.

Pelemodo leaned forward and drew his rubbery lips wide, allowing them to part just enough to show the tips of his canines. "Some of the men are exuberant. It is to be expected. It is a long time coming."

"There is talk of long pig."

Pelemodo shrugged. "That is part of our tradition. Part of our history."

"Are the men I treated involved? The Tangaroa legions?"

"I have not said anyone is involved. I said only that it is part of the fa'a."

"But you have heard the stories too?"

Pelemodo held Gastro's gaze and after a long while tilted his head once in a nod.

"The Tangaroa legions. Have they been involved?"

Paramount Chief Pelemodo lofted his chin and took on a dreamy expression.

"Why?"

Gastro measured the chief with his eyes. There were things about the change and its effect that he did not understand. Making changes to a system as complex as a human being was inherently uncertain and with no control group it was impossible to be sure whether certain outcomes were effect or coincidence. He recalled the evening eight years before when he first knew something was different about Katya. She had returned home in the early evening with her hair mussed and clothes ripped but a serene gleam in her eye. Gastro asked what had happened.

"A man tried to rape me."

He was reaching for the phone to call the island police while wondering where he could get a gun when she stopped him.

"It's alright, Papa. He didn't and he will never try again." She told him what she had done and as she did Gastro found himself slowly sinking to the floor.

The attacker was a minor but muscular chief and he must already have been so far beyond help that Gastro simply listened. On a dark forest path the chief stunned Katya with a rock to the head and when she revived he was on top of her with a knife at her throat and fumbling with her palangi clothes, while promising to kill her quickly if she cooperated and slowly if she didn't.

"Thank god for button-fly Levis," she said. When he was distracted by the buttons she punched him in the throat and dodged a slash of the blade and rolled away. Her first kick to his face stunned him and the third dropped him. She tied him with vines from the forest and used a match to bring him awake. With his knife she fashioned a wooden blade-like tool before his eyes, explaining what each notch and hook would do. Then she raised his lava-lava, pressed the point of her contrivance beneath his scrotum, and shoved and twisted. It worked as advertised. His sex organs fell into her hand.

She waved the chief's remarkably deflated dangly bits before his equally inflated eyes and then stuffed them in his mouth. He passed out and she used another match. She smiled at him and slashed again, this time from sternum to crotch, then patted him on the head, spat in his face, and left him disemboweled and with his mouth full of himself.

Tanua was a small island and the chief's ways were known. His end came as no surprise though the brutality was noteworthy. The police made a perfunctory investigation into what they viewed as direct justice rather than a crime. They assumed the menfolk of some victim had had enough.

Gastro knew that Katya's mother had also had a hot streak and that on two occasions she dropped overly frisky suitors to the flagstones, once with a knee to the groin and once with an elbow to the solar plexus. But Gastro wondered what lay within Katya. Maybe all was fine and this was only her mother's heat in a rougher world. Maybe.

But he was worried about Katya and about the others and the Tangaroa legions. All had undergone the change and so had the killer rats. He looked up to see that Pelemodo was regarding him with cool calculation.

"You are not telling me everything, little man."

"Of course I am.

"There is something about the Tangaroa legions I should know? A problem?"

"I know of no such problem," Gastro answered truthfully but carefully.

Pelemodo regarded him as a full tiger eyes a plump calf. The kill would be fun but so would a nap.

"I must question your honesty."

"Why?" Gastro challenged.

"Because I have known and watched you for years, and you are telling me something might be wrong. Perhaps not in words but you are telling me all the same."

"Not true," Gastro replied. "Now, about this unfortunately early revolution. I have thought it over and despite this change I see no reason why I can't stay on Tabu for the agreed time. We are merely modifying our agreement slightly."

"That is not up to me."

Gastro blinked twice. "Then who is it up to?"

"I am but an instrument."

Gastro stared and Pelemodo smiled animalistically before speaking.

"Tangaroa guides the legions. They do his bidding. With my help only when necessary."

"You're saying that it's up to Tangaroa?"

"It is up to Tangaroa."

A series of rapid pops sounded in the distance.

"But we cannot just leave. We need time."

"And time you have, Doctor. All the time that Tangaroa will allow."

Chapter 37

Marcus held Callie until his arms ached and his back cramped and then he held her more. At first she was stiff and both familiar and unfamiliar and then she softened and melted. Old grooves and nooks fit together and the whole was complete again. He wondered once more if any of this was real.

"I've been looking for you," he said. He felt like an astronaut who after years of training finally attains the moon but is caught without a thing to say.

"I know."

He took in the scent of her hair. Sea salt and wildflowers, as always. His fingers stroked the tight navy sweatshirt. She felt more muscular.

"Where?" he finally breathed.

Her teeth tugged gently at his skin, serving as another hand, another grip. She understood his meaning. "Here. Mostly."

He began to ask the what and how and why but she hushed him with a finger on his lips and pulled back.

"I know, I know. All the questions you must have. Too many. For some there are answers, but know that for some there are not. Some things just are. And we have to accept them."

She looked into his eyes and Marcus knew that not a moment of the six-year search had been wasted.

"Alright. Tell me what to accept."

She took a deep breath then smiled shyly. "Alright," she began, her voice a husky imitation of his and her eyes glinting with play. Callie took little seriously; it was one of the things he loved about her. Then the light faded under the weight of something heavy.

"I was dead, Marcus. Dead and gone. Then I came here and I lived, in a manner. But I've changed. I'm not who you remember, Marcus, not anymore. I don't belong to you and I don't belong to myself. I didn't mean to be here when you awoke. That was a mistake.

Understand—our meeting here, like this, can't change anything. I'm still gone. As gone as ever."

Marcus took her by the shoulders and marveled again at the substance while waiting for all to vanish as he awoke drenched in a mildewed cot on some nameless island. It would not be the first time. It would not be the hundredth time.

"Callie, what happened six years ago? Where's the rest of your crew? How did I get here? I've—"

She held up a hand and wet her lips with the tip of her tongue, a tiny idiosyncrasy he'd forgotten. "I know what you've done to look for me. Giving up NASA, back to oceanography. But Marcus, in a hundred years I don't think I could explain everything."

"Try anyway, for the next ten minutes."

She studied him for a long moment, taking in the deep tan, the blond stubble, the too-long hair still matted with sea salt and sweat, the new tattoo on one bicep. He was the same, but he, too, was different. Then she nodded once and began.

"Everything went fine until the fourth night out of Viti Levu. We were making good progress and the weather was clear when, during the midnight watch, we hit something or it hit us. The impact wasn't just hard, it was violent. We never saw what it was; it could have been a whale, a big log, or even a Navy sub. We didn't just stop, we pitch-poled. In ten seconds we were dismasted, the aerials stripped away, and sinking. Sato and Ilya went right into the water and I never saw them again."

Marcus knew the crew intimately and he could see their faces on the battered photo he still carried. The faces of Sato and Ilya, inseparable friends in life and apparently in death, too, faded at the news.

"Then . . . Kate and Sandy and Jenna are here?"

Callie shook her head.

"Just listen, Marcus. Even our lifeboat was gone. We were on the way to going under. Everyone was hurt. I'd broke my left arm and my left leg, the arm in two places and the leg in three. Couldn't swim and the others couldn't help me because they were as bad or worse. We figured we were done. I did, at least. It was dark. The seas were high. I could barely breathe for all the foam. And that's when it happened."

He waited as her mind traveled to a place it usually avoided.

"I was thinking of you, Marcus. I was thinking of you because I knew I was done. My mind tried to reach out to yours, to share a last moment together. I really tried."

Callie was not one to cry but her eyes were misting.

"Then my foot hit something. Two hours later a boat came crashing through the sea. It seemed impossible that they would see us but they drove straight up and hove to as if they'd been guided in. They put pumps on the *Nefertiti*, took us aboard and her in tow, and here we are."

Marcus looked at her levelly. "That's it?"

She smiled and smirked. "Of course not. Not by a long shot."

"It seems like you're leaving out something."

She laughed, not the tinkling peal of a delicate woman but her own deep-throated guffaw. "Marcus, I'm leaving out a lot."

Marcus edged backward a millimeter. An indefinable darkness was taking shape, a void he could see no way around.

"Kate, Sandy, and Jenna are here, he said."

"They were."

He rubbed his pounding head and studied her. Could they have returned to the States?

"No, Marcus. I'm the only survivor. They didn't make it."

"Their injuries from the accident." It was question and conclusion, an offer for her to accept.

Callie scratched at her ear in a way he had forgotten but now remembered and her voice softened as she looked sideways with eyes reddened.

"No. Their injuries were serious. But not, in the end, fatal."

He waited until it appeared that she would not say more.

"Then . . . what happened?"

A broken smile. "That's the part that's hard to explain."

Marcus rolled his shoulders, trying to shrug off the shroud of unreality.

"And what about the other ships and their crews? The *Papoose*, for example?"

"I always had a hunch you'd find those. It seemed impossible but I just thought you would."

"Yes, Callie. I found them, and you. The question in my mind is: why didn't you find me? And how the hell did I get here, wherever I am?"

She crossed the room with hands in the pockets of her loose sweatpants and pressed her lips together. "We keep coming back to the tricky part of this."

Marcus could feel the gulf separating them and knew that though he had found her, the search was not over. He went to her and gripped her shoulders and held her at arms' length and searched her face.

"Do you remember when we got engaged? On top of Shasta, on your birthday, looking down on all of California, and the clouds below us, as if we were in heaven? And you asked on the way up if your birthday present was something small and sparkly in a velvet box—joking, because you were expecting scuba gear—and it was? And you cried?"

The planes of her face softened and her voice grew husky and low. "That was so long ago."

"Eight years. Just eight years."

"Not all time is measured on a calendar. I've wanted and dreaded this, Marcus. This moment. By night I dreamed it would be you and by day I worried it would be." She took a deep and oddly ragged breath, then nodded in the way that once meant she had reached a decision and her voice took on a new hardness.

"I just wanted to see you. You weren't supposed to wake up, Marcus. But since you did, let me show you why everything is different. Why we can't be together."

She sat him on the hard bed and stepped to the sink where she filled a tall glass with water and drained half, her throat flexing.

"That is how you drink, yes?" she asked as she refilled the glass. "Now watch again."

This time when she tipped it her throat stiffened and her torso shivered and her face took an odd cast. Dark stains appeared on the ribs and sides of the blue sweatshirt.

"Callie—"

She shuddered again then relaxed. "It flows through me. Remind you of anything?" Her eyes held a calm challenge.

He didn't speak.

"Of course it does," she said. "You have to know. There's only one biological structure that water flows through like that. And that's exactly what this is: a gill. Elegantly simple, really. And you'll appreciate this: You see, by some molecular quirk we still carry the genes."

"The genes," he echoed softly.

"Apparently our cell nuclei are like rubbish heaps. We use only a tiny fraction of what we lug around; lots of ancient genes are tucked away in there. They've always been there. Vestiges. Anachronisms. Leftovers. These particular ones are a small cartridge of genes on one arm of chromosome 8, once thought to be a genetic backwater. Over so many millennia they should have mutated away but apparently they play some role in embryonic development and so are maintained by selection pressure. And if you turn them on just right in adults . . . they work."

"The vaitama," he said after a pause.

"Experiments."

"I found the gene. We got a vaitama and I studied it. Found the sequence, found what it was, but still couldn't figure it out."

For a moment the old Callie resurfaced to stroke his cheek and twinkle her eyes. "It's hardly obvious. And I did marry you for your looks, not your brains."

"The genes are active in you?"

The light-hearted Callie of old vanished like a shadow beneath a spotlight. "Oh yes."

Marcus looked from the sink to her soaked sides and touched them to feel the wet. "I wouldn't think that's possible."

"Aren't you the one who always said nothing is impossible?"

"Maybe not anymore."

"It's unusual, but no more sophisticated or farfetched than a heart or liver transplant, fetal surgery, or the reattachment of a limb. In comparison this is quite simple. Just a simple "on" switch. The genes in our bodies are constantly flipping on and off. This is just more of what's happening anyway. With a few different genes. It takes just a little drink—it used to be a series of shots—and the changes happen. The drink tastes like water, and mostly is water mixed with a modified retrovirus that delivers a cartridge of customized DNA to chromosome 8. And then you have the controlled activation of a set of ancient genes. The machinery is all there, Marcus, in all of us. It just has to be turned on. Most of our DNA is never used and this is why. It stores old, lost traits. Traits we can regain."

He ran a finger across her cheek. "Your scar?"

"I heal better too. As good as any lizard, we think. No one's willing to chop off a limb to test it, but in theory it would grow back."

He took her in his arms again then knelt and felt along her body with probing fingertips.

"The structure is all internal."

"Of course."

His eyes rose to hers. "You can breathe water?"

"I can."

He thought back to his work on the artificial gill and what he hoped to achieve. He had been beaten to the punch and roundly. He could have asked a thousand questions. But one came first.

"What is it like?"

She suddenly kissed him.

"Marcus. No one ever asks that; so few see this as a gift and not a curse. To breathe water, Marcus, to need no air supply, to be free to roam the seventy percent of the world that is underwater and the ninety-eight percent of that which is too deep for divers—it is indescribable. I've been ten thousand feet, Marcus. Others have been deeper. It's a new frontier. Giant squid, sperm whales, other things almost unimaginable. It's like Africa before the firearm. We can barely swim compared to those creatures. We're way down the food chain. But we're learning how to live. Carving out footholds. I've seen sights you can't imagine. Sunken caves. Ancient wrecks. New species. There's even talk of a party on the *Titanic*. It's opened a new world."

"At what cost?"

She held his chin. "It wasn't cheap. I wouldn't have chosen it."

"Then who chose it for you?"

She considered. "Fate, I suppose."

"I'm guessing someone more tangible. That white-haired doctor?"

"Yes. Gastro. Marcus, it takes some time to get used to. I've had six years. You've had twenty minutes. You have to remember that I was dying when his people found us. In some cultures if you save a life then that life is yours."

"Not in ours."

"It's a way of looking at it."

"Another way is to consider it kidnapping and mutilation. He's dismantled and reassembled you, and how many others?"

She looked away. "There are over a hundred of us. Mostly palangis rescued from shipwrecks. Some islanders."

"The Tabu Zone? The vanished wrecks?"

"The survivors are here. Gastro says the wrecks really happened, Marcus. Explosions and fires and collisions. A streak of bad luck. The crews were already dead, one way or another. Here, they live."

"Do they?"

"They do live, many of them. I could show—"

"I walked right past a freighter—the *Papoose*," Marcus cut in. "It didn't sink by accident. It was scuttled. The seacocks were open all the way around."

"You were gasping and hurrying and you hardly spent any time there. The damage could be out of sight underneath."

"How do you know how long I spent?"

She half-smiled. "Because I was right behind you."

He recalled the visions and glimpses. "It's quite a power you have."

"It can be. I followed you until you collapsed, then brought you through a tunnel with a lift bag. When I cracked the suit—and what a stone-age tool that thing is—you were barely alive and at first I thought I was too late. But you came back. I ditched the suit in the sea and here we are."

"Simple."

She shrugged. "Parts of it."

Marcus thought back to his own research, to the hours spent in the laboratory and to the curious nature of these genes. Activating them would be turning on the juice to a whole new circuit, which led to other circuits and in turn to other circuits. "But the side-effects—"

"Let's not talk about those," she said softly.

After ten minutes of argument about genetically modifying people who might have died anyway Marcus stood facing Callie across the widest eight feet he'd ever known.

"Callie, I've lived the last six years looking for you. And you've been here. You could have picked up a phone."

"No. I've been gone since my boat was lost. What you see now is not who I was. You have to know that accepting this now, and wanting it then, are two different things. The person I am now could not just call you."

"But you were haunting me. At dive sites."

"At first I did. I just had to see you again and I thought that from a distance would be enough. But I kept coming closer and finally had to send you a message. Some things are stronger than sense. I gave all that up a while ago, though."

He moved away and looked at her across six lost years.

"I have vowed every day that I would never let you get away again if I found you."

"The person you've been looking for is still gone. You haven't found her."

"I have."

"We can't be together."

"We can."

She was shaking her head, eyes moist and hard at the same time. "I don't know why but this is our fate. Maybe it's more cruel to have seen each other again; maybe it would have been better not to. But when I knew you were here I had to see you. And I couldn't let you die. Marcus, we're like grown-ups who had grade-school crushes on each other. We're different now. I'm different now. Life has changed me."

"The *Omega* crew? They were going to die so you brought them here?"

"Not me, but yes. The sub was trapped in a cave-in. There was no chance of a rescue and no one knew you'd show up with that ridiculously clumsy suit. We could either let them die or try to save them. Once we rescued them they knew of us and there was no choice. We chose to try life. We brought the sub here, got them out—they were nearly dead—and took the sub back. Life honors life. That's one of Gastro's sayings."

Her eyes looked far past the walls then snapped back to him.

"Marcus, you have to go. You shouldn't be here."

"After six years I get thirty minutes?"

"You get your life," she hissed with an edge that was new. Like a sword slipping into a scabbard it vanished. "Please. The halls are quiet now. I was able to sneak you in and if you go now we can avoid trouble."

"Maybe I don't mind trouble."

"Trouble for me. Please, Marcus."

She reached for his hand and he let her take it and they walked an unremarkable corridor of cheap linoleum and fluorescent lighting that could be in any third-world government building. The windows looked out on groves of coconut and mango trees.

"Where—" he started to ask.

"Tabu. We're on the island of Tabu. It's the mythological home of Tane, the Polynesian forest god. With Tangaroa out there and Tane here no islander comes around, it's forbidden. It would be stepping into a crossfire of lightning bolts."

"Is that really the myth or have the locals modified it?"

Callie shrugged. "Is there a difference? All myths start off somehow, somewhere. Who's to say what version is right?"

"The islanders must know about you."

"Of course. But our being here is, from their point of view, our problem. They couldn't care less if we stick our heads in the lion's mouth. What's the single adjective most often put in front of 'palangi'?"

"Stupid."

"Exactly."

They arrived at a heavy steel door that opened to a blast of heat and humidity.

Marcus looked out onto a flat valley planted with taro. A sky-blue pick-up rested beneath a palm. Near-vertical rock walls hid the valley from the sea and Callie pointed out the gap between two overlapping stone curtains. Beyond, the surf boomed.

"What now?" he asked.

"It once was perfect but it is no longer to be, Marcus. Go. Before we are found. Go."

"I was dying, too. Now I'm here. Why shouldn't I join you?"

"No. I found you, not them. And I don't want this for you. It is dangerous and not perfect and I've already reconciled myself to being apart. But I don't want to see you die, especially the way people die here." She glanced over her shoulder. "Please. You may not care what being caught would mean for you. But it could cost me what little I have left. I have a place and a purpose and I'm still a doctor of sorts."

He didn't move.

"Marcus. Accept that we can no longer be together. Know that I live, that I am well. Take what you can from that, for that is all I can give. It has to be enough."

"It isn't."

Her eyes flared with an anger he hadn't seen before but her voice did not show it. "At least consider it. Sleep on it, as they say."

There was only one person in the world who could have kept him away from Callie. And he let her push him out the door.

Chapter 38

Devon Lucas ran until her legs burned and her head throbbed, stopped for a few moments, then accelerated into another wind sprint. Another hundred meters, more or less, through soft but burning sand under a merciless sun. Afterwards she stood with hands on knees, panting for exactly thirty seconds while watching bright sweat splatter a white coral boulder and sizzle away.

Then she was running again. And again, after thirty more seconds of rest.

More sweat flew, again her legs burned, and now her chest ached. More than it should have, she knew.

Again she ran. She ran until she wobbled and felt faint, and then she ran more, and only when her vision began to squeeze into a tunnel with black around the edges did she stop. She was wearing most of her clothes—long sleeves and pants—even though it was the hottest part of the day; she was not just strengthening her body, she was deliberately over-heating it. Creating an artificial fever.

Her vision opened and she felt faint and dizzy but ignored both sensations as she again flew across the burning beach. The world swam before her eyes in a watercolor blur of green and blue and white and still she ran, until her stomach revolted and she collapsed, heaving, in the shade of a palm leaning picturesquely over the beach. She defied her body's urge and crawled out into the blistering sun.

Devon was fighting Gastro on the cellular level. She knew that a fever is physiological defense mechanism, and that certain enzymes and proteins are very sensitive to temperatures even a fraction of a degree above normal. Key DNA replication enzymes are among the most fragile. Thus a fever helps the body fight off invaders. Devon didn't know if it would or could work, but she was giving herself a fever.

And even if it didn't work it was not the only thing she was trying.

Less than two hours before, Devon had been walking slowly through the forest, studying the ground as she went. On her back she wore a rucksack that held a few cuttings—green and yellow leaves, bright flowers, roots.

She moved slowly and methodically, searching the world around her from mud to vine-hung trees before moving another ten steps and doing it again. Her slow pace integrated her into the forest world and the small animals had come to accept and ignore her; birds hummed and frogs chirped. It was as busy as downtown at noon.

She spotted a red-tipped curlicue of vine and carefully snipped then slipped the coil into her rucksack.

None of her finds looked particularly palatable but she was unfazed; she intended to make a tea out of every one of them and drink it down. During a morning exploration she had run across an ancient islander woman whose skin dangled from her bones like leather forgotten atop a drying rack. The woman turned out to be a traditional healer, who used potions and poultices made from local herbs and plants to treat everything from colds to fractures. Devon knew that the ancient Greeks had used willow bark as an analgesic, and that willow bark contains the active ingredient in aspirin, so she discounted nothing. She also knew that pharmaceutical companies were actively attempting to harvest and test every species in tropical forests for useful properties and hoped to do the same to the deep sea vent communities; Devon was merely following the same tactic in a smaller way.

All the plants in her pack had been identified by the healer as those that acted to clear up sniffles, aches and pains, bad stomachs, and so on. In other words, Devon had in her backpack every anti-viral compound found during the thousand years the local islanders had lived on these islands.

On the mainland, under the severe oversight of the FDA, it would take years if not decades to get approval for such a treatment. But Devon planned to treat herself. Immediately after her run.

She staggered to her feet, slung her rucksack, and set off beneath the brilliant sun.

Chapter 39

Paramount Chief Pelemodo reclined in his fale and assessed his progress. Tanua was firmly in his grasp. Many of the islanders who opposed him had left in the previous days and weeks, driven away by the stories of Tangaroa, the vaitama, the increasing earthquakes, and that final straw, the disappearance of the crew of the *Omega*. Those who remained were either hiding in the brush or cowering in their villages under watchful Matai guards. Many were also burying their dead for the Matai had not been gentle with those who denied their Lord's existence.

The palangis were also under his control, to what would be their lifelong but brief chagrin. His warriors had rounded up two hundred of them; on all of Tanua only two or three might have slipped their grasp and those would be caught soon enough. The Matai had first taken control of the island's phone system, and so the outside world knew nothing. The warriors were thrilled to have control over those who had been so condescending for so long and perhaps they were even a little too exuberant. Pelemodo had seen many six-foot earthen umus and the air carried a smell like burnt pork. It was not pork.

Two hours before he had visited the old mansion which once housed the governor and where in a happy twist of fate the palangis were now held. Patches of red-brown marked the ground and so many umus holed the wide lawn that it looked like giant dogs had been burying a truckload of dinosaur bones.

Pelemodo congratulated the men for creating the first traditional Polynesian state but he saw the need to temper their enthusiasm.

"Do not forget," he reminded them as they stood among clouds of greasy smoke that rose through kapok and guava trees, "how our ancestors kept the turtle fresh for eating on long trips. With no refrigeration, no ice, no cooling at all, in a simple canoe. Fresh for weeks."

"How?" they asked.

He smiled. "Simple. They kept the turtle alive."

He gestured at the pits and saw that they understood.

Pelemodo did not care to save palangis but if word of a widespread massacre leaked out it could cause unpleasant consequences.

Besides, this way they would have long pig for many weeks.

Chapter 40

Katya walked into the village of Sava with a backpack that held the future of the world. The batch fermenter had finished its task the night before and she had concentrated the viral brew down to ten liters and then to one. Each new dollar bill received a dip and went into its sealed envelope and here she was, with the weight of the paper on her back oddly satisfying. Beside the pack was strapped the Weatherby, its heft and balance speaking of its power. It could knock down an elk at a half mile yet beside the backpack it was like an ant by a starship.

She saw islanders staring at her and knew why. She was a palangi from Tabu and also one of Pelemodo's favorites and this combination unsettled them.

Smoke stung the air and in light of what was happening across the island they were even more unsettled. The Matai were on the loose and perhaps Tangaroa was afoot and though Sava had not yet been hit, it had been the center of palangi influence and the villagers knew the Matai would come. They did not run for there was no place to go.

From the eyes of the islanders she could see that they did not know whether to like or dislike her but they were quite sure to fear her.

At the Sava post office, known as the *fale meli*, or the house of mail, she paused to take in the murals on its brick walls. Tangaroa was gleefully dining on canoes in one while in the other, warriors were cooking someone. She knew the islanders were watching her and so she rubbed Tangaroa's belly because this frightened and annoyed them.

Despite the havoc that Pelemodo might wreak, she knew that he would keep up appearances, at least until his control was complete. When she had learned that the timetable had accelerated she sought an audience, which was automatically granted to a priestess such as herself. She suggested to Pelemodo that it would be unwise to attract international attention too soon, and so perhaps some of the banks and offices should continue to function at close to their usual slow pace. He agreed and selected the fale meli as one office that would continue. Inside she saw a clerk waiting nervously at the counter. There was no line.

Katya looked at the world that had been: the blue of the sea and the curve of the bay and the lines of palms and mangroves at the shore.

Then Katya and a trillion rhinovirus particles entered the post office.

Marcus paused beneath an acacia tree to catch his breath. His eye tracked down the jungled hillside to the beach, past the two smoking villages and across the narrow channel to the isle of Tabu, which from here appeared uninhabited. Since finding the corpses, he had moved slowly with many stops to scan his trail for pursuers.

Crossing the shallow water from Tabu at slack tide had been a simple mix of wading and swimming. On the rocky shore of Tanua he turned south and after a half mile of mangroves came to a seaside village built on once-white sand now stained red. Of a neat ring of fales, only black poles and ashes were left; all the canoes were burned save one and Marcus rested a foot on an outrigger while taking in the massacre. The villagers were not just dead but destroyed: limbs ripped from sockets, heads smashed, chunks gouged and parts missing.

It was worse in the next village. The bodies were dismembered and there were not nearly enough parts left.

Whatever was afoot, Marcus did not want it to find him. His head pounded and his body ached while in his ears boomed the dull roar of the carbon dioxide and the twisting sense of unreality at having seen Callie, as if the entire universe had moved three steps to the left when he was not looking. He hung his boots around his neck to avoid leaving palangi prints and just as he edged around a thicket of thorned vines a silence wrapped the jungle as if it were waiting for something to happen. He stopped, then slid forward and began to work around the slick folds of wet wood at the base of a buttressed looking-glass tree.

A hand clamped over his face and lifted him off his feet. He kicked and stabbed with his elbows but the grip was hard as concrete. He knew that next would come cold steel on the bulge of his throat or a wooden blade chopping into his skull.

Instead a familiar gravel voice spoke in his ear: "Is it really you?"

Marcus stopped fighting and the grip released him.

"It is," Nick said, and grabbed him again, this time in a bear hug. "How did you—why I—a group of Matai boarded the ship and cut the cable. I thought you were fish food. In a can."

Marcus rubbed his chin where the big Greek's arm had scraped, then yielded to the open arms and gave in to a fierce hug.

"You've got enough lives to make a cat jealous," Nick said. "I don't mean to sound negative—but how are you alive? This one has to top them all."

"You're going to wish you were sitting down," Marcus said, and as he was about to speak, a burst of gunfire rang out and shredded the trees above. Foliage fell and both men dropped.

"Stray shots," Nick said through a mouthful of grass, then saw the look on Marcus' face. "Pelemodo's men. The Matai. They didn't just take over the *Aurora*. They took the whole island. They've done a lot of killing and they're just getting started. They've gathered up all the other palangis in the old governor's mansion. I was on my way back there when I crossed your trail."

Nick gestured at Marcus' bare feet. Five toes on the right, four on the left. A souvenir of frostbite on Denali.

"Guess I'm a giveaway."

"It's surprising you don't go in circles."

Several distant explosions were followed by a duet of thin screams, and then voices speaking Samoan came through the brush. Nick waved and they crept into the shelter of a stand of wild banana. Beside it the bloody feet of a corpse stuck out from the cheerful spray of a fern. The bush thrashed and the voices of the Matai patrol approached.

"Whatever you were going to tell me," Nick whispered, "better wait."

Chapter 41

It hit Gastro Nister in the shower. It wasn't the solution but a road that might lead to it and so, looking like a drowned rat, he bolted across the tile floor to seize pen and paper.

The genes he had resurrected resided on the short arm of chromosome 8 and near the tip of the long arm of chromosome 9. All were riddled with introns, as are all genes. These intervening sequences spouted gibberish in the middle of a meaningful genetic sentence, as if to say *The quick brown fox jumpATCCCGTCs over the lazy dog*. The cellular machinery that turned DNA into protein dealt with the introns by snipping them out and moving on. Much of the genome was introns; there was more junk than genes.

But what if the introns on the resurrected sequences weren't all gibberish? What if after being snipped out they went on to do something? What if the introns were actually the real purpose of some genes? He knew the function of each and every gene—some controlled new proteins, while others guided the development and maintenance of the structures. It seemed impossible that any of them could have created the sub-text of violence.

But the introns . . . He had never examined them; he had assumed them to be mere garbage. But now he wondered, and it was a not just a hunch but a hunch of the sort which had felt right before. Perhaps a gene was snugged away in an intron. Perhaps after being snipped out the intron went off to cause its own havoc by expressing a secret gene. Or perhaps the intron was not snipped every time and so the gene product was sometimes different. An assembly line that sometimes made innocent crowbars and other times planed the same tools down to deadly spears.

He dropped his pencil at another thought. Perhaps a reverse-frame gene—as in English most genetic sentences form gibberish when read backward. But it could happen that when read backwards, the letters might form something both readable and very different. Reading a gene backwards might order up a product as different as a god from a dog. He had never looked for such things; there had been no need. It was enough to get the system to work at all. It was unlikely but out of the billions of nucleotides it could be expected to happen.

If the answer was a hidden intron gene, Gastro could deal with that. It could be removed or blocked or deactivated. If it was a reverse-read of a necessary gene—something hidden on the back of a page he needed. Gastro shook his head. If the DNA were necessary it couldn't be cut up, but if he couldn't attack at the DNA level, he would fight at the RNA or protein levels. He smiled at the thought. Like a tiny Winston Churchill he would fight at the DNA, at the RNA, at the protein.

He marveled at the wiliness. The gene actually seemed to be hiding. One could look right at it and not see it for molecular biology worked by looking at vast numbers of molecules and assuming all were alike. This gene would only appear in a tiny subset of these, and only occasionally. It was stealthy. It hid as if deliberately avoiding the only techniques that could catch it.

And it manifested in the organism in the same way: Those who carried it showed no sign until they erupted with bloodthirst. The gene had twin goals: to reproduce and to kill. And those who carried it had the same goals.

In a way, Gastro decided, this gene, wherever it hid, might be the ultimate survivor. It prevented the very civilization necessary to detect and eradicate it. To keep itself intact it either hid or bathed its carriers in blood.

But not anymore. Gastro's mind was already outlining the search strategy. Now that he knew what he was looking for he could find it. And if he could find it he could kill it. Someday the gene might form the basis for a study that might unravel the genetic basis of thought. Someday. But not today.

He felt like a fisherman who has gone out too far and caught too much. He had cast his net back over the eons and it had come back full of things that could not be seen but were deadly.

Still in a damp towel he sat before his computer.

Another thought reached him. His brain was old and stiff; in the sciences it was not unusual to do one's best work before age thirty. If he had figured this out it was possible Katya had as well. But if she had cracked this nut why not tell him? The only reason would be if she were doing something with the information. Something he would not like. He tried to imagine what that could be and imagined too many things.

Chapter 42

Nick let out a grunt at a fleshy squishiness underfoot then saw there was no need for an apology. The man's throat was ripped out and flies walked on his eyes. Hunks were missing from his clawed abdomen, arms, and legs, and an old M-1 Garand rifle lay in the mud.

Marcus knelt and examined the corpse as Nick hovered overhead with one eye drawn to the bloody spectacle and the other roaming the jungle. The dead man had been huge and built strong.

"Looks like a leopard mauling," Nick muttered.

"No leopards here."

"I know. That's what bothers me."

Marcus retrieved the weapon and checked the barrel for mud.

"How old is that thing?" Nick asked.

"Second World War. My granddad had one."

"Great."

Marcus searched the body and found an extra eight-round clip then pointed at a face that though disfigured by bloating was familiar.

"Nick, it's Toma. The Fijian. He was on the ship."

The Greek leaned in and studied the corpse. "He looked better alive," he concluded. "And whatever could do that to him I don't want to meet."

Nick shifted his gaze to Marcus and studied him almost as closely. "Hey. You Okay?"

Marcus came back from wherever he had been. "Yeah. It's nothing."

"This isn't the time for distraction. What is it?"

"Later. Let's keep moving."

They slipped back into the jungle and climbed through a copse of fish poison trees and past several huge banyans and kapoks. Parrots called from high above and butterflies the color of molten metal flitted past. Then Nick pointed beneath a spray of yellow orchids to where another body lay and whispered, "This whole island is going to hell."

Marcus saw at a glance that the body—a boy this time—had no weapons or ammo, and thought about Gastro's plan.

"Way past it, I'm afraid."

Above a band of wild guava and mango, Nick motioned for silence and lowered himself to the ground to creep on hands and knees through patches of hibiscus and dogbane and around a tangle of liana. He avoided a wide trail of bright red ants and a four-inch millipede that seemed to have more legs than were strictly required by its name and eased into position beneath a tamarind. He gestured.

From behind a screen of ferns they looked down on the governor's mansion seventy meters away. It was a two-story plantation home fronted by a lawn and a long curving driveway, and backed by orderly rows of coconut trees. With its portcullised entry and rows of Ionic columns, the once-white building looked torn from a Georgia plantation right after General Sherman's visit. The walls were scorched and the windows broken and swaths of paint peeled off. Matai warriors lounged on the front lawn like an occupying army, half with traditional war clubs and the rest with rifles. The lawn was pocked with earthen mounds and freshly dug pits.

"They're locked away inside," Nick said.

Marcus pointed to a circle of warriors at one end of the clearing. They stood around a black mound of turned earth from which rose white steam. A meaty scent hung on the air, brackish and oily.

Nick shook his head. "That would be Casper, I'm afraid."

Marcus looked from Nick to the mound to Nick again.

"Data-crunching Casper? Casper of the perpetually foul mouth? Curse-a-minute Casper?"

"Yeah. I saw it from here. You should have heard him."

"He's in there? In the umu?"

Nick nodded slowly.

Marcus stared at the smoking umu then shifted his gaze to the other pits. "That's what they're planning for all of them?"

"Us too if they get the chance. I have it on good authority that the eyeballs and cheeks are the best part."

The brass door to the mansion banged open and a thin scream came out followed by two sleek warriors dragging the round man who was screaming. He had light brown hair and a goatee and his heels left twin furrows in the lawn.

"That's McCormack. The Aussie herpetologist," Marcus said.

"I hate snakes," Nick whispered as the warriors turned towards a large flat stone. One warrior grabbed McCormack's body and another forced his head onto the stone. A third raised a round boulder.

"But I don't hate snakes enough for this," Nick decided, starting to rise.

The stone smacked McCormack's shoulder. His scream turned piteous and he thrashed as the other warriors jeered at the clumsiness. The round stone, now bloody, rose again.

The stone fell and the scream stopped with a hollow crunch. The black anvil was sprayed with pink and gray on a lace of red and, atop the mess like cherries on a sundae, two eyeballs dangled from stringy optic nerves. Warriors moved the trembling body to a waiting umu.

Marcus gripped Nick's arm. "We can't take them head on."

"We have a choice?"

"There's always a choice."

Nick looked from Marcus to the umu that was giving off a dark, greasy smoke and back to Marcus, then eased down.

"Alright. What's your plan?"

Marcus studied the compound, analyzing lines and forces while choreographing dances of violence and playing each one through to its end. Every time the result was two more umus hosting two more palangis. Two against a hundred. Guns—or gun—blazing wouldn't work. Sniping wouldn't work. Marcus laid the rifle sideways and set his chin on the wooden stock.

"Don't forget," Nick whispered, "I'm a lover, not a fighter."

Marcus snorted softly. The big Greek might rather be a Hellenic Casanova but he was also a gifted brawler, a skill developed during what he called his misspent youth. Five minutes later Marcus, raised his head from the rifle. The sun was lowering and the warriors beginning to relax.

"I have an idea you're going to love."

Nick rubbed his brow. "Love?"

"That heritage you're so proud of is finally going to be useful."

"It's already useful. But I don't think the locals are looking for a fountain of democracy."

"They're not," Marcus agreed while back-sliding out of the fern. "Come on. We need to find Toma."

"But he's dead," Nick said. He turned to find he was talking to Marcus' back.

The moon rose at midnight and bled cool silver over the courtyard as fox-sized bats winged across its white face. A few confused roosters crowed while, after hours of drinking, wrestling, and fighting, the warriors of the Matai lay before the governor's mansion in heaps. One stoically ignored an arm that had been broken in a clash over a fistful of kava, while another rubbed a cracked collarbone.

"You look marvelous," Marcus whispered in their post above the mansion.

Nick stood before him bare of chest and foot and with a bloodied lava-lava lashed around his waist and a crown of leaves and flowers adorning his head.

"I feel ridiculous."

"But you look native. You can thank your swarthy Greek ancestors for that."

"I just hope I don't get the chance to."

Marcus added another red hibiscus to Nick's hair. Though effeminate in the west, it was not unusual among the Matai warriors and would draw eyes from his features.

"If you do, say hello for me. Just remember, those warriors are drunk and you're drunk. No problem."

Nick grimaced. "No problem for you, you mean."

"Right," Marcus said, and checked the warriors. Some were still standing about but many were almost motionless and the open fires were burning down. "Well then. Now or never."

"I'd prefer never," Nick muttered.

Marcus took a position with a clear field of fire and laid the rifle at the ready, then gestured at Nick to go ahead.

The Greek looked at the black weapon gleaming in the night.

"If I hadn't resigned my professorship at CalTech I'd probably be dining with a young lovely right now at a sidewalk café in balmy Pasadena. Instead—"

Marcus pointed and Nick turned and sighed and hitched up his lava-lava.

"Instead," he finished.

Marcus waited as Nick vanished into the brush. It would take him several minutes to creep to the edge of the clearing that held the mansion.

A figure appeared beside him and he began to turn the gun but he saw bright teeth and a wide smile and the eyes that were the first he had seen on Tanua. She wore anklets and bracelets of leaves and her skin glowed and she carried a rifle strapped to her back. He recognized her from the sea and also as the priestess from the kava ceremony. She had made a perfect and soundless approach.

"How'd you do that?"

"Old trick." Katya's smile ratcheted up a notch then she flicked her gaze from Marcus to the mansion. "You two against a hundred warriors? I like bravery and optimism but I don't think much of foolishness."

"Which is this?"

She shrugged. "Depends on how it turns out."

"You didn't sneak up on me to tell me that."

"No. I came about Callie."

Marcus stared.

"Of course I know about her. And the others. What you're planning won't work," Katya said.

"You can't know what I'm planning."

She widened her eyes in mock surprise. "Why not? I am taupo. The priestess knows all."

"Not this time. Because I don't know either."

"Touché. But I know your objective. And you can't get back with her."

"She's my wife."

"She was. That person is gone. Now you have to be open to other possibilities." She held his gaze and he became aware of her clean girlish scent and something else. He felt a pulse of desire as if she had reached out and goosed his nervous system. Her honey flesh glowed with vitality and he imagined her dark hair arrayed on a pillow or more likely hanging around her face below a jungle palm as he looked up at her and she rose and fell and grunted.

"How are you doing that?" he asked.

Her eyes widened slightly as she relaxed the pheromone release.

"An even older trick. No one has ever noticed it."

"I'm taken."

She laughed softly. "I'm not talking about a relationship. I'm talking about a mate. I've evaluated you for preliminary histocompatibility—"

He waved a finger at her. "You'd need a sample to check that."

She caught his finger with a lightning grab and bit it. "And I took one. Remember the kava cup? You and I are an excellent match. Our offspring would thrive."

He pulled his hand back and narrowed his eyes as if in thought. "You're not much of a romantic, are you?"

"Romance is a fiction. I'm concerned with reality. Genetic reality. Sending my genes—and yours as it happens—into the future as well prepared as possible. The future is going to be a strange and exciting place."

He cut his eyes to the courtyard below and back to her. "If the future is going to be more exciting than this I don't think I could stand it."

"In ten years there will be more people like Callie and I than you. The change will be everywhere."

"I doubt you can give everyone a shot or a drink."

She looked at him with cat eyes and her eyebrows twitched up as did the corners of her mouth in an expression of faint but benevolent amusement. She plucked a few grass stems and puffed them into the air. "And we won't have to. See you soon."

She rose and firelight flashed off her eyes as she vanished around a banyan tree.

Nick crept forward until only a stilt-rooted screw pine stood between him and the warriors. Some were lying down but many milled around fires and others manned a rough perimeter. He could hear snatches of Samoan and to his ears it sounded like all the consonants had been cut from it.

He stiffened his spine and puffed out his chest and stepped forward regally. He would be a chief in the same way that a hunter becomes his prey. Two steps into the clearing something grabbed his ankle and threw him to the ground. His lungs emptied with a massive grunt and the Matai warriors turned.

Nick saw his predicament. He was a palangi who spoke not a word of Samoan lying before a hundred armed and murderous warriors. His thin chance of escaping attention was gone. What he did, he decided, didn't matter. He was headed for an umu. It was only a question of which one.

He kicked to his feet and bellowed at the vine that had tripped him then roared forward while beating his chest. He was expecting a charge but instead some of the warriors turned away and he aimed himself at the darkest area between fires and strode past the first guards. He made more noise and waved his arms and they made no challenge. The island was theirs; there was no need to doubt someone who looked and acted the part.

Nick blinked in surprise but kept his mouth and arms and stomping stride going. He was so deep among them that to be spotted would mean getting cooked though if Marcus did the right thing he would not live that long.

It was then that a scar-faced warrior on the ground squinted up at the image of a bulky, mud-spattered figure in the lava-lava of Toma, his boyhood friend who he himself had put to the blade to less than a day before. The Matai lived in a world of gods and ghosts and so the appearance of a slaughtered ghost or aitu, especially one intent on revenge, was all too possible. Scar-face rose with the realization that Toma had returned to take him to Pulotu, the Polynesian under-world. He screamed and pointed.

Seventy meters away Marcus drew a bead on the figure that was wobbling towards Nick with fists raised and eyes so wide he could see shining whites. Other warriors were turning and Nick was deep among them and surrounded. Marcus took up the trigger slack. The

M-1 was a fine weapon but to shoot would alert all the Matai. To not shoot would abandon Nick.

He felt a twist in his stomach for it was his plan that had put Nick down there and it would be his plan that put Nick in an umu. There were at least forty warriors within thirty yards of his old friend and Marcus knew he had only sixteen bullets. He also knew that he could use only fourteen of these on the warriors.

"Don't let me get cooked alive," Nick said before leaving, with uncommon seriousness and with a glance at the rifle. "Understand?"

And so the last two bullets were for Nick. One should be enough but two to be sure. Marcus drifted the open site towards Nick's back but could not hold there and pulled off. He wouldn't finish it until it was over. If he waited too long he might lose the shot but if that happened then Nick could bitch about it in the afterlife. Marcus was sure he'd be bitching about something anyway.

Scar-face closed on Nick and more warriors turned to watch. Several fingered clubs or guns as Scar-face screamed the word "aitu" through the night. Marcus saw a chance to shoot and hope Nick could escape in the confusion and he snugged the rifle in tight and willed Nick to slide to the right to open a lane to the chest of Scar-face. As if hearing his thoughts Nick edged left and blocked the shot.

"Crap, Nick," Marcus breathed, easing off the trigger and moving the muzzle off his friend's broad and muscled back. Too many warriors were watching and Marcus could tell that it was going to be very bad very soon.

Nick sensed it, too, and with a roar he ran at Scar-face. He arrived in four powerful strides and delivered a massive uppercut. The crack of the blow reached Marcus and the warrior's limp mass lifted into the air and thudded to earth. Nick howled to the sky and beat his chest again and stomped along. The other warriors turned away from what looked like one more of countless fights.

Marcus shook his head as Nick vanished into the house. Just before the door closed he saw Nick face the jungle and deliver a broad wink.

Chapter 43

Gastro barged into Katya's private lab without knocking. For a moment he stood stock still; Katya was gone but electricity hummed and gels ran and HPLCs sifted molecules. The lab felt like his own for it was operating at maximum capacity.

Worry lines etched his brow at the realization that Katya was working at such a level and he cursed himself for the thought but wondered again what she was pursuing. He eyed the electron micrograph on the wall but it was only the modified hepatovirus which had been so successful in water and which was a reminder of Katya's prowess. He looked for a lab notebook but saw none. He prowled over her desktop, looking at sequences, scanning gels, checking equipment settings. He felt vaguely guilty for checking up on her but reminded himself that he was trying to further his own work.

He turned on her computer and began prowling about. Whatever he had gone along with in the past, he could no longer ignore the trends marked by the killings among the rats, by the changelings who now lived a wild life in the deep and many of whom had once had been the crash crew tasked with subduing ships, and the cannibalism. All these things might mean nothing or they might mean something very bad.

And Katya might be working to solve the same problem but waiting until she had the solution before surprising him with it. She had surprised him with the water virus and this could be the same; he calmed at the realization that he was letting events get to him. Katya was tough and bright and precocious but she was no monster; she was only what he had made her.

Gastro always worked with a characteristic single-mindedness and now that he was on the track of the genetic source of the violence he could not turn away. He could wait to ask Katya but she might be gone all day. He had a hunch that her work would help and he tended to follow his hunches. He sifted through the drawers and files as the computer searched for key phrases. He could see that there were encrypted files and he would break those next, not out of suspicion of his daughter but because the march of science could not wait.

Then he found two documents that deepened the furrows in his brow. The first outlined a detailed and methodical strategy to hunt down the gene or genes that caused the killing, and which Katya in her notes called BTh for BloodThirst. Her plan was a solid one and Gastro was sure it would work; what was not clear was whether she had implemented it. The paper concluded with a number of possible genetic explanations and suggested counter-measures for each.

It was the second paper which froze Gastro's blood. In it Katya laid out a number of ways to amplify and spread the BloodThirst genes. Her ideas included using mosquito vectors, contaminating water supplies, or even loading the genes into plasmids that could be shared among bacteria and would eventually find their way into humans. All humans carry *E. coli* in their guts and Katya envisioned using these as messengers for the BloodThirst gene. The most alarming allusions were to creating an aerial viral vector.

Gastro could tell that the second paper was old and he pondered the contrary messages of the two papers. Perhaps the second was a joke or idle speculation or a thought experiment; as an exercise in grad school he had once figured out a way to mass produce and deliver an antibody that would target human growth hormone and thus convert humanity to a race of dwarves as a way to conserve the planet's resources. After first confirming that he had no plans to pursue such a scheme, his advisers gave him high marks.

He turned to the sector of Katya's hard drive that was encrypted and attacked it. He had raised Katya from birth and he could not believe she would work to spread the gene she called BloodThirst; she could only have been working out a thought experiment.

But her data might help. He set up a brute-force cracking program and left it to run while he returned to his own lab to search for the killer gene. Time was growing short; if Pelemodo's men came they might even have to evacuate Tabu. He hoped not, because there was nowhere to go. But regardless, for now he had a bug to chase.

Chapter 44

Devon Lucas felt strong, she felt lucky, and most of all, she felt desperate. The horrors of Tabu were too much; the awful infection, the strange people, Henry Winston's horrible degeneration, her own future.

Henry Winston had gone from bad to worse to unimaginable. He had turned into some form of mutant freak show before her eyes, a victim of what Gastro Nister called a "massive hox regulatory failure." To Devon that was like calling a bloody decapitation a "total cranial removal event."

Whatever had taken root in Henry Winston kept growing and surging until it overtook him and his systems collapsed. He had died screaming and fighting, expiring in mid-thrash, as if whatever had been awakened in him was furious at being re-submerged into darkness after such a brief glimpse of light. Devon could feel some of the same forces within her own body, but knew that in her these dark powers were being channeled in another direction. Whether that was better or worse, she couldn't say.

Which was perhaps the worst of it, and a possible explanation for the mindset of those who had gone before her. She could flee, but she could not flee what was in her—what she now was, and what she would become. You could take the girl out of Tabu, but you couldn't take the Tabu out of the girl. Though she was working on that.

She looked across the quarter-mile spit of water that separated Tabu from Tanua. At times the current ripped through it and at other times it could be waded. She was an oceanographer and a sub pilot, and in light of those accomplishments, it might surprise some to learn that she was afraid of swimming in the sea. It wasn't the swimming but the big toothy things which had to be there, somewhere out of sight. She knew all about tiger sharks, oceanic white-tips, sea wasps, marine crocodiles, and Portuguese Men-Of-War.

She also knew that she might not be able to make the swim, and that even if she did, according to everyone on Tabu, she would receive a cold reception from the Tanuans and a prompt return.

But she saw no choice. Tabu kept unfolding like a rose of horror. Every time she thought she had reached the last layer another appeared. And then another. And another.

Katya had come to view her, because of their shared scientific backgrounds, as something of a compatriot. No doubt she was swayed by her perfect record in persuading captives to take on their new lives, but Devon nonetheless found the openness of Katya and Gastro Nister to be surprising. Katya had given Devon a tour not only of the grounds and later of the tiny isle of Tabu itself—adding little that Devon had not already found in her pre-escape reconnaissance—but also of the labs. There, for the first time, Katya was less than fully forthcoming about the work she was undertaking.

Devon Lucas did not consider herself any sort of virologist, but she had done a rotation in a molecular virology lab in graduate school. It takes a special sort to work on critters so small they can be seen only with an electron microscope, and then poorly, and that defy even the conventional description of life. Nothing could ever be observed directly; it was all done on educated inference and wise hunches. Give a lab mouse a poison and you can watch it die; poison a virus and you detect it by finding that it can no longer infect cells or reproduce. Or perhaps the cells have become immune to it, or a buffer in the experiment was contaminated, or a thousand other things.

Working with such tiny things was the art of inference. Of reaching strong conclusions from a paucity of information.

Devon was working with just such a paucity. But from what she had seen and what she had observed, she was worried. And amazed.

She understood that Gastro and Katya Nister had found it unexpectedly simple to resurrect in human DNA cartridges of ancient genes which remained intact from times so ancient they predated the human species and even the rise of mammals. She knew that to be less surprising than it sounded; every person and every creature alive could in theory trace its lineage back through ages, through ever more primitive iterations, until arriving at some common single-celled creature that, through its mindless feeding and dividing, gave birth to a world. But the surprise came from the continued survival of some of these ancient genes. Perhaps not even that should be so surprising; bacteria and men used genetic codes that were largely identical, with many of the same three-letter codes for the same amino acids.

But the shocker was that genes that seemed to have been unused for so long seemed to have survived. And not just survived, but survived in perfect working condition. Katya explained that the genes had not slumbered for millennia but in fact continued to perform important tasks in fetal development; there was continued selection pressure to keep them intact.

And so, through a series of gentle genetic manipulations, Gastro and Katya were able light the fires on these ancient genes and bring them alive in a way that grew functioning gills on an adult human being. The water came in through the mouth, was shunted through a new passage that paralleled to the trachea, and passed through the internal gill structure in the chest before venting through exhaust slits on the torso. The lungs shrunk a bit but most of the necessary space came from moving things around slightly in the abdominal cavity. It seemed fantastic but Devon had now seen scores of people just so modified. And she had her very existence to prove it—without these water breathers she and Henry would still be at the bottom of the sea, dead in the oxygen-depleted submersible.

Devon and Henry had been infected in what Katya called the old-fashioned way—through a drink of water, which deposited the water-tolerant virus in their guts where it promptly infected them. This version represented an advance; in the old days it had taken a painful series of shots.

But Katya referred to even the water-tolerant version as relatively primitive, and she spoke of a time to come soon when millions of changelings would take to the sea. She spoke of the collapse of the world's countries and economy and of the rise of a brave new sea-based world. She told Devon that she wasn't ready for the rest of the story, but with a chill Devon noticed from the labeled tubes in the lab that Katya was also interested in the rhinovirus family, which she knew caused the common cold. Other tubes hinted at other things, and Devon managed to steal one particular bullet-shaped microcentrifuge tube. But it was the rhinovirus that haunted her thoughts, for Katya had demonstrated that she could re-engineer a virus. The possibility that she might do so using the common cold template was terrifying.

Devon realized that she was the only person on the planet who knew. She also realized that there was nothing she could do.

She stepped into the water—the current pulled at her even when the sea was only ankle deep—and started swimming.

Chapter 45

Just inside the massive brass door of the Governor's mansion Nick found a large sitting room to his left, a hallway to the right, and a descending stairway straight ahead. The sitting room was littered with beer cans and kava stains and in the precise center, atop a glass coffee table, an enormous pile of human dung. Nick took the stairs. The house sat on a hillside and the captives were likely below.

The first flight was carpeted with a beige shag that matched the painted mortarboards and complemented the cream walls. The stairs turned at a landing, and once out of sight of the entry hall became unfinished stone hacked from the lava of the hillside. The lighting dimmed and a dank scent rose where the stairs ended in a small room that ended at a door of bare plywood. Two alert and sober warriors stood before it and watched him.

Nick pointed at the door, grinned, and patted his belly. "Hungry," he said in English.

Neither warrior moved. The one on the right fingered an automatic rifle and the other a machete with a dull red substance clotted on its blade. Their faces said that they didn't recognize him but were slow to challenge someone who, based on behavior and size, might be of high standing.

Nick knew he didn't really look Polynesian and that the more they looked the less Polynesian he would seem.

"Boy meat or girl meat?" asked one guard in Samoan, which to Nick sounded like gibberish from which the consonants had been hacked.

"Hungry!" Nick screamed and put his hand on the knob. Turning his back to the guards was a deliberate and calculated show of dis-respect and he expected them to be too surprised to react in time.

The door was locked.

Nick turned to see the guards exchange a look. Both were young, which cut two ways. They would be reluctant to challenge established authority, but once they decided to fight, they would have no sense of their own mortality. Soon, Nick knew, they would wonder why someone they had never seen before, who on close inspection looked less and less Samoan, and who didn't appear to speak even a word of the tongue of the gods, was trying to go where he had no business. Nick interrupted any speculation by saying, "Never mind. I have a key."

He raised a foot and kicked.

The door exploded into the room and shattered on the far wall. A mass of filthy palangis stared at him from a cluster along one side. From their faces not one recognized him.

Nor did the guards. From the warrior with the rifle came what was obviously a challenge as the gun rose. The other warrior moved to flank him with his red blade coming up.

Rifles are no good in phone booths, Nick recalled. Even for a big man he had a surprising reach, and one hand shot out and ripped the gun away while his other fist delivered a light jab to the man's jaw—just enough to slow him while Nick spun to swing the rifle like a bat. It had just started to whistle when it met the other guard's skull and dropped him as if he'd been de-boned. The machete left a red smear on a wall and clattered to the floor.

The first guard was scrambling and Nick brought both hands together and accelerated his spin. The old moves of the discus came back, with a touch of the hammer throw. The warrior dove too late and took the hit on his shoulder and grunted then rolled in the dirt. Nick was sure bones must have broken but the warrior immediately gathered himself to spring with one foot braced on the far wall. His eyes glinted with a look Nick had once seen on a pissed-off tiger in the Chicago Zoo, and the set-up reminded him of a fight three years before in a bar in the New Hebrides when his opponent had coiled and braced the same way. That time Nick had held only a length of broken chair, but the same technique would work. Nick stepped forward and chopped with the gun butt in a maneuver that was, he decided, more of a very short range javelin. The leaping warrior drove his own face into the blow. His head shot back with the snap of a dry stick. Nick's hands stung.

He left the two heaps and entered the makeshift cell. It stank of urine and feces and sweat. A single bulb cast harsh light and stark shadows.

The palangis backed away. He was, he realized, dressed in native garb and covered with blood, and he had just murderously beaten two men. He saw Linc, Stanislaw, two entomologists, a lawyer, and several crewmen from the ship; they obviously saw him only as a Matai warrior. He felt the power of terrorizing the weak and helpless, the adrenal surge of the bully.

"Hungry," Nick repeated in a conversational tone while patting his belly. "Cheeseburger, anyone?"

Marcus was waiting behind the villa when Nick appeared.

"No trouble?"

"None for you, I'd wager," the big man replied evenly. He wiped blood from his hands onto the grass while the captives hurried into the coconut grove and eyed the forest like two-legged deer.

Nick vanished into the house and returned with a half-dozen rifles. They ranged from ancient Lee Enfields that could have seen action in the Second World War to a few shotguns and a clutch of modern assault rifles. He passed them out.

"Nick, you make a hell of a Samoan," Linc said. One side of his face was blackened and swollen.

Nick feigned surprise. "Why Linc, I thought you were supposed to have been eaten by now."

Linc grinned, then winced and put a hand to his face. "Same to you."

Marcus gestured at the forest. "We could all still end up as barbecue. A thought which, in the case of you two, is enough to make me go vegetarian."

"Never," Nick declared, but formed the group into a line. Marcus suggested that since Nick looked local he take the lead; the lava-lava might buy a few seconds if they hit a Matai patrol. Marcus would bring up the rear.

Before taking his position Nick studied Marcus, searching the odd look in his eyes. "Marcus, other than the obvious, is everything Okay?"

Marcus half-smiled, nodded once, and wiped his forehead. "I think it will be."

Nick gathered the group and explained that they would sneak down the hillside to the *Aurora* and escape to sea. Just like giant lemmings, he said, but no one smiled.

"It's about four miles. Silence is golden, and we'll go slow and take breaks every hour." He looked at some of his out-of-shape charges, particularly two cultural anthropologists from New York. They looked too tired to lie down let alone walk. "Make that every thirty minutes."

He turned and began to slide through the jungle, trying to pick a route that would be easy to follow with little noise.

Marcus stood watching as the last in line, a South American entomologist who always carried a personal bottle of hot sauce with which he claimed to douse even water, vanished around a banyan tree. Then he turned away.

Katya Nister slipped through the jungle in green shorts, a pair of light jungle boots, and a camo blouse from which she'd ripped the sleeves. Two throwing knives rested in belt sheaths and across her back she wore the Weatherby. For years she had roamed the jungles, sometimes staying out for days. Sometimes she spent as long in the sea. Both were like visits to an old primal self and on such trips she traveled light; never before had she gone armed. But the Matai were loose and blood was on the air.

She was looking for the fleeing Devon Lucas but she was also curious; she knew she was afoot in an open-air lab. Tanua was a preview of what Earth would become when the rhinovirus arrived. She found herself both thrilled and appalled; increasingly over the past months and years she had found herself to be of two minds about so many things. It was as if the old genes were contesting her independence and seeking to take her over. Or perhaps they had and her old self was not yet entirely quelled.

Katya had found what Gastro still sought. The genes lay on the short arm of chromosome eight and were an integral part of what Gastro had made; they were a reverse reading frame section of a gene that coded an oxygen transport protein. Sometimes the gene was interrupted by a series of repeats that read CAG over and over like a barrage of advertisements during a television show. The more repeats, the more violence. The repeats were self-propagating, as if they were tiny bunnies intent only on swelling their numbers. Darwinian selection at the smallest level.

The BloodThirst system was complex and other genes also played supporting roles. She was not at all sure that you could recapture some of the old without bringing back all of it; it seemed that there might be no way to split the violence from the abilities it accompanied. Katya had discovered the genes by serendipity when she used the wrong cutting and ligating enzymes and constructed a virus that raised the level of violence a hundred fold. The first sign came when the female test rats lost the ability to have multiple births; each would bear only a single offspring, and often a defective one. Katya found that the fetal rats were battling in the womb until there was a sole survivor.

When she first understood what she had made, part of her wanted to destroy it, but the new and louder part of her wanted to spread it. She wondered if this were the effect of the same gene within her recognizing itself elsewhere, and urging her to build it.

She had used the killer virus on some of the crew from the last several freighters and on half the dollar bills. While the old part of her wanted only to expand humanity's range to the seas, a noble goal that could help her species survive global warming, asteroid impacts, or even nuclear war, that newer side wanted so much more; it wanted to spread an old gene and bring back an ancient time of savagery and killing.

She passed a few wrecked bodies and saw that they had been weak and so did not deserve to survive. The old genes were ruthlessly effective; they culled individuals to create species that could survive for tens of millions of years. *Homo sapiens* had been around a mere hundred thousand and was already finding ways to bring all sorts of weaknesses into the gene pool. The BloodThirst gene would be a whetstone on the blade of humanity; it would chip off the weak and leave only the hard and strong.

A large pale man erupted from behind a rubber tree and sprinted at her. Although he was naked and caked with blood she vaguely recognized him as the second mate from the *Cielo di Sarona*. He had been on Tanua only eighteen months and already he had crossed over, she could see. He had been one of the first to receive her modified virus and a short time later he had become one of the ones who lived deep and wild, perhaps tottering at the edge of what was human. Gastro allowed it, interested to see what would happen with them. But she already knew.

His hands were clawed and his lips pulled back in a snarl as he accelerated through the mud.

Katya wanted to grapple with him, to beat him with her fists and kick him with her feet, but he was much bigger and stronger, and even if she could take him—and she thought she could—if another of his kind arrived it would be over.

She un-slung the Weatherby. The bolt flew and she shouldered it. She had removed the scope and no aiming was necessary but for fun she waited until the man was fifteen feet away.

The slug punched into his upper chest and blew him into the bole of a palm. He left a red mess and collapsed as Katya re-slung the rifle.

Her nervous system sang. The kill had felt good. The smell of the blood and the look of the meat and the sounds on the air all swirled around her. She felt a stirring deep within.

She turned and began to trot through the forest. She made no sound and her senses were tuned with exquisite precision and she somehow knew she would not be surprised by anyone else.

But she also knew she had to get back to Tabu. Her own change was coming and she had to get there before it was too late.

Chapter 46

It was not until the first rest break that Nick found that Marcus was gone. The exhausted and filthy captives collapsed on a mossy creek-bank beneath ferns and a tangled bird of paradise but Marcus was nowhere to be seen.

Nick questioned the two Brazilian entomologists who had been in the rear but neither had heard or seen anything, or even recalled seeing Marcus since the mansion. As the group began to grow alarmed Nick dropped it. He was tempted to climb back up and search but he knew he would find nothing. If Marcus had left on his own he'd be gone. And if he'd been taken he would be gone. Marcus knew their destination and perhaps he would meet them there. But he had already come back from the dead once and a second time might be too much to hope for.

He put Linc at the rear and moved the group out.

Minutes later shots sounded in the distance and Nick stopped his little column and crouched. The brush thrashed as though thick with warriors—which, Nick reflected, it was.

When the shots quieted Nick led the group on a traverse of a steep slope. It was another game trail but they would make far too much noise plowing through raw jungle. The path led into a ravine and back up onto the mountain flank.

A choking scream sounded from far away and right after it came another of different pitch and much closer and then a third. Nick had the awful sense that something was trying to play a tune with human screams like a street performer with soda bottles. The something was not having much success but it kept trying.

In a small glade where sunbeams shot through giant ferns and blue drifts of hungry smoke, the forest stilled. Nick half expected to see a dinosaur clomp through the preternatural ferns but knew he was likely to see something much worse.

Nick felt the prickliness of a tarantula on his spine. It wasn't from the screams or the blood on the air. He studied the play of breeze on fern and palm, listened to the rustles walk the forest, and watched a swirl of motes in a sunbeam. There was a pattern that he was slowly piecing together. He brought the column to a halt and then stopped it again thirty seconds later.

Something, he was quite sure, was stalking them.

Sweat wet his black hair and rolled down his back. He eyed the column; three people back, Stanislaw Tatum was wide-eyed and scanning the brush. He felt it too.

Nick gestured his charges into low crouches, then traded his Lee-Enfield for a coral taxonomist's Winchester twelve-gauge pump shotgun. It was a short-barreled weapon that was hardly sporting but Nick had no interest in being sporting.

He stepped off the trail and the heat thickened, and in the green grip of the vegetation, even the distant screams seemed to hush and the far-off gunfire to slacken. He looked back. From five meters away the group was invisible and he was alone. He wove between a tangle of vines specked with tiny blue flowers and past a massive banyan that dropped a forest of prop roots all around. He held the shotgun lightly and swept the barrel across his path as he slid between creepers and vines.

He had to stop several times to remove thorns from his clothes and flesh, and once a swirl of motion brought the gun up, but it was only a huge snake wrapped in a futu tree. He crept up the hillside and climbed above his invisible followers. Salt stung his eyes and the heat squeezed in and a miniature clearing appeared ahead, a space large enough for a pair of graves. He thumbed the safety off and stepped in.

From behind a *huff huff* sounded a rustle, and he spun to see something burst from the white flowers of a small dogbane—a blur of honey skin and wild eyes and a whistling black war club already at the top of its arc. Nick jerked back and raised the shotgun. Another half-second and he could have pointed it and used it as a twentieth-century firearm rather than a stone-age stick, but he lacked that half-second and so raised it sideways. The club hit and the shotgun barrel bent and the stock shattered and Nick's hands stung.

He was still falling when the warrior swung again. Shark teeth edged the inverted triangle of the club, some white and some stained crimson. Nick rolled and the club bit mud. He tried to rise but slipped and the club was coming again and he dodged. Shark teeth parted his hair. Even on land the sea seemed to pursue him.

Nick burst up. Already the club was falling but he drove inside the arc and put his shoulder to the warrior's chest. They landed in a tangle of spined vines in the throat of a forked fish poison tree. The warrior spun and twisted and Nick felt elbows and fists and teeth. He landed a solid punch to the sternum that had no effect and then felt something on the warrior's side, a long cut that did not bleed. Nick punched it and then tried to rip it open and the warrior jolted into a frenzy. Nick felt like he was fighting a cartoon creature for the warrior moved in an inhuman blur of fists and Nick took hit after hit. A stone blade flashed and Nick felt a hot line on his ribs and then the warrior was on top of him. Iron hands ripped at his flesh, working like claws and driving for his throat.

Nick locked his hands on the warrior's wrists as they slowly slid toward his neck. He knew that some combination of body geometry and genetics gave him uncommon strength, and he grunted and flexed to bring maximum pressure to bear. He felt and heard a faint crack from the warrior's left wrist and his attacker's eyes widened. Then the warrior smiled. Still his hands slid up Nick's sweat-slicked chest.

Nick brought the pressure down on the other wrist. Surely, he figured, if he could crack both wrists he should be able to gain an advantage. His garrulous talk had landed him in more than his share of bar fights but never had he encountered anyone so primally fast and strong as this attacker. Or so immune to pain. Still, Nick thought he had a chance. He always thought he had a chance.

Another warrior exploded from the brush, fell in the mud, and sat up. Nick glimpsed a round face that was hungry with bloodthirst and scarred and wearing a beautiful new welt. It was Scar-face from the mansion. Scar-face tried to join the first warrior but Nick half-rolled and blocked his way. He tried to move the other way and Nick blocked him again.

Scar-face screamed. His club cut air and Nick twisted and the first warrior took the blow on a shoulder. Then both were on him, biting and pulling and ripping. Nick swung and chopped but the tide was against him.

Nick saw the brush part and another figure appear. Three would be too many. One, in fact, was too many. He tried to crack heads together but it was like trying to smack fence posts into each other. He tried to punch both in the throat but they dodged. Hands closed on his throat, and just like that, his air was gone. He would have chuckled, had he any wind, at the irony of suffocating on land when avoiding precisely that fate was his reason for avoiding the sea. If the gods wanted you, the gods took you. He tilted left, and when his attackers braced against that, he reversed and bucked right. They hung on and grinned and Nick could see that both were seriously overdue for a trip to the dental hygienist. He was terribly disappointed that this was likely the last image his brain would record. It was a far cry from the sumptuous young blonde he had planned to view through fading nonagenarian eyes.

Then the first warrior jerked and straightened, jerked again, and twitched. His eyes crossed. Nick heard a dry tapping that reminded him of a woodpecker and the warrior toppled. A little air squeezed down his throat.

More tapping and Scar-face spasmed and gurgled. He half-twisted and Nick saw past him to Stanislaw Tatum with an upraised geologist's hammer. The sharp tip was bloody and matted with black hair. It struck again like a beak.

Scar-face leapt for the little man but Nick caught a fistful of his hair and yanked. The warrior spun in the air and landed on his back, stunned and gasping. Stanislaw swooped like a falcon and the hammer nailed away between the warrior's eyes. Stanislaw was wide-eyed and breathing hard when he rose. He eyed the quivering mass at his feet, then looked at Nick and waved his chromed hammer.

"I didn't know you had that in you, Stan," Nick wheezed as he checked his damage. The stone knife had slashed across his ribs but the cut was shallow. His neck was sore but it still connected head to body.

"I don't," Stanislaw agreed as he stared in wonder at his hammer and the fallen warriors. He looked as if he wasn't a hundred percent sure that his hammer might not turn on him next. "I don't have it in me. I tell you, between the crazy geology and the crazy people, I really think living here is making me a little crazy."

Nick heaved himself up and draped and arm across the smaller man's shoulders.

"Well. Sometimes a little crazy is good."

Chapter 47

Marcus placed one hand behind his back and with the other rapped on a door.

It opened.

"Marcus," Callie said.

He presented a bouquet of yellow plumeria, red hibiscus, and pink frangipani. "Hello, wife."

She leaned forward and looked left and right down the hall. "Marcus, you shouldn't be here."

"I should. Do you know what's going on?"

She moved as if to brush her hair behind her ear, an old gesture but one which did not work with her short hair. "What?"

He told her.

"Probably just some minor disturbance."

"More like a full-fledged revolution."

"Even if so, this place is safe."

"Not even close.

"Marcus, it is."

He reached for her hand. "Come see. Then decide."

She stepped back and crossed her arms. "Marcus, I know you don't like it. Maybe I don't either. But I can't leave."

Marcus closed the gap to her. "The Matai have been capturing palangis. And eating them. They won't stay away from Tabu because of some old myth. The myths are on their side."

She frowned. "Eating? Are you sure?"

He grimaced. "The smell is not to be forgotten."

"That's a problem."

"You have no idea," Marcus said.

"No, actually, you have no idea." She stepped forward. "Show me."

The air outside was laced with smoke and the sharp smell of burned things. Over the green wall that hid Tanua a black pall smeared the blue sky like charcoal on a watercolor. Distant screams and gunshots sounded.

Gastro Nister was loading his pale-blue pickup from a half-dozen wheeled carts that held cages of rats and racks of tubes. His jaw was slack and his eyes round and he stopped often to scan the horizon.

"This was not to happen. Not like this," he was muttering when he saw them. "Callie," he said, then he looked at Marcus. "You. I thought you might join us. But not so soon."

"He's not joining us," Callie said.

"You and I have some things to discuss, doctor," Marcus said in a quiet tone.

Gastro gestured at the smoky horizon. "If you want a piece of me you'll have to stand in line."

Marcus pulled an orange-capped fifty ml test tube from a rack and read the typed label: *K. transforma.*

"This is your miracle?" he asked.

Gastro tipped his head at Callie. "No. She is my miracle. One of them. You know of my work?"

"I've been using a similar gene to engineer an artificial gill. Like a better scuba."

Despite the situation Gastro glimmered with amusement. "How quaint. You work on Model Ts while around you are Indy cars."

Marcus tipped the tube, watching the viscous suspension roll back and forth. Gastro held up an identical tube.

"A custom retrovirus with an encapsulated retroposon that targets genes on chromosomes 8 and 9. That's what makes everything happen."

Marcus pocketed the tube. "Souvenir."

"Keep it. I cannot save it all anyway. Not with this madness."

"Is it so bad, Father?" Callie asked, and Marcus cut a hard look at her.

A group of Matai warriors appeared on a ridge a half-mile away. Rifles glinted, polished clubs shone, torches smoked. They formed in a line and gave a shout and advanced.

Gastro looked at them for a long time. "Yes, it is so bad. Go, Callie. Go before it is too late."

"Father, I can stay and help. We have a few weapons. We can—"

Gastro pointed into the jungle and his voice grew stern. "Go now. We cannot match them and you are not safe here. No one is. Have you seen my daughter Katya?"

"She's not here?"

He shook his head bleakly. "She is not. And neither should you be. Go."

Callie cast a sidelong look at Marcus and hesitated then asked, "Father, the others. Have they—"

He nodded grimly and returned to his task. "They have. They all have."

"God help us."

Gastro stopped his work and glanced skyward with a wry smile. "I wouldn't ask him."

Callie grabbed Marcus by the arm. "We have to get out of here."

Katya edged up to the bright water that led to Tabu. A tremble rippled across her body and she backed away and fell beneath a small dogbane, the suicide plant with the poisonous sap. She had never had to fight so long or so hard. It came in waves but each wave was taller and stronger than the last and she knew that eventually one would take her. The blood and killing were sounding a call and she would have to answer.

But she could not let that happen on Tanua. She could not let herself succumb for she knew enough of the biochemistry and of the behavior to know that she would become something that would not survive. And above all she had to survive. It was the only option.

She heard footsteps pass close by and dug deeper into the dogbane but did not open her eyes. If she could survive this burst she could get back to Tabu. Perhaps.

Marcus and Callie stopped after an hour of running, both panting. A group of warriors had spotted them crossing the narrow straight between the islands and chased them through the mangroves before losing them in stands of wild banana and giant fern. A wave took Marcus' rifle but they kept their skins and now they huddled in the slick folds of an enormous strangler fig hung with yellow orchids.

"We used to like hiking," Callie wheezed.

"When we weren't running for our lives," Marcus agreed. He pulled off his sweat-soaked shirt.

She leaned into him and his arm found its place along her shoulders, like machined parts snapping into place.

"We always did fit together."

Callie raised her head and scanned the forest.

Marcus tensed. "What is it?"

"Nothing," she said slyly, and then pulled away a pile of dry moss at their backs to reveal a hollow beneath the tree. She gestured at it and wiggled her eyebrows in a gesture he hadn't forgotten.

"You haven't atrophied in six years, have you?" she asked.

"Find out."

"I will," she said.

From their burrow they occasionally heard feet pound past as each of the thirty minutes passed with exquisite slowness and terrible speed.

"We have to go," Marcus said.

She touched his shoulder and for the first time she was the old Callie. "Once more?"

"Later. We'll have plenty of time later. But if we don't get to the ship . ."

A flicker of darkness crossed her face but she said nothing and they rose and dressed.

Chapter 48

Paramount Chief Pelemodo was in his royal fale dining on palusami with a side of anthropologist when a messenger ran in. Pelemodo had heard his approach and knew he came down the mountain trail from the governor's mansion. The messenger was a youth of perhaps sixteen and he kicked off his sandals and stepped into the fale with head bowed.

"Palangis have escaped!" he cried.

Pelemodo took another bite and noted that the taste was indeed porky.

"How many palangis?" he asked.

A slight pause. "All of them."

Pelemodo was on his feet though he did not seem to have moved. He was tempted to kill the messenger and could see that the young man was expecting it but that would not be a good use of resources. They needed messengers.

Pelemodo gestured and his attendants dispersed. Within minutes his warriors had gathered before the fale. Shots were fired into the air and war clubs swung in preparation. Several chiefs entered the fale.

"We will go to the governor's mansion and track them," Fuimono announced.

"No," Pelemodo said, and unrolled a map of the island on a table. Both were palangi tools but both were needed to fight the palangi. When the battle was over and Tanua theirs, both map and table would be consigned to a purifying flame.

Pelemodo tapped the map. "I understand how the palangi thinks. They will not fight. They will flee. And how can they flee?"

He looked at his chiefs and they looked at him.

"The boat," Pelemodo finished. "They will try for the boat."

"There are two. The big boat that swims and the small boat that flies," a minor chief noted.

"Yes, the plane," Pelemodo agreed. "That cannot carry all of them but let us be thorough. Destroy the plane. But leave the boat."

"Leave the boat?" said Fuimono, and Pelemodo smiled.

"What is Tangaroa's plan?" asked an old chief.

"The same plan he used against the demon octopus Rogo Tumu Here. Bait. We will draw them to the boat and catch them and hack them apart. But first send two men aboard. Tell them to leave no mark but to go into the engine room. We have someone who can find an engine room?"

"Ropati and Lio were mechanics, Lio on a ship."

"Excellent. Here is what they must do."

As the men trotted down the road Pelemodo decided that some palangi concepts were useful. Insurance, for example. He had just bought some.

Nick guided his group into the jungle above the main village of Sava and tucked them into brush and vines before crawling forward with Linc to peer down. Through the fronds of a fern they saw a village transformed. In the grassy square of the open malae, mounded umus smoked and steamed. The burnt husks of buildings smoldered. Corpses and wrecked cars littered the ground. The square gave onto the research pier where all the science buildings had been burned. On the other side of the pier the Flying Canoe tilted a wingtip into the water like a drunk duck, obviously flooded. Beyond it, the *Aurora* appeared untouched.

In the malae, guarding the only way to the ship, waited a group of warriors. They did not play or wrestle but stood patiently.

"Almost like they're waiting for us," Linc finally said.

"They are," Nick said.

Linc surveyed their little band. "We have about ten guns. Think we can get them all?"

"All hundred?" Nick rubbed his brow and pulled at his hair, not at all surprised by the white among the black. He continued.

"They have the numbers. The weapons. And the position. But there's one thing they don't have."

Linc looked at the umus. "A balanced diet?"

"Discipline. Here's what we'll do."

Nick worked his way to the north end of Sava then walked back into the square. A few of the warriors noticed but most paid no heed. Perhaps, he realized, he still looked too Samoan. That would be easy to fix.

"Tangaroa is my bitch!" he screamed.

A few of the warriors looked at him curiously.

"Tangaroa takes it in the butt from Poseidon! Tangaroa squats to pee! Tangaroa is a *fafafine*!" This last accused the sea god of being a drag queen, something Nick had found a useful insult in bars across the southern ocean.

To punctuate these declarations he leveled his rifle and fired. The warriors looked at him, at each other, and then began trotting towards him as a solid mass.

Nick turned and ran.

"What brass. That's our cue," Linc said as the square emptied. Nick was surprisingly fast for a big man. But so were many of the warriors chasing him. Only three remained behind.

Linc led the band down through the brush and into the open of the malae. The two warriors, who by chance were looking, did not call out or hesitate but immediately charged with mouths wide and hands clawed. Linc got the idea they had no intention of using their guns but he did not wait to find out. He raised his rifle and sighted as he'd been taught in the Marines so many years before and from forty meters shot the first through the chest twice.

He had heard accounts of being nauseous after killing a man or of being overcome by the enormity of such an act. Linc merely felt that his weapon was pulling to the right. He corrected his aim and shot the second warrior through the head.

Beside him Stanislaw Tatum fired five times and managed to hit the third warrior twice and drop him.

"Go, go, go," Linc screamed and saw that even the New York cultural anthropologists were managing to run. Though empty-handed, they looked like they were carrying suitcases. The group crossed the square with pale legs hurdling corpses and stinking umus and streamed onto the wharf.

Linc pulled the guns from the fallen warriors and sent most of his people onto the ship while emplacing his armed men at the foot of the pier. Their attackers would have to face a combined fire and their rear was guarded by the sea. He made sure everyone knew to keep low and silent and settled in to wait. The big Greek had gotten them there. Perhaps he'd make it back. Linc would give him the chance.

It was in an innocuous directory on Katya's computer that Gastro hit the motherlode. He had retreated inside, away from the approaching warriors, and once there he decided to continue his research into both the viciousness problem and what Katya had been up to. He crafted a quick search program to scan Katya's hard drive for certain key items and went to work correlating all the genetic variations with the levels of violence.

When he checked back, his program had snared a fish he had both hoped and feared would be there.

Katya had indeed been busy. In fact, she had been working on the same problem of the violence. At the very least, she was close to finding the BloodThirst gene. She had correlated a number of genetic markers with violent behaviors and she had a fat data set. That alone would help him and he made a copy on a diskette and returned to his lab.

He had to move fast, he knew. But though it was a race there might still be time to find the gene and stop it.

Nick pounded through a coconut grove with vines slashing at his face. He could hear his pursuers behind; they were excited and calling out to each other and a few were even laughing. They could laugh; there were at least seventy of them. Twice he paused to shoot at swift-footed attackers and though he couldn't tell if he hit them, he at least slowed them.

He hurdled the buttressed trunks of several looking-glass trees and flew around a huge fig. The understory cleared and he fired over his shoulder and accelerated down a slight slope.

He cut behind a banyan, intending to eyeball his pursuers and see if they might have lost him. But someone was already there. Automatically he reached out and grabbed and only when he heard the squeal did he realize that he had a caught a female palangi.

"You," he said to Devon when the red-haired sub pilot turned. Her eyes were wild and she was mud-spattered and scratched but it was her.

"Nick Kondos," she said, eyeing his native garb in dismay. "You're one of them too?"

"No, I just like to dress up." He glanced over his shoulder and his eyes bugged. "And if we had time for twenty questions I'd have a few for you."

She peered over the bushes up the hill. "Are all those chasing you?"

"Not exactly. They're chasing us."

He grabbed her arm and they tore down the slope, slaloming between palms and hurdling fallen trees and lava boulders. As the warriors pressed from behind, taking occasional wild shots, Devon ran strong and stayed beside him, though she wheezed loudly.

A flicker of motion appeared ahead. Uncharacteristically, this warrior ducked behind a tree rather than charging. Nick angled towards the tree, which was a wide black toa, and readied his rifle. He expected that that this warrior would add a dash of cunning to the usual mad bravado and try to hit him from behind as he passed. Nick had a counter for that: a face full of lead.

Marcus heard shots and a roar that was not the wind or sea. He looked around the black toa tree and saw one large and one small warrior sprinting for them, and leading many others. He pulled Callie into the lee and wished he still had the rifle, but picked up a heavy branch with a thick knot at the business end. It wasn't much, but he measured its balance and tightened his grip and cocked it high. The Matai had been very effective with clubs and if he hit the warrior right he would crush his skull before a shot was fired.

He edged around the tree and cocked his weapon. When you bring a stick to a gunfight you must strike fast and hard and he would.

The big warrior flew past in a dive.

Marcus took the one step he expected to need and then another two and started a head-smashing swing as the warrior rolled neatly and came up in a squat with a black gun snugged to a dark cheek.

Marcus cut his wrists and his stick took a deep bite of black earth with the wind of its passage rustling the man's crown of leaves.

The warrior's gun did not fire.

"Nick," Marcus said.

Above the black eye of the rifle barrel the Greek's eyes were wide and his breathing hard. He was looking beyond Marcus. The shouts of closing warriors rang through the trees like spears but he did not move.

Marcus looked beyond Nick and his own eyes widened. "Devon."

Nick lowered the gun but not all the way. Sweat ran down his face. He stared beyond Marcus.

"Hello, Nick," Callie said softly. "Surprise."

"Holy Zeus," Nick muttered. "Either there's a lot of dead broads here or I'm dead and the afterlife is quite a disappointment,"

Marcus peered around the tree. "No, none of us are dead, but we're not far from it. And if your friends back there catch up with us I have a feeling we're going to miss out on a really good story hour."

Nick glanced to his left and shook his skull. "Later," he agreed and shot upright. "Follow me." He slung the gun and charged off.

Paramount Chief Pelemodo arrived in the empty square at the center of Sava. The village was empty and the pier was empty and boat was empty.

"Where are my warriors?" he asked a boy who was too young to fight.

"They are chasing a palangi."

Pelemodo smiled dreamily.

"A palangi? One palangi?"

"A big one."

"Tell me what happened," he whispered. "Leave nothing out."

The boy did so.

"Is that all?"

"Yes, Paramount Chief."

Pelemodo cuffed him to the ground. This was the right of a chief and the boy accepted it. Pelemodo walked in a circle as he surveyed the square, wondering where the palangis were and why all his warriors would chase one. He knew the answer—he had carefully avoided inculcating too much discipline. As he stepped over the body of a female palangi who had worked at the bank, he glanced at the body to her right, which fittingly enough was her husband, an islander who rejected the fa'a.

With his head turned he by chance—or by Tangaroa's design—caught a glint of motion near the *Aurora*. Looking closer he saw that the cars and wreckage at the foot of the pier had been formed into barricades. His eyebrows raised, his head tilted, and he understood and nodded in appreciation. It was a good ploy. He nodded to the sea for Tangaroa had again shown the way.

He gathered the warriors of his personal cohort and gave careful instructions with his hands painting delicate pictures in the air. He made it simple. That might be costly but it was necessary.

The warriors were moving out when one of the brown nuts around his neck exploded. The shot rang out a moment later.

"Damn. Missed," Linc said. Pelemodo had dodged out of sight with shocking speed for so large a man and Linc's second shot had drilled through the air four feet above where his bulk must have lain prostrate. Just for good measure he sent another bullet through the space, but lower. Maybe the big bastard would at least feel the wind.

Linc decided to save his ammo when he saw the warriors advancing on the wharf. They were at least fifty in number and more would come. But the advantage was to the defender and Linc had picked and fortified his position well. He and his men were secure behind barricades that faced a naked forty meters. It was a fine killing ground.

Ten warriors charged. Linc and the others put up a barrage and cut them down. Linc noticed that an Australian botanist had fired a full clip into the air over the warriors' heads and reminded him to conserve ammunition. And to aim.

Another ten warriors launched. One of these managed to crawl back to safety, although judging from the dark trail of blood on the packed sand he would not last long.

Across the malae Pelemodo was ignoring the small wounds from the shrapnel of the exploding nut and watching in dismay. He prided himself on not over-training his charges for such was a hallmark of hated western ways. But ignoring basic tactics was proving costly.

As the guns rang again and another group fell, he called together his legion leaders and sketched in the dirt with a broad and bloody finger.

"Watch," he said, showing them how to flank the position. "This is how to do this thing. Alamana and Luka here and here. Fuimono, from the rear. The water. Fuimono, use the Tangaroa power. You understand?"

Nods of obedient assent.

"Now do it."

Four Samoan legions approached the head of the pier. Two held the center while two went wide to encircle the flanks. Unlike their predecessors they moved cautiously and used the cover offered by their fallen comrades, the burnt hulks of buildings, and the ruined cars. They began a steady fire from long range and slowly advanced.

Meanwhile, a half-mile south, Fuimono's legion entered the sea with their rifles wrapped in plastic. As leader, Fuimono was first to call on the power of Tangaroa. Fuimono walked into the water until it was shoulder high, then dropped out of sight. Below the surface he swam until he found a large coral boulder. He wrapped his arms around it and held on as he felt the hunger for air burn in his chest. He fought the urge to surface. He had been told that with time the transitions would become easier but, for Fuimono each was still awkward in a way that was not painful but somehow worse than pain. It had been less than a year, though.

His vision began to tunnel and his chest to hammer. He could hold out no longer. With his own men above he could not return for another breath of air for that would be a shameful show of weakness. He opened his mouth, exhaled the last of his air, and inhaled the sea.

As the water washed in, ancient instincts fought modern ones in a battle for control. The palangi doctor had loaded the dice in favor of the ancient and so the water coursed onward to wash through the fork in his trachea and across gill arches and lamellae before exiting back to the sea through the slits that now flared on his abdomen.

Fuimono continued the gulping motion that drove the water though him and felt his nervous system settle into new rhythms that were old. He could not feel his lungs fold but knew they had. Or would as he dove deeper.

Fuimono reversed course and swam to where the legs of his legion stood. He stuck a hand above the water and gave the command and the warriors began submerging themselves. Several of the men were new and had only gone through a few transitions and Fuimono hovered by these. As usual they panicked and tried to bolt for the surface but Fuimono wrapped an arm corded with muscle around each and held them until they yielded and crossed over.

Within five minutes it was done. Each warrior blinked and squeezed in the way the doctor had taught and corneal membranes lowered into place to give water vision. The legion formed into battle array and swam twenty-five feet below the surface, their passage unmarked by bubble or splash as they turned north.

Fuimono felt hungry. He did not want to use the plastic-wrapped gun for it was far too antiseptic. Even a knife would be too remote. He had teeth to slash with and hands to rip with and those were the tools he wished to use. But the dim call of his forebrain instructed otherwise. They had a mission. He was the leader. He must bite down and quell the urges. Gastro Nister had recommended him to lead and he wondered if the palangi knew of the urges. Perhaps the palangi knew that he, Fuimono, would be able to control them. Not everyone could, he knew. He glanced to his left where the sea dropped off to purple depths. Down deep lived the wild ones. The ones rarely spoken of but often thought of.

Fuimono believed that all who went through the change felt the pull of the deep. He did not know whether it was stronger in some than others or if over time it became harder to resist. He knew many who had gone deep and he had considered it himself. The pull was similar to the one he felt on land, the one that made him hurt and kill and that made him so useful to Pelemodo. But it was not yet time to give in and go deep. Not yet.

His hand tightened on the rifle. Ahead and above, through a cloud of angel- and unicorn fish, appeared the black stripe of the pier on the blue back of the sea.

Linc peered from behind a barricade formed from two junked mini-buses, each garishly painted and now sprayed with blood. At least fifty warriors, spread in a wide half-circle, were methodically approaching. They were barefoot and half-naked, with only woven mats wrapped round their waists. Many also wore headbands, anklets, and bracelets of twisted pandanus. Their oiled bodies glinted like bronze statues and the blue-black weave of their body tattoos seemed to coil and shift in the smoke-shot sunlight.

They had learned and now they sought cover and protected each other, and it was strange to see men in stone-age garb carrying rifles and trying to move with modern military tactics.

Linc gave the men fire zones and each plinked away at any warrior within his zone. Every shot drew a furious return and few hits were scored.

The last forty meters to the wharf were empty of cover and the warriors would have to charge exposed. He waited and they waited and he began to wonder what their strategy might be. Then they came. On some unseen signal fifty screaming warriors rose and charged and then behind them another fifty and behind them fifty more. Volley after volley rang out. Blood sprayed and bodies fell.

They would not be able to hold, Linc saw. They would take many of their attackers but they would not hold. This time some would make it over the barricades and put their machetes and clubs to work.

He was sighting on the muscled chest of a warrior when it vanished in a pale streak. He lifted his eye from the sight to see an eruption of things burst from the bush and sweep into the warriors. The things were men, Linc saw, but barely. Some were islanders and some palangi but they seemed to have more in common with Neanderthals than *Homo sapiens*. Most were naked and all were smeared with blood and mud. They swarmed onto the Matai center and destroyed their charge. A few of the palangi ones kept running for the barricades. They were naked and blood-smeared and their eyes were hollow and their jaws worked soundlessly. When it was clear that they were attackers of another stripe, Linc waved and the men shot.

The Matai warriors were fighting the new attackers hand to hand. Two of the new attackers worked together to finish a Matai then turned on each other. They sought only the kill and Linc was tempted to try to shoot all of them but there were too many.

For now the attack was blunted and Linc turned to check and congratulate the men. He had not expected them to survive this long.

They hadn't.

Four lay in pools of blood that dripped through new holes in the planking. Gunfire rang and more holes appeared.

The Matai, he realized, had gotten under the pier.

"To the boat," he screamed, hoisting a plant biologist who looked wilted and was either dead or dying. The others joined the retreat with the wounded in their arms and on their backs. Linc twirled his hand over his head, yelling for Cork to start the engines.

Chapter 49

Marcus panted after Nick, with Devon and Callie in tow. The Greek repeatedly tried to turn back towards the main village of Sava and the bay where the ship lay, but each time was either cut off by pursuers or stopped by terrain. Marcus shot a warrior who got in close and Nick clubbed another who slipped in front.

Three more times they tried to reverse course without success.

"Not working," Nick gasped.

"Other way?" Marcus suggested.

Nick hesitated. The path to the right was thick with vines and low brush that brimmed with warriors; to the left lay an open descent with a clear understory. Where it led was another problem.

"Why not," he agreed, and plunged downward.

They stopped ten minutes later for a short rest beneath a mango tree.

"What's the plan?" Marcus asked, leaning against a prop root.

"The ship," Nick replied. "The *Aurora* is the only way out. The others should be on board. I was decoying a few warriors away."

"That's more than a few."

"I underestimated my popularity."

"What about the plane—"

A shake of his head threw sweat droplets through the air. "She sleeps with the fishes."

The women were eying each other.

"You shouldn't be here," Callie said in a cold tone. "You are still in process."

"I changed the process," Devon countered. Her nostrils flared and her eyes glinted.

Callie took a half step forward.

"Callie," Marcus said, edging between them. "Do you know this part of the island?"

Her eyes stayed on Devon with a strange hunger as one brown arm pointed down the slope. "That's the only way. The way we've been going." Her arm aligned with the looming black spire of Tabu.

"But that's the wrong direction. We can't get back to the ship that way," Nick said.

The distant rumble of diesels vibrated the air and Nick's shoulders slumped a millimeter. "Well maybe it doesn't matter. That's the *Aurora*."

"This way," Marcus said, starting down the hill and towards the spire of Tabu.

"Towards Tabu?" Nick asked. "They're already there too."

"I know. Hurry."

Gastro hovered over his lab bench with a micropipette in one hand and an eye on a computer screen. Deep in his main lab all was calm for it was a steel-walled underground room built into the basement of the old colonial.

The lab had only one obvious door and that was four inches thick and secured by steel pins worthy of a bank vault. It had been Katya who had suggested fortifying the lab. Gastro had assumed her intention was to protect it from the authorities in case of discovery, but she pointed out that if one was going to experiment on the most dangerous and lethal creature known to man—namely, man himself—one ought to be able to stay safe. Just in case.

From the violent hammering on the door Gastro was thankful. Gastro had no doubt that whoever was battering so powerfully would eventually get through. But not for a while. And by the time they entered he would be gone through the old tunnel built a half century before in anticipation of a Japanese invasion that never came. The tunnel surfaced two hundred feet away in thick jungle.

Which gave him the chance to try to figure out how his crop of gold had turned to pure shit. He had seen the evidence first hand. It was the same as in the rats. It was, he knew, as if he had pulled from the ancient mists of time more than the ability to sift oxygen from water, more than renewed healing abilities that eliminated scars and most degenerative diseases.

Ironically it was these scientific failures that had saved him. As the Matai warriors advanced on his compound, Gastro had seen a line of men rise from the sea to attack the warriors. He wondered what the Tangaroa-worshipping Matai must have thought when they found themselves attacked by sea creatures with brine still upon them. The deep ones had come back and in force; they were not organized and they were not on anyone's side nor were they defending him; they were simply partaking of the violence. In any event they had broken the attack and bought him some time though not a lot. Many things were afoot and the islands were not safe. Everything, he knew, involved the old genes.

The genes stemmed from a time alien and remote, a time when a pure savagery was the norm. Many genes serve multiple functions and Gastro now knew that the ones he had activated must have a hidden behavioral component.

It was just the kind of thing the gods would do, Gastro thought. Tie the good and bad together. Yes, you can breathe water and heal like a salamander, but in return, you must eat your own kind. Capricious sons of bitches. There was a reason the old legends were the way they were: because that was how the world worked. Maybe, Gastro mused, you could fly if you didn't mind sleeping upside down like a bat.

Gastro searched the strands he had changed, examining every shift and resurrection. He had already correlated the level of resurrected violence with each version of the change, and from the small but genuine variations he knew that the effect was linked to what he had done—and more specifically, to what he had done in certain areas.

He examined the differences between the versions causing the greatest and least Affiliated Violence, as he was dispassionately calling the problem in the best scientific tradition. For the first time he added in the data from Katya's secret experiments. She called the same gene the BloodThirst gene, a name which wouldn't work for publication though some flippancy was permitted among molecular biologists; Gastro knew of a fruit fly longevity gene named *INDY* for *I'm Not Dead Yet.*

Katya's data was detailed and went further than his, and he used it to compare the sequences base by base.

And there it was. A series of small tags of DNA, of unknown and presumably no function, but within the packets of genes and therefore included. The more violent rats had more copies. Gastro studied the tags and saw that they had the ability to replicate themselves. And they had done so. Repetitive sequences were a common feature of the genome and made up a large piece of it. But these played their own role. Just as genes could be said to look out for themselves, these tiny subunits, mere fragments of genes, also sought to reproduce. And they did. Somehow they had unleashed themselves to make copy after copy. And with every generation there would be more and more of them.

"If only I had known," Gastro sighed to himself. "I could have stopped all this. I could have saved them. Maybe I still—"

"It is too late," came a whisper.

He spun. The apparition spoke with a familiar voice but was an unrecognizable mass of hair and mud and blood.

"Ekaterina?" Gastro murmured, flashing back to the wife who looked so similar in that emergency room at Stanford so long before.

"No, Papa," came the soft correction.

"Katya." Gastro shook his head. "I'm sorry. I—"

She swallowed hard and when she spoke her voice rasped. "We are all going through a lot right now."

"Katya, the blood, the mud. You too?"

She nodded wearily. "One of the first."

"And you never told me?"

"I thought it was just me. At first I didn't have any idea it was your work. And I learned to control it, somewhat."

"How?" he asked, hoping she might provide a clue to a cure more expedient than the vaccine he pondered.

She grinned, then grimaced as the stretching of her face cracked the layers of dried mud and blood.

"I would come here, Father. When I felt it coming on I would come here." Her eyes were flinty in a way he had never seen. He lay one hand on a bottle of ethanol and the other on a sparker and took a step back.

"I didn't know you ever came to this lab."

She glided forward like a cat. "Only when I felt it coming. It seemed safe here and in the clutch I wouldn't leave. I don't know why."

The battering at the door stopped.

"You have it now," Gastro said simply. "You are in the throes of it. What is it like?"

"I don't have it all the way, not yet. Or I wouldn't be able to talk to you. It's . . . being an animal. Pure in spirit and purpose. Wonderful, really. A simple, single, overwhelming urge to survive. To kill and eat, to eat and kill. Every other creature is either competition or food or both. The long-ago time where these genes come from, it was an age of total war; there were no truces or ecological balances or symbiotic systems as there are now. No limits. No restraint. Everything took and ate and killed as much as it could. Despite the appearances of human history, this quality is very suppressed in humans. Maybe what these genes do is take away the restraint that accreted over eons. It's the only thing that separates us from the animals, and also from something more vicious and more pure than any animal today. Except maybe some sharks."

"Which evolved long ago."

"Exactly. They are also of that time but they too have learned control. Usually. In a feeding frenzy their old true selves show."

Gastro's pale brow furrowed. An intellectual puzzle was before him and though the battering of the door started up again, more loudly than before due to the use of some tool of destruction, he could not resist it.

"This restraint. It serves a purpose?"

She raised to him eyes that were colder and harder and she seemed to struggle to speak as if drawing back from some brink.

"That depends on your definition of purpose. To me, it enabled civilization. Civilization itself is merely a tool for the creation of better killing tools. Those groups with that little bit of restraint known as civilization were able to make better tools to kill those groups without it. You see the irony? The fundamental purpose of civilization is uncivilized."

"Why is all this happening now?"

"Violence begets violence. It triggers it. This revolution with all the blood and killing and the return of long pig has brought it out. Do you remember when I changed the group's diet to vegetarian?"

Gastro nodded. "You said it was more cost effective."

She trembled and for a moment she seemed not to be there and then her eyes cleared and she returned. "A plant diet is less of a trigger. Blood . . . blood is a catalyst. The chains that hold us dissolve very quickly in blood."

"Did you make another virus?" Gastro asked suddenly.

She tilted her head and seemed to fight her tongue. "I did. From a rhinovirus." She smiled with her eyes.

"A rhinovirus? My god. Where is it?"

"Everywhere. Courtesy of the U.S. Post Office. I mailed it. You've created a new world, Father."

His face was frozen, his eyes blank with shock. "You mailed it?"

"I did." She swallowed and with effort described the batch fermentation, the junk mail scheme, the dollar bills. How it would go out on the next day's ferry. She told him how the two of them had changed the planet. Then she described the world of pure savagery and selection that would come. "It is the way things are to be," she finished.

"I've opened Pandora's box," Gastro whispered. His face was drawn and white.

Katya grunted and took a half step and dropped to one knee. Her body trembled and flexed and her breath came in gasps and Gastro could see she was fighting something. Gastro uncapped the ethanol bottle with thumb and forefinger and readied the lighter. The tin cap tinkled on the linoleum.

When Katya rose her eyes were harder still and her tongue oddly active in her mouth.

"Can't close it now," she rasped, and sprang.

Gastro saw her lift into the air, saw her eyes fix on his throat and her hands sculpt into claws and hair flow into a bloody comet. He saw her the day she had come from the hospital, swaddled in pink and white with big blue eyes studying the world. He saw her in the hospital again nine years later, dying. The perfluorocarbon. The years with flooded lungs. The first experiments. The failures. The success.

Gastro knew he had time. A splash of ethanol and a jab with the sparker and she would be aflame. He knew there was good reason; the sacrifice of Katya might enable him to treat and save the others. In a purely intellectual corner of his mind Gastro was fascinated by the multilayered difficulties of the choice before him. On the one hand, his survival instincts should force him to battle any threat, even one from his daughter. But it was not that simple. Survival instincts were designed and intended to protect an individual's genes, and so a mother bear's famous willingness to sacrifice herself for her cub. But Gastro's genes lived on in Katya. Would his genes attack themselves as embodied in Katya? It would be a sort of genetic cannibalism. If it was only an experiment it would be very interesting.

It was not an experiment. This was Katya, the Katya he had spent much of his life saving.

He flung the ethanol to the left and the sparker to the right and Katya slammed into him and drove him onto the lab bench with his back arched and his arms stretched out as if on a cross.

With a howl that echoed off steel cabinets and resonated glass chromatography columns her knees pinned his arms and her hands shoved his chin back and her teeth dove for the throb of life in his throat.

They stopped a millimeter short as if a physical force prevented her and her head cocked to contemplate or perhaps listen to a distant noise though only the methodical battering on the door could be heard.

A different sound rasped from deep in her throat. It sounded like "Papa."

White teeth met white skin. Red gushed.

Chapter 50

The coughing diesel had driven the *Aurora* a quarter mile from shore when Cork ran onto the bridge. "Vessel off the, uh, right side. Starboard bow I mean. Canoe, actually."

Linc grabbed a rifle and headed for the bridge wing. An outrigger canoe was paddling straight for the ship. He recalled his last encounter with a war canoe and raised his weapon. It happened to be a scoped Winchester .30-06 and under the crosshairs he saw four figures raise their arms and wave. Linc placed the crosshairs on the first figure's chest and tightened on the trigger then paused. He slid the crosshairs to the second, third, and fourth figures then exchanged the rifle for a pair of binoculars.

"Unbelievable. Pick them up."

Devon was receiving disbelieving hugs from the *Aurora*'s crew when Nick stepped slowly onto the steel deck. "I'm not sure I can believe any of that," he said to Callie as Marcus shoved the outrigger canoe away.

"It takes a while," Callie agreed. "It's been a giving and a taking. It saved me and it saved Devon, there. But it has taken a lot. Don't forget the village where we got the canoe—the sheer savagery."

She swallowed and looked at her hands. They were trembling and curved. Her face was flushed and her pupils wide.

"Animalistic," Nick said. "But that's an insult to animals. No animals are so brutal."

"Primeval," she murmured.

Marcus looked at her. He knew from her tone that it was no innocent quip, no remark in passing. Her lips were pursed and lines creased her forehead and her eyes glittered like glass. She was fearful, and Callie was one of the most fearless women he had known. It was not what they had seen and been through; that was a lot but this was something else. Something deeper.

Five hundred yards from shore the diesels gasped and caught and gasped again then went silent. The bubbling wake turned clear and the ship coasted. In the sudden quiet gunfire rang from the island and bullets hit the ship with sharp spangs and whirring ricochets.

On the beach warriors were forming in ranks and pretty tinkles sparkled, each one hurling death. Some of the warriors splashed into the water and vanished.

"Linc?" Marcus said to the little man as he flew from the bridge.

"Dunno," he answered. "But there's plenty of steel on board so I'd get behind some while I figure this out."

"Be quick," Nick suggested.

"No duh," he called over his shoulder.

Callie took Marcus' arm and guided him down a passage. Her eyes darted, her cheeks flushed, her tongue seemed active.

"This is no good, Marcus. I can't stay."

He put his hands on her shoulders in a gesture that was as much restraint as affection.

"I didn't look for you for six years just to let you go again."

"You didn't find who you thought. You know that. I'm not who I was. Sometimes, sometimes, I think I'm becoming one of—them. The old ones. The vicious ones. I have strange urges, Marcus. I—"

Cork poked his head in. "Hey where's Linc, Marcus?"

"Engine room."

Cork vanished then reappeared. "Then could you look at something? Nick says you should see it."

Marcus took in the firm set of Callie's lips and chin, a stubborn and familiar cast, before stepping to the bridge. "You're fine. We'll finish this later."

By the time Callie whispered her reply he was around the corner. "No. It's finished."

In the sonar cubby Cork pointed at a blue screen with a swarm of green blips.

"I don't suppose you're telling me the fishing is good," Marcus said in dismay.

"Only if you want to boat a bunch of six-foot-long, two-hundred-pound fish," Nick replied.

Cork tapped the screen. "The sonar was on so I was watching. And I noticed all these. They were on the bottom but they're moving up. Never seen anything like it. What are they? Nick said you might know."

"Did he."

"It's them," Callie said.

"Who?" Cork asked.

"Your people," Marcus said.

Her lips compressed and she shook her head wearily. "Not these ones. These aren't anyone's people. I don't know how much Gastro knew but these ones went off the deep end long ago. Some of them palangis, some Matai warriors. All of them nuts. Most of them used to be the crews that would take down new ships but now they're completely disconnected from our version of reality."

"Throwbacks."

She smiled ironically. "They would say we're the throwbacks, and they're the future."

The blips multiplied.

"Almost a hundred contacts," Nick breathed.

Cork twisted a knob to adjust the resolution. "No. More."

The swiftest shimmers passed through five hundred feet. Behind them others were strung out to the bottom.

"This could be close," Nick said. "I hate when it's close."

"Hopefully we'll be going again any second," Cork said, eyeing the throttles and putting his hands in his pockets as if to stop himself from shoving the chrome levers.

Linc stepped onto the bridge with blackened hands and a grease smudge on his brow. "Some ass pumped water into the fuel tanks. Forgot this," he said, pulling a huge crescent wrench from a tool box. "Gimme thirty minutes to drain it."

"What?" he said to the transfixed stares.

"We need to be going. Now," Nick answered while pointing at the sonar screen. "We have visitors."

"How fast can you start up?" asked Marcus.

Linc leaned to the sonar then looked to the skin of the sea. "If I do it wrong and dirty, fifteen minutes. Maybe ten. What are those?"

"There's not time," Marcus said as the first contacts broke four hundred fifty feet. From below the ship's hull would be a dark patch on the lit sea. He pushed Linc.

"Can they hurt us?" Linc said.

Callie spoke. "They can. They have. They will. They'll have grappling gear. And mines. What do you think happened to the freighters? These are the ones who live deep. The wild ones who have given over to the old ways. You saw them on the island; all are savages." She looked downward, as if she could see through steel and water to the rising attackers.

"What I would do for a depth charge," Nick muttered.

"Were you doing seismic surveys this trip?" Marcus asked.

Cork nodded. "The geologists always do."

"With what?"

"Pentolite, two-pound survey packs. Why?"

Marcus was straightening.

"How many are left?"

"Several hundred, in the aft locker."

Marcus and Nick were already running.

Three minutes later a pile of marine-rated Pentolite packs sat on the deck with Marcus and Nick taping them together like lethal sausages.

"Are you sure we should use all of these?" Nick said.

"I'm sure you shouldn't," put in Stanislaw. "The geology—"

Marcus cut him off with a hard glance while taping charges together and lining them beside the rail. "Let's anyway. I just wish we had more."

"And to think I passed up a nice safe career in the family grocery for this," Nick muttered while struggling to lift an assembly of inter-connected charges without letting any hit the deck while Marcus hoisted another armload. There were five bundles.

"Different depths?" Stanislaw asked.

Marcus nodded and shoved a homemade bomb over the rail. "We set the timers so the first should go off at two hundred feet. Then four hundred, six hundred, and the last two on the bottom."

"The timers may not be that accurate, you know," warned Stanislaw. He was standing on a bollard as if scary mice were about. "They weren't meant for this."

"You already said that," Marcus noted as another bundle splashed into the water.

"Based on my research I'm a little concerned," Stanislaw said in a voice that indicated he was very concerned. "The island—"

"Hush, Stanislaw, unless you prefer being eaten."

Stanislaw fell silent.

"Two hundred feet. Right under the ship," Nick said skeptically. "Are we going to be swimming?"

Callie looked over the rail. "If so, the water looks fine."

Marcus flipped the next packet into the water.

Paramount Chief Pelemodo surveyed the wreckage of his personal guard. Ripped and torn and shredded. Pelemodo himself bore a bloodied shoulder; he had been attacked and had to kill two wild palangis with his bare hands. At least he knew he still could.

He gathered together his remaining soldiers into a ragged cohort and began marching them west.

"We are going to Tabu," he announced, and some of the men blanched. "Do not worry, Tangaroa himself orders this. There is a palangi there that I must discuss matters with."

Pelemodo smiled at his men. There was a new flint in his eyes. He had already killed two palangis with his bare hands. It was time to add a third.

Linc ran onto the bridge, soaked with sweat, panting, and stinking of diesel. He stabbed buttons and threw levers and the engines rumbled and strained and then died.

"If they ever want to make me a saint, if this works I'll be one miracle down the path," he muttered while trying for a restart.

"Any second now," Marcus said with an eye on his watch.

Linc gave up and swore and ran below again.

The skin of the water heaved, bulged, and shattered.

"Holy Poseidon," Nick breathed as torrents rained down. The water exploded again as another charge detonated, and then again.

"What's the sonar show, Cork?" Marcus called.

The reply from inside the bridge was muffled. "Nothing but foam. It'll take a bit to clear."

More rumbles shook the ship.

Nick looked at Marcus. "You don't think they could have survived."

Marcus stared at the sea. "I wouldn't have thought they could have existed."

"Looks pretty good," Cork called. "No big parts, anyway. And none moving."

A deeper rumble sounded and the island seemed to ripple. A column of white smoke rose from the green peak and clouds of parrots blew into the air. The smoke turned to black.

"Uh oh," said Stanislaw Tatum.

"Uh oh?" Nick repeated, looking from Stanislaw to the island.

"Movement!" Cork called from inside the bridge.

The sonar screen showed three ghostly figures rising under the ship, around a large bright object that was metallic and about three feet across.

"That has to be a mine," Marcus said.

"If we get out of this I'm definitely retiring," Nick announced.

"We need some more Pentolite."

"There is no more," Nick said sadly.

"Then I'll need something else," Marcus said.

Cork shrugged helplessly.

"Get me a mask, fins, and a spear."

The mask leaked and the fins were loose and the small thiry-cubic-foot tank was only half full, but two minutes later Marcus was hovering beneath the crimson keel of the *Aurora*. He realized that it had been a long time since he had been able to enjoy being beneath the sea; the muffled sounds and slanting rays of light and the velvet feel of warm water on skin. There was no time for savoring on this dive either. Three shapes rose out of the blue mist below like a developing photo. The three were each the point of a star; at the center was a round black object attached to yellow lift bags.

Marcus kicked over and piked downward. He let the air flow from his lungs and felt the pressure build as he slid downward, stooping like an underwater hawk. The three creatures below him wore no tanks and had no breathing apparatus; they wore only thin rubber thermal suits. He'd expected it, but nevertheless, to see a man breathing water was startling. It was what he'd been seeking for years; it was an amazing triumph.

And he had to kill it.

One of the men looked up and fixed dead eyes on him and he knew what was coming as the creature released from the mine and sprang at him.

Marcus had seen sharks and jacks move so fast that thick water seemed thin as air. But he'd never seen a man move so fast.

The creature pulled a black stone knife from its waist and reached for Marcus. Marcus fired the spear at the creature's throat and scored a direct hit. Blood spurted and the creature thrashed and the others stopped to stare at the coils of blood loosening in the water.

Marcus revised the old admonition about not bringing a knife to a gunfight to cover spear fights as well.

As the first creature began a lazy spiral downward, with small fish nipping at the comet tail of blood and gore, Marcus angled towards the other two. They waited expectantly, if not eagerly. Both were deep chested and heavily muscled; both moved with tremendous ease underwater.

Marcus approached the larger one from behind. The creature turned to face him but rather than advance, like the last had, it waited. Marcus came in over the top, tipped down, then cocked his spear and kicked hard, aiming the three rusty but sharp points at the creature's head.

The creature flicked out of the way and Marcus moved almost as fast but in a different direction. He drove the spear into a lift bag, loudly exploding it into a swarm of bubbles that danced up through blue rays of light.

Both changelings were surprised and neither reacted before Marcus drove his spear into another lift bag. It banged into another hiss of bubbles. The mine began to sink away, one creature hanging on gamely with one hand and flapping in the underwater breeze as the blue folds of the sea were drawn over the mine and its passenger.

The other swam at Marcus with an odd but powerful combination of kicks and dolphin-like waist thrusts; the creature swam faster than a man could run. It circled him once, then in a flash, reached out and ripped the spear away.

A heavy burst of bubbles rose from below and Marcus thought he tasted sulfur but ignored that as the creature snapped the spear over a muscled thigh and dropped both pieces. They chased each other in a spiral down into the depths. The creature looked at him with lips pulled back in something far colder than a smile. Then it moved in.

Marcus dodged and fought down to a hundred feet, then a hundred twenty. Below, in the fine blue mist, he glimpsed a black round shape, and realized the mine was coming back, with two fresh lift bags. He kicked and punched but it was like fighting an otter. The creature twisted and contorted and flowed; he was above and below and all around and Marcus knew he was in trouble. As if to prove it a moment later his mask was ripped away and then his regulator.

Marcus blinked against the salt sting and grabbed for his adversary. He found an arm as hard as polished wood and tried to bend it. The creature flicked him free. His lungs hammered and he reached for the mouthpiece hanging behind him. He sucked in one deep breath before it was ripped away and this time, for good measure, tore off the hose. The hose whipped and snaked as it spurted bubbles for five seconds, then the tank was empty.

Marcus kicked upward and one fin was stripped off. The sky was a bright ceiling of air far, far away. He locked his ankles and tried to kick with the one fin and then that one was gone too. The weight of the water above seemed to hold him down and he felt his chest squeeze. He turned to find the creature and it was closing on him and then in his sea-blurred vision he saw a strangely familiar figure swimming straight down in that same hip-flexing way until it stabbed out to wrap an arm around his attacker's throat.

Suddenly the sea exploded; the two were welded as one and the sea ripped and tore into bubbles and thrash. Marcus could hear grunts and screams but could do nothing but kick upward and wonder where the mine was.

His vision was a dark tunnel looking up the last ten feet of blue water, a distance which seemed insignificant except to one to whom it was too far, to whom it was very significant, when he felt a push and broke the surface. They were below the bulge of the ship's hull, just aft of the port waterline access hatch and out of sight of the crew.

"Callie," he gasped.

"Even changelings need oxygen to the brain," she said. Her mouth moved stiffly, as if she had to force the words out.

"The mine?"

"Heading down." She tilted her head at the yellow lift bags floating nearby and waved a stone knife; she'd cut the mine free.

"Let's go." He kicked towards the boat.

"No, Marcus. I'm already home." She smiled but there was a hard glint to her eyes.

"Come on."

"This is me, what I am. I'm not what you knew." Her tongue moved strangely again. "I'm not even what I knew a few days ago. I am continuing to process."

"I won't leave you."

"You can't stay with me. Don't. I beg you."

They drifted along the steel wall of the *Aurora,* beneath the rust-streaked hatch.

"Marcus, you have to go. Now. Ten minutes ago."

"You killed that man underwater, didn't you?" he said slowly.

"You would have."

"Yes. But the killing is affecting you, isn't it?" He stared at her with cold dread and fascination. Cords of muscle stood out on her neck; her eyes narrowed to slits against the sun. Her voice became strained.

"I'm still changing, Marcus. Get away fast. Get away while you can."

"You're my wife."

"Your wife is gone."

"No—"

Abruptly she vanished downward. Marcus waited until an uncomfortable time had passed. He realized that she wouldn't have to breathe but the wait seemed wrong. He slowly kicked backward until he could feel the steel of the ship behind him.

Another thirty seconds passed and he began to wonder if she was gone. He stuck his face in the water and searched the blur but saw nothing but the gold specks of tropical fish.

He had just raised his head when Callie exploded out of the water. She flew up until her feet rested atop the sea then crashed back down. Her hair was a wild mane and blood and gore streaked her cheeks. She stabilized waist-deep, her body resonating with the powerful strokes necessary to keep her elevated in the water.

"What's happening, Callie?" Marcus whispered, though he knew. She had saved him and because of that he had lost her.

Her eyes were cold stone but somewhere deep in them he saw a flicker of the Callie he knew. Then it was gone. Her mouth worked and a hand bent like a claw wiped hair from her face. She swept back and forth as if compelled to try to circle him. Then she stopped and sank into the water, head bowed. Her body trembled and when she rose again the wildness had taken hold. Marcus could see that she no longer knew him, perhaps no longer knew anything. She was a simple creature of old. She knew only one thing.

She fired across the water like a lunging crocodile and Marcus stiffened himself to meet her charge. He did not want to but he knew he would defend himself as best he could, but he also knew he stood little chance against a brutally strong creature that could breathe water. He had just time enough to appreciate the irony—he had changed his life and even risked it countless times over long years in a search for the one who, it turned out, would kill him. With her bare hands and teeth, most likely. It was not the reunion he had planned.

Callie was leaving a powerful wake, her legs churning and her hips flexing in a blur. She dipped beneath the surface and then fired out of the water like a cruise missile aimed at his head. Her eyes had gone flat and glittery and he could see that the Callie he had known was gone as he tried to dodge, knowing it was hopeless. He felt like a staked goat awaiting a tiger. From her arc her teeth would find his neck.

A metallic clang and then an explosion and another. Callie was thrown back, thrashing and clawing at the water and her chest. Blood leaked from her mouth and tinted clear water and her cold distant eyes fixed on him and again she came.

A black rifle flew past his head and splashed into the sea and then Marcus was rising until his feet cleared the water and then rising more. He landed on the deck of the ship with Nick's big hands under his arms. The hatch slammed shut and a few moments later there was a soft thunk as something struck the ship and a faint sound like claws scraping metal. Nick wheeled the hatch shut.

"I'm sorry, Marcus. She really is gone."

Marcus stared at the hatch but made no move towards it.

Nick continued. "And we have another problem."

Paramount Chief Pelemodo and his personal legion traveled a rocky path with the violet chop of the sea on their left and the emerald pitches of the forest to their right. Ahead, beyond a green stripe of shallow water, rose the black finger of Tabu.

The air was smoky and greasy and they passed many who had felt Tangaroa's wrath. The villages were burned and the ripped bodies left strewn like the toys of an evil child at an infernal playground. At first the men only glanced at the human wreckage but soon they stared, as if the bloody spectacle had a growing power of compulsion.

The march took an eerie turn. Several of the men were walking stiffly and a few were stumbling, with eyes that had gone glassy. Stranger still was the island, which thrummed beneath their bare feet with vibrations as if it were a great beast waking from an ancient slumber. Strangest of all was the water, for all along their march Pelemodo felt that they had been watched from the sea. Heads like periscopes seemed to rise every hundred meters or so and then recede when he turned to them. He never got a clear view but he felt something was there. The men seemed to sense the same. They became unusually quiet.

It almost seemed as if they were waiting for something to happen. As it turned out, they were. It happened at the beach that led to the crossing to Tabu. Just off shore were a large number of rocks that had not been there before. The rocks rose into men, dripping with brine and wild of eye. They were decorated with starfish and the spiny skins of pufferfish; several had capes of purple sponge. One wore a cloak of lobster carapaces stitched together and a crown of flame-red coral that jutted like bloody antlers. They waited patiently, shuddering gently, and then as one began to move forward. He saw to his surprise that some were pale as palangis.

Pelemodo knew that his men would be moved by beings who seemed so plainly to have been sent by Tangaroa. But he did not like the way these had stalked them from the sea and he did not approve of the way they now approached. Yet he knew enough of the ways of the wild not to show fear.

"Brothers," he called out. "Join us in our sacred mission."

They answered with a charge. Pelemodo, fascinated, watched as the first attackers were repelled by his guard, who were far more organized. War clubs sang and heads popped like melons and the rich scent of fresh blood colored the air. Soon more of the newcomers rose from the sea and then a strange thing began to happen. The new ones were not just attacking his men but were attacking each other as well. It quickly became a frenzy of chaos.

And it was spreading. Pelemodo's own guard began to turn on itself. At first it was a few men, mostly close to the front, but it spread quickly. Pelemodo glanced backward and found a riot. Two even attacked him; his skills remained and he ripped the war club from one while fending off the other and then savagely killed both with overhead blows.

Pain lanced his calf and he found that one of the new ones from the sea had actually bitten into his leg. Blood was pouring before his club flew again and he felt fury. How dare they. Already bodies littered the sand and three more came at him, followed by three more, and behind them even more. He fought and twisted and swung and eventually bit, but finally he went down on the sand. Some of those atop him began attacking each other but most continued to stab and bite and gouge at him. He battled but the hot press of animal fury was too much. The blood of the Paramount Chief mixed with that of commoners, and the sugar-white sand drank it all. He felt the earth below bounce up and down, as if they all rested on the chest of a cruel and laughing father.

On the bridge, still dripping and with a thousand-yard stare, Marcus said: "What's the problem?"

Stanislaw and Nick pointed at Tanua. "That."

Marcus nodded. "You're right. We have to get back to the island. The post office. There's a load of junk mail laden with viruses and we need to have a bonfire."

Stanislaw was shaking his head. "I don't think so. How much explosive did you put in the water?"

"All of it."

The little geologist flinched. "And how much was that?"

"Who cares? Six hundred pounds, give or take. Now let's get back and hijack some mail. Commit a felony and all that."

The little geophysicist was gripping the rail and gazing at the peak with his head cocked. Black, white, and gray billowed against a topaz sky.

"For six months I've been studying Tanua's fragile geology," Stanislaw said. "And six hundred pounds of explosive on an underwater fault may have lit a fuse. I was never able to research the submarine fault zones because the locals were so touchy. But let's wait here a bit. Just a hunch."

"That looks like more than a hunch," Nick said.

The engines came to life and the ship began to cut a white wake across the bay of blue glass.

"If something happens we're safe here, right?" called Linc, turning the wheel to aim them at the mouth of the bay.

Stanislaw shot a picture. "Safe? Mount St. Helens was lethal out to fifteen miles just from blast effects. Pyroclastic flows can go further.

Basically we're a bug and that there is a giant boot. Whether it squishes us is entirely up to it. Because it certainly can."

Behind the ship the green peak hung over the white wake that lay on blue water. The wake was a crystal road straight from peak to ship.

The smoke and steam abruptly cut off and the peak stilled.

"Does that look different to anyone else?" Stanislaw asked after a few moments.

"The clouds are gone?"

"No, not that."

"The mountain looks swollen," Marcus said. "Bulging."

"To me too," added Nick.

"Right," Stanislaw said, then straightened and turned away from the rail. "We're too close. Much, much too close."

Palms were swaying and falling on the island as if giant gophers were attacking their roots. Landslides coursed down the peak like make-up sliding off in rain. Deep bellows and thumps coughed through the air.

"If I'm even half right," Stanislaw said, "we may not survive even behind cover. But we definitely won't out here."

Linc got on the PA system and ordered everyone below and the ship's inner spaces filled. Marcus and Nick remained clustered on the center of the bridge with a few others. Stanislaw peeked around one bridge wing, watching Tanua as if it held a sniper rifle on him.

"What are you looking for, Stanley?" asked Cork.

Stanislaw stared for a moment, one hand raised, then turned. "It's like that saying about pornography. I'll know it when I see it. If it holds off for thirty minutes, we can—"

Stanislaw snapped into the bridge and pressed his back against a bulkhead. "Damn," he breathed.

The sky flashed pure white and there was a moment of stark and eerie stillness in the bright light, and then came a roar that was no mere vibration of molecules but a thrashing of atoms and seven hundred tons of ship rolled like a toy smacked by a rough hand. The windows blew out and the sky went dark and waves of sulfur and steam wrapped the ship as if she were sailing across the mouth of Hell and being washed by its breath.

Flaming rocks began to fall, throwing up geysers of steam and, when they hit the ship, punching holes in the hull and ripping off pieces of superstructure. A car-sized boulder glanced off the port bow and left a boiling hole in the water.

Stanislaw staggered to Linc and pushed him away and twisted the ship's wheel while pressing the already-firewalled throttles, laughing as if on a rollercoaster. The roar and din went on and the ship rang and shuddered under a barrage of boulders.

The rotten egg smell of hydrogen sulfide gas swept the bridge and Stanislaw turned the wheel further. Later they would learn that he had saved all of their lives. In a moment's glimpse he had seen the direction of the pyroclastic flow descending upon them and his turn moved the ship to the edge and then out of the footprint.

The smallest flaming boulders were now the size of cars. The impacts shook the ship though they could not be heard over the roar.

The ship began to lean further and further to starboard. Her deck was holed by the barrage of rocks and the paint along her port side scalded and blackened. The stern edge of her top deck was peeled up and chunks of superstructure had been blown off.

"We're listing," Nick yelled.

At seven knots, then four, and finally at less than two, the ship crept from beneath the reach of an angry Tanua.

By the time she was out of danger she was half-flooded, listing nine degrees, and capable of barely two knots.

It took six hours of scrambling with pumps and buckets to stabilize the ship; Nick had almost insisted on building an Archimedes screw to pump water, and had even scavenged a cylinder and tubing to wrap around it before Linc repaired a bilge pump and they began to win the battle against the sea. The ship moved with an odd corkscrewing motion; somehow she was fundamentally bent. Tanua lay wrapped in steam and smoke and they could hear rumbles and roars but see nothing until they were ten miles away. It was as if a secret construction crew was at work and when the blanket lifted, Marcus trained a pair of binoculars on the glowing rock.

"Good god."

He handed the glasses to Nick and Linc raised another pair. They looked onto a new world. The top half of the peak was gone and the rest of the island was beneath smoking mounds of hardening lava, some still incandescent. The island had consumed itself and left in its place a new and lifeless rock. Both Tanua and Tabu were gone.

"Maybe too much explosive," Nick said.

Marcus rubbed his chin in thought. "No, just enough."

He felt both stricken and more at peace than he had been in years. The search for Callie was over and with the Flying Canoe gone the Ocean Sciences Institute was also gone or at least on hold. A future once packed with struggle and work had suddenly opened up. He now knew that Callie had been gone ever since she vanished; what so many had said turned out to be true. He had been permitted to see her one last time and he would view that as a small victory. He still felt a pain but the pain was a different pain; the certainty of knowing displaced the uncertainty of the last six years. And this time he would heal.

He climbed atop the bridge and leaned against a burned bulkhead and looked at the scorched island and towering plume. A fine ash began to fall and the waves were coated with gray. He suddenly realized he was so tired and sore that he did not think he could stand. Which was fine because he didn't care to.

Devon climbed up stiffly.

"Marcus, I never thanked you."

He slid his eyes to her lazily. "I never did anything."

"You came for me. And you found me."

"And I found what was left of Callie. Will you become like her?"

Devon shook her head. "I'm sorry about her, Marcus. But no. I was going to become like her but I won't anymore. I tried fever therapy and native medicines to combat Gastro's virus and finally found something that definitely works." She held up a plastic tube.

"Antisense DNA," she continued. "From Katya's lab. It deactivates the old genes, and shuts down the virus."

"You're cured."

"I will be."

"And the air virus?"

"Boiled and sealed under lava. It was far too fragile to survive that."

Marcus slumped in fatigue and Devon lay her head on his shoulder and closed her eyes. Nick arrived and collapsed to the deck, streaked with grease and grime and with lines of exhaustion cut into his swarthy face.

"Marcus, next time I say I have a bad feeling about a place, please listen to me, Okay?"

"Deal," Marcus agreed.

"You know we're due in Tuvalu in a week," Nick said slowly and with his eyes closed as he took the sun.

"But we've lost our plane and all our equipment," Marcus pointed out.

"So maybe its time to head back to the States," Nick suggested. "Clean sheets, soft beds, running water . . ."

"You'd get bored."

"I'd love to get bored," Nick lied.

"I know a guy in Hawaii with an old Grumman Albatross. You'd love it—two big engines, tons of space."

"Can't I get bored for a little while first?"

"It'll take us a couple months to outfit it."

"And then?"

Marcus shook his head. "Maybe we need a change of scenery."

"Palm Beach? Santa Barbara?" guessed Nick hopefully.

"How about the Aegean?"

Nick frowned in mock anguish. "You know I can't refuse the Aegean."

"I know."

"At least the old gods there are my friends," he murmured, then he looked at Marcus. He was sound asleep in the sun, his face more relaxed than Nick had seen it in years.